THE PRODIGAL SON

Also by
Chris Bishop

The Shadow of the Raven Series:
Blood and Destiny
The Warrior with the Pierced Heart
The Final Reckoning
Bloodlines

THE PRODIGAL SON

CHRIS BISHOP

Red Door

A RedDoor book
Published by Ember 2023
www.emberprojects.co.uk

ISBN 978-1-7392844-3-5

A CIP catalogue record for this book is available from the British Library

Cover design: Patrick Knowles
www.patrickknowlesdesign.com

Map design: Joey Everett

Typesetting: Tutis Innovative E-Solutions Pte. Ltd

Printed by Severn, Gloucester

'There is rejoicing in the presence of the angels of God over one sinner who repents'

Luke 15:10

In memory of Ted and Emily Hull

Such lovely people. I hope only to be remembered in the way that I remember them

A glossary of some of the terms used in this story
can be found at the back of the book

The story so far…

Having been sent to Wareham for his own protection, Edward established himself by successfully training Fleet, Governor Osric's magnificent black stallion, thought to be unrideable. He then proved his worth still further by stampeding the horses and cattle during the battle near Twynham and driving them into the heart of the Viking ranks. In so doing, he turned a near disastrous defeat into victory and saved the lives of many Saxons who would otherwise have been slain. His quick thinking persuaded King Alfred to at last publicly acknowledge the stable boy's true lineage, thereby making him heir to a significant fortune but also putting him at risk from those who might seek to exploit him or, worse still, wish to see him killed.

One such person was the boy's treacherous uncle, Edmund, who stood to inherit the entire family fortune if Edward died. He hired an assassin to kill his nephew but, when he mistakenly thought the deed was done, he murdered the assassin rather than pay him. He then fled without realising that his plot had been foiled and that Edward still lived.

Meanwhile, a huge fleet of Viking warships was patrolling the south coast looking for a place from which to launch their invasion of Wessex – with Wareham being an obvious target…

When the rain has washed the blood from this field and all the dead have been counted, who will remember what happened here?

Such is the way of wars. They pass like storm clouds across the sky, but the dead are still dead, their deeds are forgotten and it seems that even those who swore never to fight again whispered their promises to the wind.

C.J.B

THE PRINCIPAL CHARACTERS FROM BLOODLINES (BOOK 4) WHO CONTINUE TO PLAY AN IMPORTANT PART IN THE STORY

EDWARD – The bastard son of **Matthew, christened Edward** (known as the Warrior with the Pierced Heart who died whilst defending the settlement at Leatherhead and serving the Saxon cause with distinction)

EDMUND – Edward's treacherous uncle. Having been enslaved by the Vikings for over fifteen years, he has returned to Wessex determined to reclaim his inheritance

ALFRED – Having restored himself as King of all Wessex, Alfred is now fighting on all fronts to preserve his Kingdom

LORD ETHELNORTH – An old but much-respected warrior and a close friend of Alfred

OSRIC – Once chief of Alfred's personal guard, Osric is now Governor at Wareham with responsibility for keeping it secure at all costs

OSWALD – Osric's nephew who is Commander of the Garrison at Wareham but has yet to prove himself following a series of near disastrous military decisions

SIGBERT – A carpenter and trusted member of the fyrd at Wareham who is charged to watch Edward's back at all times

WULFRIC – Second in command of the fyrd at Wareham

ODELIA – Governor Osric's young daughter with whom Edward has fallen in love. Is she more knowing than her years suggest?

FATHER EMMETT – A priest at the Minster of the Lady St Mary at Wareham

The Author's Impression of the Burh at Wareham

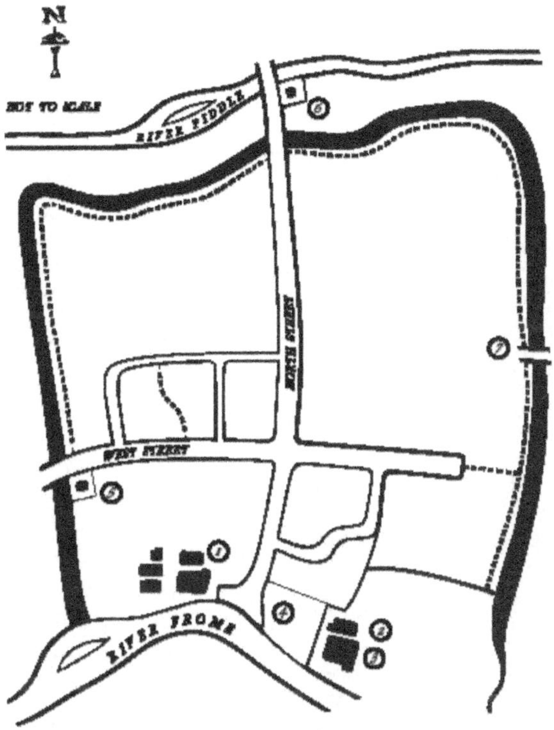

THE BURH AT WAREHAM

Most of the people would have lived around the crossroads and the quay

KEY

- - - - - FOOT PATH

1. THE VILL WITH ANCILLARY BUILDINGS AND STABLES
2. MINSTER OF THE LADY ST MARY
3. NUNNERY
4. THE QUAY
5. WEST GATE
6. NORTH BRIDGE
7. GATE TO PASSAGE AT BELL'S ORCHARD

Prelude

WAREHAM FOREST – 893

The figure of a man passed like a shadow through the forest, easing his way between the tall stands of oak, beech and hazel. He moved quietly and carefully even though he knew he was being followed – he had caught an occasional glimpse of his pursuers who had otherwise kept themselves well hidden. Afraid lest whoever they were should realise they'd been seen and give up the chase, the man stopped when he reached a small clearing where he hurriedly checked that he still had the knife he'd used to kill a man in Wareham. With that he made himself an obvious target by kneeling down to drink from a small spring, scooping up handfuls of cool water as he waited for whoever was following him to reveal themselves. When they did, the man calmly got up then turned to face them.

'Ha! So there you are,' he said, smiling benignly. 'You're very hard men to find.'

The man who confronted him was a burly fellow with long black hair that was braided, suggesting he had once been a warrior. 'That all depends on who's looking for us,' he replied, toying with a seax with just enough menace to suggest that he meant to use it.

'Well, my name's Edmund,' he said, stepping away from the stream. 'And I've been looking to find you.'

'Have you now?' asked the stranger. 'And why would that be?'

'Because I've a proposition for you,' explained Edmund. 'Something which may be of benefit to us both.'

Sensing no danger, the man signalled for two others to join him. They emerged from within the trees, one of them carrying a spear and the other a bow. Both looked similarly dishevelled and Edmund overheard one of them call the first man by the name of 'Byram', though he was quickly rebuked by the others for doing so.

'A proposition, is it?' asked Byram. 'Well, given there's three of us, my friends here think we should start by offering you something instead. How about you give me that purse you have tucked under your belt and, in return, we won't slit your throat? Does that not sound like a "reasonable" proposition to you?'

Edmund laughed. 'Oh, I had in mind something far more profitable for you than the few coins I have in my purse.'

'And what might that be?' demanded Byram.

'First, do you know who I am?' enquired Edmund.

'Should we?' answered Byram.

'Not really, but it might help if I tell you. You may not yet have heard that a man was killed in Wareham a few days ago. A wretched fellow who had just murdered my nephew.'

'So, what has that to do with us? We don't even know you, never mind your nephew.'

'Exactly,' said Edmund. 'Which is why you can help me.'

'And why would we do that?'

'Because it could be to your advantage. You see, in killing my nephew the rogue did me a great service. Which is why

I paid him to do it in the first place. Mind, I then killed him as well.'

Suddenly the robbers were all ears. 'You paid a man to murder your nephew then killed him for doing so?' repeated Byram, clearly intrigued.

'Aye, that's about the strength of it,' admitted Edmund. 'But all with good cause, you understand.'

'That's as maybe but, like I said, what has that to do with us?'

'Well, you see I was then obliged to leave Wareham in haste and now have need of a place where I can lie low for a while. I've heard tell that you have a hideout in this forest, a camp which no one has yet managed to find.'

Byram looked pleased with himself on hearing that. 'That may well be so,' he said proudly. 'And believe me, many have tried.'

'Which is why I want to join you.'

Byram laughed then looked back at his two men who were similarly amused. 'Friend, the pickings here are meagre enough as it is. Why the hell would we want to share them with you?'

'Because if you do, I can make you all very wealthy men indeed.'

'Could you now?' queried Byram, looking Edmund up and down. 'And just how would you manage that?'

Certain that he had their full attention, Edmund moved across to stand in front of a large oak, seeking protection in case there were others who might come at him from behind if they didn't believe what he was about to tell them. 'Some fifteen years ago, I was taken captive by Viking raiders and held as a slave. When they decided to come here to raid, I was forced to come with them. Unlike most of their band, I somehow managed to survive the recent fray near Twynham but was taken prisoner and, in order to escape being put to the sword, revealed who I am. In so doing, I thought that I might also reclaim my just inheritance but found it had already been dispensed to the bastard son of one of my dead brothers, a wretch who'd done nothing to deserve it save being born of the same bloodline as myself.'

'So you had him killed?'

'Exactly. What else was I to do, for he was all that stood between me and my inheritance? No one knows of my hand in his murder, so all I need to do now is lie low long enough for the dust to settle then reclaim what's rightfully mine.'

'What sort of fortune are we talking about?' queried one of the robbers.

'I am the eldest son of Lord Edwulf who was both an Ealdorman and also a close friend of none other than King Alfred himself. It would thus amount to lands and riches beyond reckoning. If I can remain with you until such time as I can secure what's rightfully mine, I'll share it with you. You can then divide your half between yourselves as you see fit.'

The men all looked at each other, hardly daring to believe what Edmund was offering.

'How do we know you're telling the truth?' asked Byram.

'You don't. But you no doubt get word from Wareham from time to time so will soon learn that all I've told you is true. The fools there will be speaking of little else.'

'Even if we agree to let you join us, you'd need to prove your worth and also earn your keep,' warned Byram. 'Or is that too distasteful for the heir to a great fortune?'

Edmund shrugged. 'I have no objection to soiling my hands. Believe me, to survive being held as a Viking slave I was forced to do far worse than rob a few strangers.'

The three men then drew closer together so they could discuss Edmund's proposal without him hearing. Having finished their deliberations, it was Byram who then continued to speak on behalf of them all. 'Very well,' he agreed. 'We'll take you to meet the others so you can tell us more. If all agree, we may then come to some sort of "arrangement". If not, we'll kill you – or perhaps drag you back to Wareham and claim whatever price has no doubt been set upon your otherwise worthless head.'

'And you'd do that?' asked Edmund. 'Even to a fellow fugitive?'

Byram just laughed. 'Oh yes, my friend, make no mistake about it. From all you've told me so far I judge you to be a treacherous rogue and that makes me ill-inclined to trust you.'

Edmund looked him hard in the eyes. 'Then it sounds like I shall be in the sort of company I've become well used to these past fifteen years or so.'

* * * * *

Edmund was blindfolded and, with his hands tied behind his back, was then led through the forest at spearpoint. He had no idea where they were taking him but, so far as he could tell, they were headed roughly north and following a path that was not well travelled. He was certain he could hear running water from time to time, so assumed they were following a small river or perhaps a stream but, apart from that, there was little to help him know where he was and even less that would enable him to retrace his steps. The latter didn't trouble him unduly. If all went as he intended, he'd join the band of robbers but, failing that, finding his way back through the forest would be the least of his worries.

They eventually stopped and, when his blindfold was removed, Edmund found himself in a clearing encircled by a wicker fence. Looking around, he could see four more men, all of them looking both wretched and dirty from living rough in the forest and some of them carrying the reminders of wounds. There was also a woman with them who was presumably preparing food for the others as she was tending a large pot which had been suspended over an open fire. As he hurriedly surveyed the camp, he noted that it included a cluster of crude hovels plus a makeshift shelter which was open at the front. The shelter contained a pile of firewood and a barrel but little else of interest apart from the carcass of a deer which had been hung up by its hind legs. The deer had been skinned and was being butchered by an eighth man he hadn't noticed at first who was dressed in the shabby habit of a monk, his tonsure still shaven and with a large wooden cross hung about his neck. The monk stared at Edmund but otherwise kept his distance even as all the others crowded round, anxious to know why a stranger had been brought into their camp and, more particularly, why he'd not been relieved of his knife – or indeed the purse still tucked under his belt.

Byram stepped forward to address them all. 'Well, what would you have me do with this wretch?' he asked aloud. 'He has a proposition for you but I insist that you hear it from his lips, not mine. Will you let him speak or shall I just kill him now and be done with it?'

There were several murmurs and mutterings but all there knew that Byram had already decided what they would do. 'So,' he said returning his attention to Edmund. 'It seems these good folks would hear more of what you have to say.'

If Edmund felt any fear at that point he was careful not to show it. With his hands still tied, he started to explain his proposal but didn't elaborate any further than he had to. 'So, you have two choices,' he announced once he'd finished. 'You can kill me now or you can accept what is probably the best offer you're ever going to hear. One which will see you all safe, warm and well fed for the rest of your days.'

'Well, luckily for you, we're not well disposed to killing men without good cause,' mused Byram.

'That's very noble of you,' conceded Edmund.

Byram sneered. 'It has nothing to do with being "noble". We have a good trade here from robbing travellers and suchlike who use the forest tracks. But if we go killing them, Governor Osric will have something to say about it and would likely send the fyrd from Wareham to come looking for us. As it is, they leave us alone for they know full well how hard it would be to find us.'

Edmund nodded as if to acknowledge the point. 'So then, what's it to be?' he asked.

'How much are we talking about?' queried one man, raising the question others were almost itching to ask.

'A lot,' said Edmund bluntly. 'My father had lands and wealth beyond reckoning. Also, two of my brothers were warriors who both amassed a good hoard of booty whilst they were alive. That should, by rights, revert to me as well.'

'Having been away for so long, how will you convince others that you are who you claim to be?' asked a brutish fellow who had only one eye, the other having no doubt been lost in a quarrel.

'Alfred himself questioned me whilst he was at Wareham and was minded to acknowledge my bloodline,' lied Edmund. 'I don't think others will argue with that.'

'If that's so, then why do you need us?' pressed another.

'Having fought with them against him,' explained Edmund. 'Alfred offered to pardon me only on condition that I return to the Vikings as his spy but, having lived with the bastards for all those years, I know full well that only a fool would agree to do that. I've seen what they do to spies. They've devised ways for dealing with any who are caught, inflicting agonies so dreadful that you'd not even want to imagine them!'

'Ha!' said Byram. 'Or is it because you now have a price on your head for killing that assassin and for plotting to have your own nephew murdered as well? If so, the fyrd could come looking for you and thus you could bring them down upon us all.'

'There's nothing to link me to my nephew's murder,' Edmund assured them. 'As for killing the assassin, I could hardly be blamed for avenging what he did to my kin. Besides, if they'd caught the wretch they'd have hanged him anyway; all I did was save them the trouble. Hence they won't bother to come looking for me on his account, you can be sure of that.'

They were all quiet for a moment, mostly trying to decide whether the risk was one worth taking given they knew nothing about the events in Wareham and had never seen Edmund before, although some of them said they had heard of his father, Lord Edwulf. It was Byram who then spoke. 'We'll see how this turns out,' he decided. 'We have friends in

Wareham who will no doubt confirm what transpired there but, if your story is found wanting…' he left the rest of his words to remain unsaid.

Edmund smiled to himself, by then certain that the greedy fools would not be able to resist the chance of earning a share of such a large fortune. Not that he had any intention of honouring his promise in that respect. All he needed was a secure place in which to bide his time as he planned how best to restore himself. After that he would betray the robbers to Governor Osric and, in so doing, prove himself to be a "true and loyal Saxon" after all. Of course, they would pay with their lives for all the crimes they'd committed, and deservedly so. Doubtless they would curse him and try to embroil him as being part of their band, but they could say what they liked. No one would pay much mind to any accusations made by a few worthless thieves, particularly those they uttered just before being dangled from the end of a rope.

*****

WAREHAM – LATER THAT SAME DAY

Alfred had sent word to Governor Osric and to his nephew, Oswald, asking them to attend him at his lodge at the Vill. When they arrived, the place seemed a hive of activity. Two of Alfred's servants were busily packing the King's personal belongings into several chests whilst he remained seated, sorting through a pile of documents he had yet to construe.

The King looked up and stopped what he was doing as soon as they arrived. 'My friends,' he announced by way of a greeting. 'I regret that Lord Ethelnorth and myself have no option but to take our leave of you. We both of us now have more pressing duties elsewhere.'

'My Lord,' asked Oswald. 'Has then the threat from the Viking fleet abated?' As the Garrison Commander at Wareham, he had been much concerned with ensuring that they could deal with over one hundred Viking ships which were known to be patrolling somewhere along the south coast and might well deign to strike at any time, with Wareham being an all too obvious target.

'No,' said Alfred bluntly. 'I regret that's not the case, although I wish it were. In fact, I fear we may all be sorely tested in the weeks and months to come. Lord Ethelnorth is even now preparing my personal guard to break camp. We intend to rejoin my army which is still camped beyond the marshes and march out from there at first light tomorrow.'

'Where to, Sire?' asked Osric.

'I've received word that a large Viking warband has left Essex and is now raiding seemingly at will across the north of my realm. The fyrd should deal with them well enough but I would have Lord Ethelnorth command them. For my part, I must march to support Exeter which is under the threat of imminent attack.'

Neither Osric nor his nephew took much comfort from that. 'But surely, my Lord, you'll be splitting your forces?' suggested Osric.

'Regrettably that's true,' admitted Alfred. 'But I have no choice. I'm obliged to cover both threats as best I may.'

Having once been head of the King's personal guard, Osric had more he wanted to say about that but left it to his nephew to speak instead.

'Sire, this arrangement worries me greatly given the reported size of the fleet,' said Oswald, his voice filled with concern.

Alfred got up and placed some of the documents in one of the chests. 'The fleet could strike anywhere and you're no more at risk than any of the other settlements that have sheltered harbours large enough to accommodate so many ships. We can't cover every possibility, so just hold yourselves ready. I shall be within a few days' march from here so can reach you readily enough if needed. In the meantime, I would advise that you train men to sail the two captured longships as they could prove useful.'

'Sire, will you then return to Wareham once the threat in Exeter has been averted?' asked Osric.

'No, my friend,' said Alfred. 'I thank you for your hospitality, but I must go wherever I'm needed most. In my absence, I'm most anxious that you continue to look out for young Edward.'

'Of course, my Lord. As we agreed whilst in Winchester, I'll ensure that he learns the ways and skills of a Saxon nobleman as now befits his new station.'

'I was thinking more of his personal safety as I fear that his treacherous uncle doesn't yet know that the assassin he sent to the stables failed and that Edward is still alive.'

Osric had to admit that was something which greatly concerned him as well. 'Do you think he'll try again, my Lord?'

'I'm sure of it,' stressed Alfred. 'Or more likely he'll have others do so on his behalf.'

Osric considered that for a moment. 'Then I'll alert our permanent guard to keep a ready lookout for any strangers,' he offered.

'Do that. But it won't be near enough. Don't forget that there could be other rogues who may try to use Edward to their advantage or attempt to relieve him of his great fortune.'

Osric remembered all too well what Lord Ethelnorth had said about how a fool and his money are soon parted. He also recalled what he and Ethelnorth had discussed about the risk of Edward being used to usurp Alfred as King, the consequences of which were, in such troubled times, too dire to think about. 'Then what more can we do?' he asked.

'I recall that you said you've charged the carpenter, Sigbert, to look out for Edward at all times?' said Alfred.

'That's true, my Lord,' agreed Osric without hesitation. 'Although one of the oldest members of the fyrd, he's served us well enough and is also one of our most experienced men.'

'Good. In the meantime, I've advised Edward to confine himself to Wareham and warned him to be wary of anyone else who tries to befriend him.'

Osric looked worried. 'Sire, all that should help to keep him safe from those who might seek to use or exploit him, but there's little we can do to guard against his uncle's murderous intent. A stray arrow loosed from behind a tree or an assassin who strikes when Edward least expects it – those are surely the greatest threats and yet are also the ones which we can do little to protect him against.'

Alfred didn't answer at first. 'Yes,' he managed at last. 'I fear that's true. But you can do no more than try. That and pray that God will see him safe, although with all that which now threatens this pious realm, the good Lord may well have more immediate concerns than the plight of just one boy.'

Chapter One

WAREHAM – A FEW DAYS LATER

With the prospect of an imminent attack from the Viking fleet looming large in everyone's thoughts, Governor Osric summoned the three most senior men in Wareham to join him at his Vill for what he intended would be a regular meeting to review and monitor their position in King Alfred's absence. When they arrived, they were each immediately shown through to his Hall and there offered seats at a large table which had been cleared of all save for some refreshments and several documents he felt he might need to refer to. As Governor, he took his place at the head of the table with his Reeve, Ulrich, to his left and his nephew, Oswald in his capacity as the Garrison Commander, to his right. Edward was the third person invited to attend and was seated opposite Osric as befitted his new status as a nobleman, although being so young he expected to play little part in the discussions.

'Uncle, have you further news for us?' asked Oswald impatiently.

'I have,' said Osric, choosing his words carefully as he was anxious not to cause undue alarm given what he was about to tell them. 'I fear that the Viking fleet could soon be even larger than we've been led to believe. Before dying of his wounds, the last of the three prisoners we took at the battle near Twynham implied that the ships which have been ravaging the north coast of Devon may soon sail to join it. If they do, the fleet could then comprise near two hundred vessels all told.'

All present were silent for a moment, hurriedly doing the calculations for themselves. It was Oswald who spoke first, his voice etched with concern. 'Uncle, if that's so, then it means the fleet could be carrying an invasion force of anything up to six thousand men!'

'Not all the ships will be fully manned,' said Osric, anxious to reassure them. 'Remember, this is an invasion fleet, not just a few raiders out for what they can pillage. As such, some ships will be carrying supplies and others may even have their women and children on board, not to mention various skilled tradesmen. But you're right, we'd be facing a sizeable and potentially overwhelming force. I've of course sent word to Lord Alfred to advise him of this very worrying development. In the meantime, we'll continue to monitor the position as best we may.'

It was Ulrich who spoke next. 'My Lords, since the King and his army left Wareham, the mood within this settlement has become one of fear and foreboding. Many have grown restless and, with this news, I fear panic may soon set in.'

'Then we must do what we can to reassure everyone,' said Osric firmly. 'Once camped in Exeter, Alfred will be just three or at worst four days march from here, so can be summoned readily enough.' Even as he said it, he was all too well aware that it would be of little or no consolation given what they now feared they would be up against.

They all looked to Oswald in the hope that he, as Garrison Commander, would be able to allay their fears. Inevitably, they were disappointed. 'There's little enough that Alfred can do wherever he is,' he warned. 'He has but half his army with him as the rest are with Lord Ethelnorth chasing the other warband across the north of Wessex. If this fleet becomes as large as you now fear, he'll need many more men than he has with him at present.'

'Then we must look to ourselves and to our own resources,' insisted Osric. 'What numbers can we count on?'

'We lost many men in the recent battle,' reported Oswald. 'That included several good warriors like Aelwyn who played a crucial role in our shield wall, plus there are many others who received wounds from which they've yet to recover. There are three boys who might now be considered old enough to serve as replacements in the fyrd but even so, our resident force here will remain depleted.'

None of that was news to Osric who had already made a point of establishing for himself what reserves they could rely on. 'I've sent word to Ealdorman Aelfric asking for some men to be sent from elsewhere within the Shire but he has not as yet replied,' he informed them.

'Could we not draw replacements from the local fyrds?' suggested Oswald. 'After all, the protection of Wareham is for their benefit as much as our own.'

'No,' said Osric firmly. 'Raids are likely to continue unabated as the Vikings seek to furnish their ships with supplies, so we should leave those members of the fyrd who reside in settlements outside the burh to protect their own homes and farmsteads. Besides, bringing men into Wareham will mean they must move their families here as well, which would place an even greater strain on our already limited reserves of food. It's therefore best that we try to manage with what numbers we have.'

Ulrich nodded as if to confirm the sense of that given that all the provisions he, as Reeve, was stockpiling would be stretched as it was. 'My Lord, I'm also worried for the families of the men who were killed in the recent battle,' he said, showing his concern for the less fortunate members of their community.

'I've spoken to Father Emmett about that,' advised Osric. 'He has asked the nuns at the nunnery to offer charity where they can, but I'm bound to ask what became of the booty that was taken from all the Vikings we killed? Has that not yet been distributed?'

Oswald frowned. 'There was precious little of it. I can only surmise that they must have buried their loot somewhere to keep it safe, probably long before they reached us here. I fear that many of their personal items of value were stripped from their bodies but then not shared.'

The thought of that clearly angered Osric. 'If you suspect any man of having taken spoil and then not declared it, he's to be brought before me,' he ordered. 'In the meantime, you must ensure that the families of the dead at least get what would have been their due had their husbands or sons survived.'

'Of course, Uncle,' agreed Oswald. 'But it's food they'll need, not booty.'

Osric acknowledged the point but there was little he could do to resolve that beyond the charity already offered by the nuns. Instead, he turned their attention to another matter. 'What about the two ships we captured?' he asked.

Oswald knew that his uncle was not going to be best pleased by what he had to say on that point either. As Governor, Osric had long argued that Wareham needed ships to form part of their defences and had hoped that the two they'd captured might suffice for that purpose. However, it was quickly becoming clear to Oswald that they would prove far from effective. 'Well, for a start, we lack men who are able to sail them,' he explained.

'Surely that's easily remedied?' protested Osric. 'There are men enough in Wareham who must know the way of it. After all, they managed to sail them back from the site of the battle with our dead and wounded on board.'

Oswald was quick to answer. 'Yes, but they rowed them all the way from there and even that proved difficult enough, despite having the tide in their favour. What's more, they arrived all but exhausted and also sustained some damage along the way.'

'How the hell did that happen?' demanded Osric angrily.

'Uncle, from what I saw of it, as the ships came through the narrow harbour entrance they encountered a confused tide and, with so few men on board who knew what they were about, the helmsmen were unable to keep control of their vessels.'

'Then I would hear more about that! What damage was sustained? I assume it's being made good?'

Oswald confirmed that was the case. 'It was only slight and Sigbert has all but finished making the necessary repairs. Of more concern is that if we're to use these ships to any effect, the men will first need to learn how to handle them, particularly whilst using the sails. That's easier said than done and I'm coming to the view that given the confines of the harbour, it's not a suitable place from which to deploy them. Much of it is too shallow at some stages of the tide and it sometimes all but empties of water completely.'

'What do you mean?' demanded Osric, reacting exactly as Oswald knew he would. 'Have I not said it often enough? Ships are crucial to the defence of this burh.'

'I agree, Uncle. In theory that would make sense if we could use them to sail out and intercept the raiders whilst they're still weary from having been so long at sea,' conceded Oswald. 'But without using the sails it would take far too long to even cross the harbour in order to reach the enemy, never mind engage them. What's more, our men would arrive all but exhausted from rowing so far.'

'But that's not the point!' stormed Osric. 'As you well know, the Vikings avoid fighting at sea as the risks for them are too great. If their vessels are damaged in a battle they might not be able to use them to sail back to their homelands. Therefore, we don't have to engage them. The mere presence of the two ships should serve as deterrent enough.'

Oswald still didn't agree. 'Yes Uncle, that may be so,' he said as respectfully as he could. 'But at least thirty men are needed just to row one of these longships – even more if we're to provide a viable fighting force on board as well. That means that near a hundred men would be needed if we launch them both. We can't afford to deploy that many men until the fyrd has fully assembled, by which time it would be too late as the Vikings would be already upon us. Besides, it would be a lot of men to lose if there was a battle at sea which didn't go well or if one of the ships foundered. We can't possibly take that risk if it means losing so many. What we really need are faster, lighter craft, manned by just ten men at the oars and able to carry half a dozen bowmen. After all, we saw the value of using fire arrows plainly enough at the recent battle.'

Osric was about to protest when he realised that his nephew was right. 'So, what would you have us do?' he asked.

'I think we should offer the ships to one of the burhs that have direct access to the sea,' suggested Oswald. 'They can then deploy them more readily when needed. We'll still benefit from whatever deterrent that affords us, as will others all along this part of the coast. What's more, if we are then attacked via the harbour the ships could be summoned to seal off the entrance, thereby trapping the bastards inside where they would be at our mercy when the tide falls. If we could manage that it might well serve to convince Alfred that you're right and that a fleet of ships is needed to cover all the coastal settlements.'

Osric was surprised to find that his nephew seemed to have considered the matter so thoroughly. It was almost as if he was at last thinking like a true warrior and taking a wider view of his responsibilities. 'Perhaps you have a point,' he acknowledged. 'Alfred is already designing special ships we can use. I'm told each will have sixty oars so should be faster and more stable than anything the Vikings have at their disposal.'

Oswald was tempted to point out that such ships would still require a lot of men to sail them. As he'd already said, in his view what they needed was smaller and faster ships – and lots of them but, having made his point, he decided to let the matter rest.

'Very well,' agreed Osric. 'Deploy them as you see fit. Now, regarding our defence of the settlement, what arrangements have been made?'

Knowing that his uncle was no stranger to the logistics of defence, Oswald chose his words with care. 'As always, we're relying on the watch towers on the cliffs to give us warning if the fleet approaches,' he said. 'All the people from the smaller settlements and farmsteads will then come in to share the safety of the fortifications here, which would mean that the fyrd will then be at near full strength.'

'Bringing their livestock with them?' asked Osric.

'Yes, if they can and have the time to do so.'

'Good, for if this becomes a siege, as is likely to be the case, we'll need all the provisions we can get in order to withstand it.'

'My Lord,' said Ulrich, 'I've already begun to stockpile food to ensure we'll have enough. We'll also have access to fresh water from both rivers and a limited supply of fish and eels.'

Osric seemed satisfied with that. 'Then what about the defences?' he asked.

'Well, Uncle,' said Oswald, hoping he was on less contentious ground. 'For a start, if the fleet is sighted, we'll pull up the chains across the rivers to stop any ships from sailing this far upstream.'

'Chains can be cut or breached,' observed Osric.

'Of course,' acknowledged Oswald. 'But as you know, there are several sets which should at least delay them. We can make things even more difficult for them by deploying bowmen along the banks of both rivers who will fight a rear-guard action all the way back to the settlement. It's a long way by river, so they should be able to reduce the Vikings' numbers and also buy Alfred more time in which to reach us with reinforcements.'

Osric considered that. 'That's to the good,' he acknowledged. 'Any delay will work to our advantage. My concern is that the Vikings may well realise that and try to probe the fortifications for any weak spot rather than wait.'

'They'll lose a lot of men trying if they do,' said Oswald firmly. 'To reach us by land they'd first need to traverse the marshes, so we'd see them coming long before they reach our fortifications and thereby have time enough to focus our defence on where they're intending to strike. With that in mind, I'm planning to double the guard at all the known weak points such as the north bridge, the west gates, the quay and at the entrance to the path at Bell's Orchard.'

'That should work well enough,' conceded Osric. 'And once those who live outside Wareham start to come in you should have enough men available for duty at any one time, day or night.'

'Exactly,' said Oswald. 'The roster for that is already in hand. I've also ensured that we'll have a plentiful supply of arrows as they'll be what's needed if this does become a siege.'

'That all seems adequate,' conceded Osric. 'But remember, no matter how vigilant you are, there's always a weak spot somewhere in any defence system. So, check the fortifications again. The Vikings can spot a potential weakness and exploit it, even where none is thought to exist.' He then turned to Ulrich. 'If this does become a siege, they'll try to starve us out, so I would have you organise rationing. For that we'll place some members of the permanent guard at your disposal to maintain discipline in case people panic.'

Ulrich acknowledged the order.

'In the meantime, what about attending to any raids?' continued Osric, concerned that they would not have enough men to assist if any of the outlying settlements or farmsteads were attacked. 'Oswald, your plan to use horses for an elite squad to reach the site of a raid more quickly looked promising but, assuming we ignore Fleet, we now have but two horses we can use, the rest having been killed in the battle or put down afterwards.'

'Then we must find more,' stressed Oswald. 'To re-establish my squad I'll need ten more good mounts at least.'

'I can't afford to buy that many,' said Osric emphatically. 'My purse is already stretched with all the extra provisions and weapons that are needed. Edward, you had a plan to round up some from the moors, did you not?'

'Just so, my Lord,' said Edward, at last having something he could contribute to the discussion. 'But it'll require men to do it and even then the horses will need breaking and training before they can be ridden.'

Osric considered that. 'We may be able to manage that in time but, for now at least, we dare not risk distracting men from their other duties and obligations.'

It was Ulrich who answered. 'With respect, my Lord. We also need to replace the two farm horses, both of which were also killed in the battle. That could prove to be a more immediate concern.'

'That's true,' agreed Osric. 'We'll surely need to replace them when we can. Edward, perhaps you would help with that as well? There may perhaps be some we can borrow from one of the farmsteads.'

'Of course, my Lord,' said Edward. 'In the meantime, we still have the oxen at the farm, which we can use for any heavy work if needed.'

Ulrich looked far from being at ease with that but could see no alternative. 'Then, my Lord, that will have to suffice for now,' he acknowledged. 'But with Edward's promotion, we also lack a stable boy.'

'I thought you had someone in mind for that?' queried Osric.

'I do,' said Ulrich. 'But he's very young and, as yet, much too small to handle the horses, never mind the oxen.'

'Then why the hell are we using him?' demanded Oswald impatiently.

Ulrich looked to Osric before answering. 'My Lord, his father was one of those killed in the battle so his mother is now a widow struggling to raise five children on her own. If we employ him here at the Vill, she will at least have one less mouth to feed.'

'What do you think?' asked Osric, looking at Edward.

'I think the boy may struggle to manage at first,' noted Edward. 'But I would be happy to help him. After all, I first started tending to the King's horses at Winchester when I had but five years of age, albeit under the watchful eye of Old Colbert.'

'Then that's decided,' announced Osric. 'Ulrich, see the boy again and let's at least give him a chance to show us what he can do. After all, we have cause enough to remember that stable boys can sometimes prove very useful – even when it comes to a battle.'

Chapter Two

LATER THAT MORNING

Having finished his morning ride, Edward dismounted from Fleet whilst still in the pasture and, without bothering to tether him, removed his saddle and bridle. That done, he playfully chased the magnificent black stallion off, thereby allowing him to run free for the remainder of the day.

At Osric's suggestion, Oswald had ordered a member of the permanent guard to be stationed in the stabling area to keep watch in case another attempt was made on Edward's life. Edward acknowledged the man on duty then set about mucking out the stables and refilling the water troughs before wandering down to the quay where Sigbert was completing the repairs to the two captured longships.

'How was your ride?' asked Sigbert as Edward joined him.

The boy grinned. 'I'm sure Fleet gets faster every time I take him out.'

'Well, you take care. That wound to your shoulder you suffered during the battle wouldn't benefit much from you taking another fall.'

'It's all but healed,' Edward assured him. 'What have you left to do here?'

Sigbert pointed to the ship he was still working on. 'Some of the timbers in the hull of this one have been parted and there was damage to the prow of the other one,' he explained. 'I think there was some sort of incident as they were sailed back here after the battle.'

'But you can mend them?'

'I can mend anything,' boasted Sigbert, grinning. 'Besides, these ships are so well made they'll survive almost any amount of abuse.'

'Except being set afire,' mused Edward.

Sigbert recalled seeing the burning ship at the battle. 'Aye, that's true,' he acknowledged. 'Anything except being set on fire.'

'So what's left to be done?'

Sigbert explained that he needed to finish prising some of the overlapping strakes back into place, then secure them with rivets before filling any gaps with animal hair and sealing them with pitch. 'I've already repaired the one over there so I'll soon have them both as good as new, but the womenfolk will need to repair some rips to the sails. That's skilled handiwork which is well beyond my ability. We may also need to replace some of the rigging as some of it has seen better days.'

'That assumes they can find men who can sail them,' said Edward, recalling what had been said about that at the meeting earlier.

'Good point,' replied Sigbert. 'Personally, I'd rather keep both feet on dry land as I'm sure will most of the other members of the fyrd. Mind, some might see it as better than serving in the shield wall.'

With that, Edward noticed that Odelia had come down to the quay and seemed to be looking for him. He was surprised to notice that she no longer wore her hair tied back in plaits and had covered it with a headscarf, something her mother had probably insisted upon to signify that she was now of age. There was something else about her that was different but Edward could not decide what it was – she just seemed to carry herself in a way which made her look older than her years. When she saw him, she wandered across to join them.

'It's a nice day so I thought we might take a stroll beside the river if you have the time,' she said invitingly, her smile shyly betraying her true intent.

Sigbert waited to see how Edward would respond.

'I'd like that,' replied Edward.

'You just be careful if you do,' warned Sigbert, who was concerned as he'd been charged with ensuring Edward's safety. 'Just remember that you're supposed to stay within the confines of the settlement.'

'We weren't planning to cross the river,' said Edward defensively.

'Aye, well be that as it may, a good man with a bow could cut you down even from the far bank and be gone before anyone could stop him.'

'Don't worry, I'll be watchful,' he promised.

Sigbert glanced at Odelia then at Edward. 'Yes, but somehow I have a feeling that you'll both be all too easily distracted.'

*****

As they walked along a narrow path beside the river, Odelia seemed strangely quiet.

'What's wrong?' asked Edward.

'Nothing, it's just I hadn't realised that your life is still in so much danger.'

'Don't worry,' said Edward consolingly. 'My uncle will be far away from here if he has any sense. There's nothing for him in Wareham except perhaps a rope around his neck for having killed that assassin.'

'Is that true?' asked Odelia. 'My father doesn't seem to think so, nor my great uncle. They both fear he'll try again to kill you.'

'Let him try,' said Edward boldly. 'In fact, I rather wish he would.'

Odelia looked shocked. 'You mustn't say that!' she scolded.

'Why? I should like to meet him. I'm sure that if I did we could manage to reach some sort of arrangement whereby we share my fortune. From what Alfred has said, there's much more of it than I'm ever likely to need.'

With that they stopped beside a willow that was growing close to the water's edge and which they had come to regard as their "special place", being well away from the settlement yet close enough to ensure that he was not at undue risk. Nonetheless, despite his bravado, Edward kept the tree positioned between them and the far bank as he and Odelia embraced.

'So, what's to become of you?' she asked coyly. 'Will you remain here in Wareham once you are fully restored and receive your inheritance?'

'I'd like to,' said Edward. 'Although Alfred may have something to say about that. Presumably it will all depend on what lands he decides to award me.' Even as he spoke, he couldn't resist the chance to tease her. 'Of course, it will also depend on who I eventually marry. After all, as you once said,

I am now "eligible" and can therefore take my pick of all the beautiful ladies throughout the realm.'

Odelia frowned. 'Well, that may be so, although I doubt whether they'll be quite so keen to wed a boy who still smells of horse sweat all the time.' With that she got up and ran back along the path by which they'd come.

Edward caught her up just before they reached the quay and, as he turned her to face him, they kissed again, this time more passionately. For once, Odelia seemed not to care who saw them.

*****

WAREHAM FOREST

Set on the edge of an extensive open heath, the forest at Wareham had originally been vast but, over many years, had been gradually reduced in size to make way for land which could be used for grazing. Nonetheless, it remained as a large area of dense woodland, significant only because a well-used track which ultimately led to Winchester passed through it, thereby avoiding a much longer journey around the edge of it. The robbers had established their camp in one of the more remote parts of the forest so they could take advantage of unwary travellers.

Edmund couldn't help but be impressed with all he could see of their camp. He'd expected it to be a temporary site which could be hurriedly moved in the event of it being discovered or threatened, but soon realised it was a much more permanent arrangement. Looking around the clearing, he found that it was not unlike a small settlement with several more hovels than those he'd originally seen. None of them were substantial, being just big enough for one or perhaps two men to sleep in, plus there were some which had been abandoned, presumably because their occupants had died as the robbers wouldn't have risked allowing anyone to leave the band for fear of betrayal.

He also noticed that the wicker fence which encircled the camp was actually more like a barricade, being interwoven with thorns and brambles to make it difficult to breach. Several gaps had been left to afford access, although even those were closed off at night to ensure it presented a formidable barrier for the protection of all who resided within. Apart from that, the main focus was a large table where all the robbers took their meals together, seated on fallen logs which served as benches. There was also an open fire that was used for cooking set to one side of the table and carefully tended at all times lest the smoke from it betray their location.

All in all, it seemed that the robbers fared well enough. They drank water from a stream which passed through the camp and used the open shelter as a store to stockpile supplies and provisions – notably game, dried herbs and such like, plus several sacks of grain and the barrel which Edmund had seen when he first arrived and which he soon realised contained ale. The deer he'd seen being butchered was gone but its pelt had been scraped and was stretched out on one of several frames to dry, its antlers having no doubt been added to a small pile of others to one side.

So far as he could ascertain, two men were required to hunt and fish to feed them all, or were occasionally despatched to various local markets to secure what additional supplies were needed. All the others were set to the task of ensuring that any traveller passing through the forest was stopped and relieved of whatever he or she was carrying which might be of some worth or use. Edmund assumed he would be required to form part of the latter group but thus far had barely spoken to anyone.

'I've been here for several days now,' he complained aloud whilst seated at the large table with some of the others. 'Yet I don't even know your names.'

'That's as some of us would have it,' said Byram bluntly, answering for them all. 'Those who are happy for you to know who they are will doubtless introduce themselves in their own good time, but only once they're sure it's safe to do so.'

'For God's sake, what are you all so afraid of?' challenged Edmund.

'We none of us yet know you so, for now, it's safer that way,' advised Byram. 'After all, you can't betray a man you cannot name.'

'But I already know your name,' said Edmund pointedly.

Byram glared at the man who had given that away when they'd first met Edmund in the forest, but said nothing.

'I also know that you were probably once a warrior, although how well practised I couldn't say.'

Byram shrugged. 'Most able-bodied men can claim some combat skills as all are likely to have served in the fyrd at one time or another.'

'Yes, but as your hair is still braided, I fancy you were more than a man obliged to serve in the fyrd,' noted Edmund.

'How do you know I'm not still a warrior?' asked Byram.

Edmund wasn't sure how he could best answer that. 'I can tell that just by the company you keep,' he revealed in the end.

At that, all stopped what they were doing and were suddenly silent. Clearly offended, Byram, who always sat at the head of the table, got to his feet and walked around to the side where Edmund was seated and stood behind him, towering over him like a tree. 'So, what's wrong with the company I keep?' he demanded, his hand fingering the hilt of his seax.

Edmund knew better than to get up to confront him. 'Nothing,' he said weakly. 'It's just that in my experience, warriors keep the company of their own kind. Like birds of a feather, they roost together, and I see nothing to suggest that these rogues are warriors, nor ever have been. Mind, I'll confess that I've supped with worse company than this.'

Byram seemed to settle for that. 'Warriors they're not,' he acknowledged as he returned to his seat. 'But I rate these "rogues" as you call them to be better company than most. They've proved themselves to be true. Not to some rich lord or money-grabbing priest, but loyal to each other. And more importantly, loyal to me. I'd therefore take their company over any you're ever likely to come by.' With that, he sat down, his seax still undrawn.

'Yet they fear even to tell me their names?' pressed Edmund. 'I've not been shy in telling you mine, nor indeed about saying who I am or what I've done.'

At first no one spoke, then one of the men broke their silence. 'Some of us still have friends or kin living nearby, perhaps even in Wareham itself,' he explained. 'We fear lest by virtue of them knowing us they're put at risk; hence we keep our names to ourselves.'

Edmund hadn't thought of that. 'So how come you all live like this?' he asked.

'What other choice do we have?' said Byram. 'Most here are fugitives of one kind or another. Some have stolen to feed themselves and their family, others have committed more serious crimes which they dare not so much as mention. Here at least we all of us live as free men.'

'We do until we're caught,' quipped one of the others. 'Then we get to die as free men. And I can see little consolation in that!'

Edmund looked at each of them in turn. It was true that several of them bore scars. He'd already noticed that one of them had lost an eye and another a hand, although whether the latter was whilst serving in the fyrd or from an accident, a quarrel or even a punishment wasn't clear. Looking around, there was also a young boy who, although able to speak, seemed to have very little to say for himself.

'I assume you simply rob strangers for a living?' said Edmund.

'We're not averse to that,' admitted Byram. 'Although we don't rob all travellers. We tend not to trouble those who are bearing arms or are too well guarded.'

'I should have thought those were the very ones likely to be carrying something worth taking,' suggested Edmund.

'Perhaps, but like I told you, we don't do anything which is likely to bring the fyrd down upon us.'

One of the other men spoke up at that point. 'Aye, we steal where we can. But mostly we take what the forest provides and trade for whatever else we need. Unlike you, we none of us were high born to a life of wealth and privilege.'

'Perhaps not, but like I told you, I spent many more years than I care to remember as a slave to the Vikings,' said Edmund. 'That was a harsh life and having been "high born" made it even harder for me to endure than it was for others.'

'So, what did they have you do as a slave?' asked another man.

'I was lucky in that respect,' said Edmund. 'As the eldest son, I managed my father's estates so, once captured by the Vikings, I was taken overseas and put to work on a farmstead. Mostly I was set to hard graft such as ploughing, shovelling shit and digging latrines. In fact, anything which the Vikings didn't want to do themselves.'

'But you have more years under your belt than most of us,' noted Byram. 'So you can't have fared too badly or you'd have been dead long ago if, as you say, the work was so hard.'

'Exactly,' agreed Edmund. 'Most of the men taken when I was were sold abroad in the slave markets and died within months from being overworked, half-starved and harshly beaten. The women lasted an even shorter time. Some were traded many times and most were ill-used, including my sister who was put to work as a whore and died riddled with disease. I knew my time was growing short and that they'd kill me when I wasn't worth the cost of feeding, but instead they brought me here as they needed slaves to row their ships – men who they could afford to lose. Ship slaves seldom live very long, hence I took my chance to escape when it came.'

'How did you manage that if all the other members of the warband were killed?' queried Byram.

'I feigned an injury and held back whilst the rest of the greedy bastards tried to extract as much blood and booty as they could. The battle then turned against them and I simply retreated with the others and managed to climb aboard one of the ships. When that was set on fire I swam ashore where, as I told you, I revealed who I am to avoid being put to the sword.'

Well then, it's as well for us that you did,' said Byram, changing the tone of the conversation. 'For we all of us now have many years in which to enjoy our share of your wealth. Longer than you at any rate, or so it would seem given your age.'

Edmund smiled to himself. 'Perhaps,' he muttered quietly under his breath. 'But I wouldn't be too sure about that.'

*****

WAREHAM

'Well, it's all right for some,' teased Sigbert when Edward returned to the quay. 'Whilst the rest of us work for our living it seems others have the time enough to go courting.'

Edward looked surprised. 'We weren't…'

'Weren't what?' asked Sigbert, still teasing him.

Edward looked away shyly. 'You know,' said Edward.

'Aye, well maybe I don't. See, I never was much of a one for the ladies.'

'Nor me,' admitted Edward. 'I mean, just as I think I know what's expected she either cajoles me for being too reticent or tells me off for moving too fast.'

Sigbert laughed. 'Like I say, I can't help you much in matters of the heart.'

They walked back together towards the stables which Edward had asked Sigbert to look at with a view to possibly extending if and when they acquired more horses. When they got there, he started by pacing out the existing building to get a rough estimate of its size, then examined it closely to see how it had been constructed. 'It's not an easy job,' he announced once he'd looked it over. 'If we enlarge the building we'll have to extend the main roof as well. That will take men and resources that I fear we don't have at present.'

'Would it be easier to build a rough shelter within the pasture instead?' suggested Edward. 'We could then keep the horses belonging to Governor Osric and Oswald in these stables together with Fleet and perhaps even the new farm horses if and when we get them. The rest are likely to be horses rounded up and taken from the moors, so they'll be accustomed to staying out in all weathers.'

'That could be done,' agreed Sigbert. 'I'll assess what's likely to be needed.'

As they spoke, Fleet was getting very friendly with a bay mare, one of the two horses that had survived the battle.

'And there's the answer to what you were asking about earlier,' remarked Sigbert. 'That mare seems as much set on what will transpire as is the stallion! With horses as with other creatures, there's none of this playing hard to get that we mere men have to put up with if we're minded to go courting!'

Edward was well used to seeing a stallion selecting a mare, pursuing and then mounting her but, for some reason, had not made the connection between that and his courtship of Odelia. 'You mean that's what…' he stopped short of saying more.

Sigbert grinned broadly. He realised then that with no friends of his own age to confide in nor parents who might have explained things to him, Edward had no idea about such matters. 'Aye lad,' he said kindly, putting his hand on the boy's shoulder. ''Tis the same for us as it is for horses and for every other creature under God's heaven. A little more gentle perhaps, but it's basically the same.'

'I'm not even sure I know what... you know, what a man and a woman are wont to "do" together.'

'I can see we're going to have set things to rights in that respect,' said Sigbert. 'I know of a woman who, for a few coins, will teach you much more than I could even begin to tell you. I'll take you to see her if you like.'

'Will you?' asked Edward excitedly.

'Aye. And from what I see of things between you and Odelia, the sooner the better, although I'd need to secure Oswald's permission before doing so. He may not like the idea of his daughter's suitor consorting with a whore.'

*****

WAREHAM FOREST

After supper that evening, Byram took Edmund aside to speak with him.

'You must understand that these are all desperate men. They do what they do here to feed themselves, but the shadow of the noose hangs over us all every day of our lives.'

Edmund nodded to show that he understood that only too well. 'So, where did you all go to earlier?' he asked, wondering why he hadn't been asked to join them and had been set to chopping firewood instead.

'Most of the men went hunting and foraging. You weren't invited as you don't yet know the forest well enough and I wouldn't want you to get lost, not with so much riding on keeping you alive long enough to claim your inheritance.'

'But you didn't go with them either?' said Edmund.

'No, instead I went to meet a "friend" – he told me that there's a priest headed this way who will likely pass through the forest sometime tomorrow.'

'And you plan to rob this priest?'

'No, not on this occasion,' said Byram. 'I plan for you to rob him. I warned you that you'll need to earn your keep and now is the time for you to show us what you can do.'

Edmund was not particularly perturbed by that. 'And is this priest travelling alone?' he asked.

'No, I'm told he'll have a guard with him, so you'll need to know what you're about. I and two others will wait nearby in case things don't go as planned.'

'I take it you have other "friends" who keep a lookout for likely targets such as this priest?' ventured Edmund.

'Aye, but as to who they are is a matter only for me. All you need to know is that their information is usually sound.'

'How does that work?' asked Edmund, genuinely impressed by how well organised the band was.

'Suffice to say that they tell me all I need to know and, in particular, warn me about the ones we should avoid, either because it's thought that they're not carrying anything of worth or because they're too well armed or protected.'

'But how do you know where and when to strike?'

'That's easy enough. No traveller will want to spend the night in the forest unless he has to for fear of wild beasts, so they time their journey to start as early as they can manage. The fools who travel from Winchester or are returning from there tend to keep to the main track because they think it's safer. Obviously, we wouldn't want to disabuse them of that.'

Edmund saw the funny side of that. 'So, when will we take this priest?'

'Tomorrow. It'll take him several hours to get to where we normally intercept travellers, but we'll be in place before he does. Then all we have to do is wait.'

*****

WAREHAM

Sigbert waited outside the Vill where he'd gone to report progress on repairing the ships to Oswald. When at last he was shown through, he was obliged to remain standing even though he was a much-respected and senior member of the fyrd, and also well thought of enough to have been assigned to the important task of looking out for Edward.

'So are the ships now fully repaired?' asked Oswald as he hobbled towards a chair, the wound to his leg which he'd sustained from an arrow during the battle still causing him pain.

'Aye, sir. Both are now seaworthy, although personally I wouldn't want to venture too far from land in either of them.'

'We won't have to,' Oswald advised him. 'It's been decided that this is not the best location for them to be moored. More likely they'll be taken to one of the settlements which has direct access to the open sea where they will be of more strategic value.'

'That's probably as well,' agreed Sigbert. 'We don't have men here who have any experience of fighting at sea.'

'Exactly. Although I had hoped we could train enough members of the resident fyrd to keep at least one ship here.'

'Well, sir, if it helps, I know of two fishermen who live not far along the coast who might be tasked to teach us how to handle the ships,' he offered.

'My uncle would like that, but I've told him it's not yet a feasible option. What we need are smaller, faster vessels. If I can organise that, would you then be inclined to be one of those who sail in them?' asked Oswald. 'To have a carpenter on board who could carry out any immediate repairs would be useful, particularly as you also happen to be one of our best bowmen.'

'Sir, I have duties enough already,' replied Sigbert as tactfully as he could. 'As you know, I've also been charged to look out for young Edward. I can hardly do that if I'm at sea.'

Oswald acknowledged the point. 'Do you want me to inspect the ships?' he asked, realising that Sigbert was waiting as if expecting something more.

'No, sir, not unless you have a mind to. The repairs were simple enough. I would leave it to those who are to sail them to ask for any further work or improvements they feel are needed. Mind, I reckon some of the ropes and the sails may need repairing. Perhaps you could have the womenfolk look them over?'

'Then is there something else you wanted to discuss with me?'

'There is,' said Sigbert tentatively. 'A somewhat delicate matter.'

'Well, get on with it, man.'

'Sir, young Edward seems keen on your daughter and I believe he has already suggested courtship.'

'He has. What of it?'

'He is a boy who knows nothing of the ways of men. I think your daughter might thank you for letting him learn a little of such matters should they ever desire to wed.'

Oswald was not quite sure what he was saying, then suddenly caught on. 'You mean…'

'Aye, sir. That's exactly what I mean. He's lived all his life as a stable boy so, with neither father nor friends to guide him, has no idea what might eventually be expected of him in that respect. I could take him to see the whore who resides near the north bridge if you like. She could teach him what's what as I'll warrant she's done with others before.'

At that, Oswald looked bemused and in no small way offended. 'You would have a whore teach him how to despoil my daughter!' he stormed. 'I should have you flogged for even suggesting it!'

'Sir, that's not what I meant. I would have the whore serve to satisfy his manly urges and his curiosity. Perhaps he would then find it easier to respect your daughter, particularly if it was made clear to him that he should treat her "differently", despite what he learns from the whore.'

Oswald calmed down long enough to see the sense of what Sigbert was suggesting. 'Perhaps you're right,' he managed at last. 'But I'd have you go with him. He's still much at risk so you must remain on guard outside at all times whilst he's there. I don't want to report to the King that his newly created noble was murdered whilst in our care, particularly whilst visiting a whore!'

'So, do I have your permission?' pressed Sigbert.

'Aye, you do,' he said somewhat reluctantly, then took some coins from his purse. 'This should suffice to cover the cost but I would have Edward speak with me first, just to make sure that he knows that my daughter's reputation must remain intact, particularly given what tricks and notions he's likely to learn from a whore.'

Chapter Three

Edward went to the stables early the following morning intending to ride Fleet but, when he arrived, he was surprised to find Ulrich already there together with a young boy of scarce seven or eight years of age.

'Caelin is to be our new stable boy,' explained Ulrich. 'Although as you know, he has no experience of such work.'

Edward was surprised to see how small and slight the boy was, so much so that he was sure the lad would struggle to manage much of what he'd be required to do. 'So Caelin, do you know anything about looking after horses?' he asked.

The boy was slow to answer. 'No, sir,' he said, his voice not much more than a whisper.

'Speak up boy,' insisted Ulrich. 'Have you nothing more to say for yourself?'

Caelin seemed almost too frightened to answer.

'Can you at least ride?' asked Edward.

Clearly afraid to admit as much, Caelin simply shook his head.

'Then we'll have to teach you,' said Edward trying to reassure him. With that, he took Ulrich aside. 'This is not going to be easy,' he told the Reeve. 'He can probably clean the stables and put out feed and water and suchlike, but he's going to need help with the heavier work.'

'I'm sorry,' said Ulrich. 'I know he's not well suited to the job but he's all we have given that all the men have other duties or are needed elsewhere. Besides, as you'll recall, we're obliged to find him something to do in order to help ease the plight of his poor mother.'

'He'll be fine,' Edward assured the Reeve. 'As I told you yesterday, I was even younger than him when I started work as the stable boy at Winchester. And there were many more horses there than the few we have here at present.'

'But how will he manage?'

'He won't, at least, not on his own. As I said at the meeting yesterday, I'll have to help him for now and perhaps we can then find someone to do the heavier work once this threat of an invasion has passed.'

'Thank you,' said Ulrich, clearly relieved. 'I've told him to make his bed here and arranged for him to eat with the other servants. May I leave you to outline his various duties?'

Edward agreed and set about that at once. 'Well Caelin, let's see if we can make a proper stable boy of you.' So saying, he put his hand on the boy's shoulder and took him into the stables so he could meet the horses. 'We'll start by letting them all out into the pasture and then we'll put out water and also feed for them. We keep them unbridled in their stalls so all you have to do is open the doors and they'll go out of their own accord when they're ready, but make sure the gate to the pasture is then closed behind them. We don't want them running loose about the settlement.'

'Sir, why do we put out feed if they have all that grass to eat?'

It was a good question and Edward was impressed that the boy should raise it. 'Because the grass would soon become depleted if we didn't,' he explained. 'Next, I want you to use that shovel to start picking out the horse shit from the straw in the stables. Put it in a pail and tip it onto that muck pile over there. It'll then be used by the farm who will send a cart to collect it from time to time. When you've finished that, put down a few handfuls of fresh straw and I'll be back later to see how you've managed.'

*****

WAREHAM FOREST

Although the forest was quite densely packed with trees, there were many small clearings which had been formed when a larger one had fallen, thereby disturbing much of what was growing around it. There was thus only limited cover for a group of men such as that led by Byram who were seeking to conceal themselves. Nonetheless, Edmund, together with Byram and two others, hid themselves as best they could beside the main track and waited for the priest and his escort to appear.

'They'll be travelling by cart as the Church doesn't waste its money on extravagant transport for ordinary priests,' explained Byram. 'All it can extract from the poor deluded fools who are in fear for their souls is needed just to line the pockets of the senior clergy.'

Edmund scoffed. 'So, I take it you're not well disposed towards our so-called holy men?'

'Oh, I like them well enough, particularly those who travel through my forest whilst carrying a few precious relics or, better still, a purse filled with silver. But these "holy men" as you call them are devious bastards, well adept at relieving the people of their hard-earned coin – but in return for what? A few mumblings and empty promises of salvation in the life to come? In fact, come to think of it, we could learn a thing or two from them about thieving.'

It wasn't long before the boy from the camp, who had been posted a little further along the track to keep watch, returned to say that the priest was on his way.

'Here,' said Byram, handing Edmund a spear. 'I assume you know how to use one of these?'

Edmund looked at the weapon disdainfully. 'Being of noble birth, I was trained to fight with a sword,' he complained.

'Well, we don't have any of those so you'd best do what you can with a spear. Do you know what you have to do?'

'I assume I just step out and tell them to hand over their coin or whatever else they're carrying?'

'That's about the way of it.'

'So, I'm on my own?' noted Edmund, trying to hide his concern. 'What do I do if they resist?'

'Don't worry, they won't. Priests are easy pickings and the guard won't risk his neck for it's not his property you'll be stealing. But we'll be ready to step in if needed.'

As the small party rounded the bend, Edmund could see that, as predicted by Byram, it comprised just two men – a fat priest who was seated in the cart, moaning and complaining loudly about the state of the track, and his only guard who walked ahead of him.

'That's not even a proper guard,' sneered Byram dismissively. 'It's just some ruffian he's hired to escort him.'

'Perhaps, but he's armed nonetheless,' said Edmund, noting that the man had a seax tucked into his belt.

As they made their way towards where Edmund and the others waited, the guard was trying to ignore the priest's protestations and grumblings so was paying little mind to their path, thus he seemed not to notice as Edmund stepped out to block their way. When he did finally look up, he immediately realised what was happening. 'Step aside and let us pass!' he demanded, fumbling as he drew the seax, then anxiously looked about him as if expecting there to be others with Edmund as well.

The priest seemed unafraid at first. 'Get out of our way, you idle wretch!' he shouted. 'I'm here on God's work so it'll count as a sin if you detain us.'

Edmund laughed. 'But then Father, are we not all of us miserable sinners? If so, another stain on my soul won't count for much when I stand before St Peter to be judged.'

At that, the priest seemed to realise his predicament. 'What do you want with us!' he demanded.

'Well, what have you got?' asked Edmund.

'Nothing for you, you idle wastrel. So, leave us be.'

'I would if I could, Father, but you see it troubles me that you carry such a heavy purse and, being the good Christian that I am, I should like to ease your burden if I may.'

With that the guard stepped forward and closed on Edmund, his blade poised and ready. 'You insolent bastard! You'll have first to treat with me,' he challenged, making it clear that despite what Byram had said, he was prepared to defend his charge.

Edmund didn't hesitate. Using his spear like a staff, he knocked the guard's weapon aside then, without saying so much as a word, brutally stabbed him in the belly, driving the point of his spear home as hard as he could, twisting the shaft and then withdrawing it. It all happened so fast that the guard could scarce believe it. Clutching his wound, he looked down at the blood which was welling out from between his fingers, then sank to his knees before folding forward to lay face down on the muddy track. His body was still twitching as he endured his final agonies, groaning with the pain until finally still.

'I'll ensure you rot in hell for that!' screamed the priest, distressed by what he'd seen.

'Don't worry, my place in hell is already assured,' said Edmund. 'It's my time on this Earth which concerns me. So, let's see what you have in your cart which may make my remaining time here a little easier to endure.'

'Like I said, there's nothing here for a wretch like you!' protested the priest.

'We'll see about that. Now get down from the cart – unless of course you'd like me to help you with that?'

Trembling, the priest did as Edmund ordered but, with his bloated body and short fat legs, he struggled to climb down on his own. Once he'd managed it, he handed over his purse. When Edmund looked inside to see what the purse contained, he found nothing more than a few coins, none of them of significant value. Instinct told him there had to be more to justify employing the guard, therefore, although disappointed, he went to the back of the cart and raked through the few odds and ends which had been placed there. There was precious little of interest other than a beautiful reliquary, the lid and sides of which had been decorated with a relief in silver depicting scenes from the Bible. It had been draped in a green silken cloth which Edmund carefully removed before opening the casket to reveal a small shard of ageing bone which had been placed inside.

'That's a bone from the finger of none other than Saint Augustine himself, one of our most revered saints,' protested the priest. 'I'm taking it as a gift from my bishop to the Minster of the Lady St Mary at Wareham.' He seemed to think that would be enough to dissuade Edmund from taking it but, if so, he was mistaken.

'Then I'd best make sure that it reaches the Minster safely,' teased Edmund, then wrapped it in the cloth again and put it down on the ground to one side of him.

'It's a holy relic and not intended for the likes of you!'

'The likes of me? And what makes you think you're more "holy" than I am?'

'Because I'm a man of the cloth,' intoned the priest. 'Can you not see as much for yourself or are you blind?'

'Ah, a man of the cloth is it?' queried Edmund. 'Then no wonder you have such a fine cloak and robes. Perhaps it's best you give me them as well.'

'What do you mean?

'I mean that I want you to give me the very clothes from your back. Dirty and soiled they may be from your journey, but they must be worth more than the miserly contents of this purse. I'm not best pleased with such meagre pickings and am bound to think that you may be carrying something of more significant worth.'

For a moment the priest could hardly believe what he was hearing but, with that, Edmund used the blunt end of the spear shaft to prod him in the belly, albeit not hard enough to cause more than a bruise.

'Get them off!' ordered Edmund. 'I want every stitch. If you're too shy to remove them I can do it for you, but I would first need to kill you and it would be a shame to despoil them with even your no doubt holy blood.'

Red faced with embarrassment, the priest started to do as Edmund had ordered, carefully laying each item of clothing over the rail of the cart to avoid getting them dirty. Eventually he had stripped off everything and stood there, completely naked.

Edmund found that amusing but had watched carefully enough to know that one of the robes contained something more. He rifled through the pile of clothing until he found what he was looking for – another purse which had been stitched into the hem of his outer robe. He ripped the stitching apart and held up the purse for the priest to see. 'There,' he said, sounding very pleased with himself. 'I think you'll find it much easier to travel from here without having to carry this and worrying about being beset by thieves.' He then peered inside the purse and found that it contained a dozen coins, the value of which still didn't amount to a hugely significant sum but was a reasonable haul nonetheless. 'There's so little here that I think I best have that ring you have on your finger as well if only to make robbing you worth my while. And, whilst we're about it, I'll have the gold cross you wear around your neck.'

The priest was visibly shaking as he tried to pull the ring from his podgy finger, clearly in fear for his life. Once he'd done so, Edmund then examined the robes more closely. 'No wonder you call yourself a man of the cloth,' he joked holding up one item of clothing. 'There's enough of it in this garment alone to clothe two men and still have some left over.'

The priest scowled as he tried to cover himself with his hands as best he could.

'Right, now get back in the cart. You can ride bare-arsed to Wareham from here – or walk if you prefer. Either way you can finish your journey as you came into this world – as naked as Adam and Eve in the Garden of Eden. But don't worry, we'll find your guard a nice quiet grave somewhere in this forest. You can pray for him when you reach Wareham, although I fancy you'll find it best to borrow some robes before doing so as I'm not sure how the good people there will welcome a naked priest into their midst. Now be on your way before I change my mind and send you to meet your maker instead.'

'You wretch! You'll burn in the fires of hell for this!'

'Aye, well that's as maybe,' acknowledged Edmund. 'But I reckon you thieving bastards who screw everything you can from the poor in return for nothing but a few worthless promises will be roasting beside me soon enough.'

Still naked, the priest clambered inelegantly back into the cart, took up the reins and then urged the horse to move off. As soon as he was gone from sight, Byram stepped out from the trees together with the two other men and the boy. All except Byram had clearly found the whole episode highly amusing.

'You fool!' scolded Byram, ignoring the others. 'I told you, we don't kill travellers here for fear of repercussions!'

'Yes, I recall you did say that,' admitted Edmund calmly. 'But I couldn't risk him taking me on for, like I told you, I'd have been no match for him using a spear. Besides, I was beginning to enjoy myself.'

'Well, you can enjoy yourself all the more by burying the poor sod you've killed. But dig deep, we don't want his body to be unearthed by wolves. Strip him first of anything we can use. And bring that seax he was using. As for the spear I gave you, you can keep that for yourself, although for all our sakes, I'd suggest that you get one of the men to show you how best to use it.'

*****

WAREHAM

Having shown Caelin what needed to be done at the stables, there was no time for Edward to ride Fleet that morning. He therefore went next to the Minster where he found Father Emmett who had been charged with teaching him how to read and write. The Minster was one of the few places it was felt would be safe enough for him to visit without a guard, particularly as it was so close to both the nunnery and the quay, and also not too far from the Vill itself.

It was Edward's fourth lesson but they'd got no further than the basics and already he was finding it hard. Having never been required to formally study anything before, to him it all seemed an almost pointless effort.

'Ah,' said Father Emmett. 'There you are at last. I'll start today by reading aloud from the scriptures as at least you'll then already know the stories by heart so will be able to follow them in the Latin text more easily.'

Edward looked bewildered. He'd had nothing in the way of spiritual guidance and had never been to Church except for funerals, and even they had been held mostly at the graveside.

'Surely you know your Bible?' pressed Father Emmett.

Edward shook his head. 'No one thought that a stable boy would ever have need of it,' he explained.

'We all of us have need of it,' Father Emmett assured him. 'And more often than you might think, for it teaches us so much about what we need to do in order to live our lives as God intended. Besides, I have it on good authority that your father was a spiritual man and even trained as a monk when he was about your age. Did he not instruct you in these matters?'

'I never knew my father,' said Edward feeling embarrassed.

Father Emmett then recalled all that which Governor Osric had explained to him about the boy. 'Then we must needs set that to rights,' he announced, delighted at the prospect of having every reason for preaching to Edward and, in his somewhat naive view of things, thereby saving an otherwise neglected soul.

*****

Having spent almost the entire morning being lectured to and cajoled by Father Emmett, Edward was delighted to escape and went straight to find Sigbert. When he did, his friend advised him that Commander Oswald wanted to see him.

'I expect that'll be about the horses,' said Edward.

Sigbert didn't attempt to correct him but knew well enough that what Oswald had to say would both surprise Edward and almost certainly embarrass him.

It took a little while to find Oswald but he eventually managed to locate him at the Vill where he was working on what he planned for the next training session of the fyrd. He greeted Edward warmly enough and showed him what he was intending to do. 'As you've no doubt gathered, without more horses the elite squad cannot be used to deal with any raids beyond this settlement. We'll therefore revert to the old way, although I grant you it had been found woefully wanting in many respects. For that, we'll need to get you some war gear.'

'Will I then need it?' asked Edward, not keen on the implications of that.

'Aye, as like as not you will. There was a lot of gear stripped from the bodies of the Vikings we slew, so I'll see what we can do to get you properly equipped. Mind, most of the mail vests will be much too big; I'll have the blacksmith adapt one to ensure it's a better fit.'

'Thank you,' said Edward. 'Although I don't think a mail vest would be ideal to wear whilst riding. I need to be able to move more freely than it will allow.'

'Well, it will be a good while before we can replace the horses so, until then, you'll need to fight on foot like all the other men. In the meantime, I'm calling for a training session for the resident fyrd for tomorrow.'

'Is that so we can do more practice for fighting in the shield wall?' asked Edward, not relishing the prospect.

'Of course,' said Oswald. 'But you'll be pleased to know that as a nobleman you won't be required to serve there; rather you'll stand behind it to relay any instructions and messages between me and the men actually fighting.'

Edward acknowledged that gratefully, feeling that he'd never contributed much to the shield wall anyway and could well remember the first time he'd been part of one – and the mayhem which had followed when he tripped and fell.

'I shall also teach you more about swordcraft as I gather Lord Alfred will soon be sending your family sword for you to use.'

'Yes, but I don't know when that will be,' Edward advised him. 'He implied he would first need to return to Winchester to collect it but, from what Governor Osric has said, I assume he'll be obliged to remain in Exeter for the time being at least.'

'Then I'll lend you one of ours to practise with. Now, have you thought any more about how to replace the horses we lost in the battle?' he asked. 'I'm keen to restore my elite squad as soon as I can.'

'Yes,' said Edward. 'Once free of this threat from the Viking fleet, I could take a small group of men to round up what we'll need from the moors. I'll then help the men to train them to the saddle and the bridle.'

'And where will you keep them?' asked Oswald.

'They'll be used to being out all weathers, so can be left loose in the pasture,' suggested Edward. 'That means we won't need to extend the stables, but I'd like to provide some sort of shelter for them.'

Oswald considered that. 'The settlement here is spared most of the really cold weather but, if you say a shelter is needed, that's good enough for me.'

'Thank you. I was also going to ask Governor Osric for permission to improve the area where the new stable boy sleeps. At present its damp and open to the weather.'

Oswald seemed none too interested in that. 'Very well,' he said. 'But is the stable boy up to the task of looking after the horses?'

'Not as yet, but I'll be happy to help him for now. I'll show him what's what, but we'll need someone else to work with him, particularly once we get more horses.'

'Ah,' said Oswald. 'Speaking of knowing what's what, I gather Sigbert is taking you with him tonight so that we can make a proper man of you?'

Edward was embarrassed. 'Yes, but…'

'Don't worry, it's only right that you should know what transpires between a man and a woman, and who better to teach you than one who surely knows the way of it? But you must remember that what you learn there is not something you can share with my daughter.'

Edward had only a vague idea of what he was talking about as he had thought that was the sole purpose for him going there.

'You must give me your word that you will continue to treat Odelia with the respect a lady in her position is entitled to expect. If not, you'll have me to answer to. Do I make myself clear?'

Edward nodded although was still confused.

'I'm sending you there for good reason. Think of it as like breaking in a horse. At first you'll be allowed to succumb to your wildest ways but, once trained and schooled, you'll know how best to treat a lady.'

*****

WAREHAM FOREST

Once back at their camp within the forest, Byram called his band of men together and emptied both the purses which Edmund had taken from the priest out onto the table. All told, it didn't amount to much but, as was their way, a share was first set aside for food and payments to their various informants and the remainder then distributed between them so that everyone got a share, including Edmund. Inevitably, Byram got the largest share whilst the boy, Iden, was given little more than a token for acting as their lookout.

'What about the reliquary, the ring and the crucifix, not to mention all the robes the priest was wearing?' asked Edmund, partly to ensure that everyone was reminded that the haul was better than it seemed.

'Each of us can take what robes they would find useful. The rest will be unstitched and cut up to be sold as cloth,' said Byram. 'They're of good quality so should be worth something. The crucifix we'll give to you as a reward for your part in securing the spoils. Hopefully it'll help to redeem your soul from all the killing you've done of late.'

As the others laughed, Byram held up the ring, which looked to be quite valuable. 'This I shall keep for myself,' he announced. 'For it looks well enough on my finger. The reliquary I'll place in our store for we dare not try to sell it just yet lest it be recognised.'

That all made sense and the band settled down for the afternoon. With Edmund having proven his commitment, all of them seemed a little easier in his presence. Even so, he went to sit a little way apart from the others, preferring to keep his own company whilst he considered the implications of robbing the priest who he feared would describe him to the authorities at Wareham. His main concern was that Osric would recognise him from that and thereby know where he was hiding.

Despite what Byram had said about not using names, Edmund decided that, for his own protection, he should now learn as much about the other members of the band as he could. He had heard some of the men call the boy by the name of "Iden". From what he'd gleaned, the lad was an orphan who seldom seemed to speak, although was not actually mute.

The woman who attended to their needs in terms of food and suchlike seemed to have no fear of allowing him to know her name and had readily introduced herself as 'Winifrid'. She was about his age and therefore older than the rest of the robbers and he noticed that she received a small part of the "spoils" for looking after them all, which seemed only fair. Although of a jovial nature, she was quick to speak her mind and, unlike most of the men who seemed to be in awe of Byram, quite ready to rebuke or correct him if she saw fit, sometimes sharply, having no regard for her lowly station within the band.

The only other person Edmund knew anything about was the monk. He was called Brother Linton and, whilst an odd character who played no part in the robberies, he seemed to have his own views about how a monk should behave – paying little mind to the strictures of his calling.

'You seem well set here,' said Edmund, when Byram came across to speak with him, thereby interrupting his thoughts.

'Aye, we fare well enough,' replied Byram. 'We look out for each other and use what skills we have for the benefit of us all.'

'So, having now killed on their behalf, have I yet done enough to at least know their names?' asked Edmund.

Byram thought hard before he answered. 'Perhaps you have,' he said at last, then sat down beside Edmund. 'But first you must tell me what you did after you left Wareham. By my reckoning it was several days before you reached us here, in the forest.'

'Ah,' said Edmund. 'Well, having killed the assassin, I left Wareham in haste via the west gates as that was the quickest way for me to escape and avoided me having to pass through where Alfred's men were still camped at that time. To get past the guards at the bridge, I mingled with a crowd of others and then simply followed the road. I was seeking somewhere I could hide but, finding nowhere I could be sure I'd be safe, I decided to join you instead.'

Byram seemed satisfied with that. 'Very well, then I'll tell you what you need to know about the others here. As you've probably already learned, the boy is called Iden. He's an orphan although we know little more about him than that. He arrived one day seeking food and shelter and has never left.'

'He follows that giant like a shadow,' observed Edmund. 'Not surprisingly given that the fellow's as tall as a tree and looks to be as strong as an ox!'

'You mean Oswin? He's actually a good-natured soul and not near as fearsome as he appears. He was a labourer who fell on hard times but also has other skills, most of which he learned for himself. In fact, he built most of what you see here,' he added, his hand sweeping round to indicate the various buildings which formed the camp. 'I think he has family in one of the settlements nearby but won't say which one. In fact, I doubt that 'Oswin' is even his real name. I always jest and say that if he doesn't tell me who he really is he could well be buried with the wrong name above his grave, but that doesn't seem to trouble him unduly.'

'What of the man who has but one eye?' asked Edmund.

'He goes by the name of Godwin. He lost his eye in a scuffle whilst stealing bread. He would have been punished as well if they'd caught him so he joined us instead. All told, it was a heavy price to pay for trying to feed his family, was it not?'

'The one with the long black hair looks as if he could be a Viking. I've seen his type many times before and know better than to trust them.'

'Aye, well all I can say is that he calls himself Radnor or something like it. We believe he was wounded and left behind after the Vikings raided a farmstead somewhere north of here and somehow managed to survive his many wounds. He doesn't speak our tongue but seems to understand enough of what we say to know what we're about.'

'And the other one who came with you today?' asked Edmund.

'That's Cedric, a forester by trade but, more importantly, he's an expert bowman whose aim is as good as any I've ever seen. He jests that you should never fear a good bowman, for if he kills you it'll be because he means to. It's the man who is not so skilled you should be wary of, for he's likely to kill you by mistake.'

That just leaves the man with one hand.'

Byram nodded. 'Ah yes, poor Duncan. He was a potter by trade and a good one by all accounts, but his tale is not a pretty one. He cruelly lost his hand whilst serving in the fyrd but it's not something he ever wishes to speak of. Obviously, he can no longer ply his trade but does what he can, although frankly that doesn't amount to very much. By rights we shouldn't let him stay here but…'

'So, a motley band if ever there was one. But what do you do for women here?' asked Edmund, keen to continue the conversation and learn as much as he could about the way of things within the camp. Also, it had been a long time since he'd had the company of a woman, for although the Viking raiders had raped several during his time with them, as a slave he was not given the chance to take his turn before the poor woman was either killed or, more usually, took her own life.

'We fare well enough in that respect,' said Byram.

Edmund looked at him coldly, then at Winifrid.

'No, not her, you fool!' laughed Byram. 'Although feel free if you are so minded. But if I was you I'd wait a day or two longer. There's a whore in Wareham who takes it upon herself to visit us from time to time and look to our needs in that respect. She comes with her much younger sister, but I warn you not to make the mistake of thinking she is also free with her favours. The two of them are as different as chalk and cheese in that and in other ways as well.'

'What do you mean?'

'Hild is a willing whore, as plump and jovial as her sister is thin and mean. She sees no sin in plying her trade whereas Mayda will have nothing to do with men. In truth, she's like a little vixen when roused and once held a knife to a man's groin just for trying to persuade her to lay with him whilst he waited for Hild to finish with another man. By all accounts she pressed the blade home so hard that he was lucky not to lose his manhood!'

'Then why does she come?' asked Edmund.

'She looks to her sister's needs in more ways than one.'

At first Edmund wasn't sure what Byram meant by that but then realised. 'Oh, I see. She's of that persuasion.'

'Is that surprising given that she sees all her sister is obliged to endure?'

Edmund shrugged. 'Either way it's of no concern to me so long as they can both be trusted for I'd as soon that no one knows that I'm here.'

'It's a bit late for that,' said Byram. 'By the time that priest tells all at Wareham about what happened to his guard, everyone will know exactly where you are. Mind, they'll still have trouble finding you, so you've nothing to fear unless we betray you.'

Edmund then realised that Byram had known all along that the priest's guard would resist and that he'd be forced to kill him. Having done so, any thoughts Edmund might have about betraying them were lost, for if he did, he'd be hanged for murder along with them all. 'I take it that was your plan from the start, was it not?' challenged Edmund.

'What do you mean?' asked Byram feigning innocence.

'All that crap about not killing men without good cause, you knew I'd have to kill that guard.'

Byram smiled knowingly as if to confirm the point. 'Let's just say I knew that if what you'd said about being high born was true, you'd have little skill with a spear because you'd not have been trained to use one. I also knew that even a ruffian would spot that weakness in a moment and try your hand. Which is exactly what happened. Obviously, you couldn't risk him getting the better of you so had no option but to kill the bastard before he killed you.'

'Then it seems I'm now committed to you and to this band whether I like it or not,' mused Edmund, realising he'd misjudged Byram who he now knew to be as artful as a fox.

'And there was me thinking that you were always committed to us and are here for the pleasure of our company. Just as you're committed to sharing your vast fortune with us all.'

Edmund had nothing more he could say about that and so changed the subject. 'How can you be so sure these two women you mentioned can be trusted?'

'Don't worry. They'll both keep a still tongue in their head for if they betray us, they'd have to watch their mother swing from a rope alongside the rest of us.'

'Why, who's their mother?' he asked.

'That old wanton crone over there you seem to have taken such a fancy to. Winifrid is mother to them both, though I warrant they don't share the same father.'

Chapter Four

WAREHAM FOREST

All at Byram's camp seemed to be in good spirits as they sat around the table partaking of an early supper. The fare on offer was basic but plentiful, including a large crust of bread each and as many bowls of venison stew as they could manage. As they ate, Cedric once more recounted how Edmund had robbed the priest and killed his guard even though all within the camp had no doubt heard the story several times already.

'The fat bastard was made to strip stark bollock naked and then travel like that all the way to Wareham!' he said, laughing loudly.

All there enjoyed the humour until Byram stepped in. 'Edmund did well enough,' he announced sounding serious. 'At least he had the nous to realise that the priest had more coin about his person, albeit hidden within the hem of his outer robe. But think on this: once word of the guard having been killed gets out, every traveller from now on will be minded to seek protection before venturing into this forest and likely be carrying arms. That's not good news for us and, what's worse, Edmund may well have done enough to bring the fyrd down upon us all. At the very least it means that we must now lie low for a while so as to allow things to settle. Hopefully, if the fyrd are dispatched, we'll hear about it soon enough, in which case we'll have to leave this camp and go to the glade.'

'What the hell is the glade?' queried Edmund.

'It's a clearing where we go to if we're expecting trouble or if the fyrd are getting too close for comfort,' explained Byram. 'It offers little in the way of comfort, but it's even deeper within this forest and is therefore even more difficult to find than our camp here.'

'So where is this place?'

'Don't worry. If we need to go there we'll take you with us, but you'll be blindfolded if we do.'

Edmund realised he was not going to be told anything more. 'I wouldn't worry,' he said trying to assuage their concerns. 'The man I killed was not even a proper guard, he was just some worthless wretch posing as one. Those at Wareham won't give his loss so much as a second thought.'

'That's true enough,' agreed Cedric. 'But what about the priest? Will he not try to stir up trouble? After all, he'll prize his dignity over the death of some hired ruffian. What's more, arriving in Wareham without so much as a rag with which to preserve his modesty will hardly impress the good people there or enhance his reputation!'

Most of the men found that amusing but Byram remained anxious about what he saw as the real problem. 'Cedric is right,' he warned. 'Thus we may not have heard the last of this so can't afford to relax our guard even for a moment.'

'Then perhaps I should have killed the priest as well?' said Edmund. 'If I had, we could have buried him with the other poor wretch and no one would be any the wiser.'

'If you had, you'd have needed to dig a much bigger grave for that fat bastard,' quipped Godwin.

At that, even Byram raised a smile. 'But look, that's not the point. Killing a guard is one thing, but murdering a priest would have been a much more serious matter. They'd hunt us down for that and we could expect no mercy if they managed to find us.'

And what difference would that make?' asked Edmund. 'The punishment for killing a priest is much the same as for stealing a pig. And, given all your other crimes, they'd surely hang us all anyway. But look on the bright side, they can only kill you once!'

His attempt to lighten the mood was lost on Byram. 'That's as maybe,' he said sourly. 'But I'll have no more killing, do you hear me? We may well get away with it this time as they won't spare men to come looking for us whilst there's any prospect of the Viking fleet attacking the burh. But once that threat has abated, they'll not let this pass, you mark my words. So, from now on, sleep with your weapons beside you, just in case. Also, we'll take turns to watch the main track, even through the night.'

Edmund sneered. 'Fear of the Viking fleet may well keep them off our backs for now, but they'll soon realise that's just a distraction.'

'What do you mean?' asked Byram.

'Don't forget, although I was just a slave on board one of the Viking ships, even we knew that the fleet was not intending to strike at Wareham, for it's far too well defended. We came ashore purely to take on fresh water and wait for a third ship to join us meaning to then plunder Twynham which our chieftain, Borg, reckoned was an easier target.

However, as it turned out, he misjudged the strength of the local fyrd from Wareham, which proved more able than he expected, thanks largely to my little sod of a nephew.'

'From what I heard of it that was because Borg had just three ships at his disposal,' argued Byram. 'Had he waited for more of the fleet to arrive it would have been a very different matter.'

Edmund shook his head. 'No, that's not the way of it. Their plan is to create distractions wherever they can, thereby drawing Alfred and his main army first to one place then to another. Once the Saxons are weary of that, the Vikings will strike with all the force they can muster – but where and when that will be is anyone's guess. In my view, it will most likely be London or possibly Kent, but it won't be here. The Vikings once took and held the settlement at Wareham for a time, thus they know that whilst the harbour is large enough to accommodate their ships, the tides are such that it sometimes all but empties of water completely. That could mean they'd be left beached and stranded in the shallows.'

'Are you're sure of this?'

Edmund shrugged. 'You can never be sure of anything with the Vikings, but that was always their plan.'

All were quiet for a moment as they considered what Edmund had told them. It was the giant Oswin who then spoke. 'So tell me, having killed yet another man and in so doing told those at Wareham where you're hiding, how will you now further your claim for your inheritance?' he asked pointedly.

It was a good question and one which even Byram had somehow overlooked.

'The priest doesn't know me, so they'll have no proof it was me,' said Edmund, struggling to answer.

Byram wasn't quite so sure about that. 'He'll have given them a good enough description. After all, he saw you plain enough.'

'Perhaps, but having lost the reliquary he was supposed to present to the Minster, he won't tarry long in Wareham and, once he's gone, the matter will be quickly forgotten.'

It seemed a lame explanation for something which could well threaten the lives of them all and so, as they each considered their position, Edmund realised he needed to change the subject. He looked at the coin that he'd earned by robbing the priest. 'In the meantime, I propose to invest this wisely,' he announced. 'When does that whore come to the camp?'

Byram grinned. 'Tomorrow,' he advised. 'Although as we all of us now have coin to spend, I fancy she'll find herself kept very busy when she does, so you'll have to wait your turn with the rest of us.'

* * * * *

WAREHAM

'Sir, should we now round up the horses?' asked Caelin.

Having understood little of what Oswald had said about him visiting a whore, Edward's mind was distracted by thoughts of what was likely to occur later that evening. Even so, he'd gone to the stables to help the boy settle the horses for the night. 'No, leave them a little while longer, they'll come back when they're ready,' he decided. 'Did Fleet give you any trouble?'

'No sir, except that he came back to see me several times. He's a very big horse. Is he hard to ride?'

Edward didn't answer but was pleased to see that Caelin seemed to have managed well enough in looking after the horses on his own for most of the day. 'Have you yet made yourself more comfortable in the stables?' he asked.

Caelin seemed a little troubled at that so Edward turned to look back at the building itself. As he'd said to Oswald, it was an unpleasant place in which to sleep but, having never been used to anything better, it had never troubled him unduly whilst he was the stable boy – but then he'd never had any choice and no one had ever shown much concern for his welfare. 'I'm going to have Sigbert improve the arrangements for you. He should at least be able to find a way to keep out the worst of the wind and weather.'

The boy looked at him, hardly daring to believe what he was hearing. 'Thank you, sir,' he managed.

'In the meantime, you should sort out some dry straw and make a bed tight in the far corner.'

With that, Edward went to the pasture and whistled for Fleet to join him. The big stallion came at once and Edward offered him a handful of feed then petted him as usual. The other two horses took their lead from Fleet and also trotted over, hoping to be fed as well. As Caelin could barely reach up high enough to secure a tether to each of them, Edward did that for him then led them over to stand in the yard so he could show the boy how to rub them down and groom them.

'Is it true, sir, that you were once stable boy to the King's horses?'

'I was. I started when I was even younger than you are now.'

'I've seen the King,' boasted Caelin. 'He was here in Wareham a short while ago.'

'I know,' said Edward.

'Then did you meet him, sir?'

'Yes, I've met him many times.'

'Did you look after his horse when he was here?'

'No,' said Edmund, getting weary of so many questions. 'He brought his own groom who stayed with Lord Alfred's personal guard and camped with them in the main pasture attached to the farm. It wasn't my place to interfere, although I did go to see the horse. I think he remembered me well enough.'

'Do horses remember things?' asked the boy.

'Yes, I'm sure they do. Particularly people who are kind to them. Now that's enough grooming for now. Go back to the stables and fill the troughs in the stalls with fresh water. I'll then bring the horses inside.'

Once the horses were all back in their stalls, Edward could tell that Fleet was expecting to be ridden. 'Don't worry, I'll come again tomorrow and we can ride together then,' he promised, as if the horse could actually understand him. 'For now, there's something very important I must do this evening, although I'm not entirely sure what that entails.'

*****

Having done all he could at the stables, Edward returned to the Vill for supper. He now slept in one of the small lodges which were attached to the Vill and set aside for important visitors – indeed it was one such lodge in which Lord Alfred had stayed whilst at Wareham, as had Lord Ethelnorth. Like them, Edward now dined with the family in the Hall and was seated next to Odelia, opposite her parents, with Governor Osric at the head of the table.

'You seem a bit distant,' whispered Odelia.

Knowing what he and Sigbert had planned for the evening, Edward could barely look her in the eye. Instead, he glanced awkwardly at Oswald who seemed to find that amusing. 'I'm sorry,' he replied. 'It's just that there's been much to do today and I'm tired.'

'Are you riding in the morning? If so, I'd love to come to the stables and watch.'

'Er, no. Not tomorrow,' replied Edward, anxious to avoid having to confront her so soon after going with Sigbert to visit the whore. 'There's a new stable boy there and I need to show him what to do.'

'How's the boy getting on?' asked Osric.

'As you said, my Lord, he's very young and very small even for his age. He couldn't yet manage on his own but he seems keen enough.'

'But will he do?'

Edward couldn't resist a faint laugh.

'What's the matter?' asked Osric.

'Nothing, my Lord. I'll continue to help out in the stables for now, but it's just that he asks so many questions.'

'But surely that's to the good,' replied Osric. 'It shows that he's eager to learn. And don't worry about him being small. We were all of us once small. In fact, when we first met, I thought the same of you.'

They all laughed but, surprisingly, it was Oswald who then spoke. 'His size is of no importance,' he stated firmly.

'It's heart that matters and a boy who has his heart in his work will always find a way to get the job done.'

'Surely, father, not if he can't reach up high enough to tend the horses?' suggested Odelia.

Oswald looked at Edward. 'Don't worry, boys of his age grow quickly so he'll soon be tall enough.'

'That's true,' said Osric wisely. 'But there is a simpler and more immediate solution.'

'What's that my Lord?' asked Edward.

'Give the lad a stool to stand on,' he replied. 'Surely that's not beyond the wit of man?'

*****

After supper, Edward found Sigbert waiting outside the Vill to collect him. As they walked together towards the north bridge, Sigbert carried a purse which contained the coins which Oswald had provided but which he knew were intended for Edward's benefit, not his own. He was to introduce the boy then remain on watch outside in case anyone took the opportunity to attack Edward whilst he was thus "distracted".

When they reached the north bridge, they turned towards the training area where there was what appeared to be a somewhat untidy camp with a crude hovel, outside which was a large box and a few upturned logs. Two girls were there tending to an open brazier.

'Is that it?' asked Edward nervously.

'Aye lad. And they're the two women I told you about. They come here for three or four days most weeks then move on to where their presence is wanted, but don't worry, there's no one else here tonight, all have been ordered to stay away.'

One of the women got up to greet them. She looked to be about five years older than Edward and rake thin, dressed in a plain tunic tied at the waist with a belt to which a small purse was attached.

'This is Mayda,' said Sigbert by way of introduction. 'And that's her sister over there. She answers to the name of Hild.' As he spoke, he indicated a woman who was wearing nothing but some sort of rough shift which gaped open at the front and which she hadn't bothered to properly fasten.

Hild got up and also stepped forward to greet them. She was certainly the older of the two and not overly attractive. 'Well, well my lovely,' she cooed. 'You just come with me and I'll teach all you need to know. And don't look so worried. Once I've shown you what goes where you'll be back for more, you just wait and see if that's not the way of it.' With that she put her arm under Edward's and led him towards the hovel. Once there, she pulled back the ragged and threadbare drape which covered the entrance and let him enter first.

Once inside, Edward was surprised by how small it was. He recalled seeing the large box on the ground outside which, he realised, contained the girls' clothes and their few belongings which had no doubt been cleared out to make more room. In fact, little remained inside the hovel except a wide cot that had been placed against one wall, virtually filling the entire space.

Hild followed him then pulled the drape across behind her. It was dark except for a solitary taper which flickered lamely in one corner so that Edward could barely see her. She told him to remove his clothes and lie down on the cot. As he did so, she slipped off her shift and stood naked before him. 'So, I'm to make a man of you,' she said softly.

The only naked woman Edward had ever seen before was the one who had been raped and butchered at the raided farmstead he'd attended with the fyrd.

'Sigbert told us that you answer to the name of Edward,' she said putting her arm around him as she settled down beside him.

Edward nodded.

'Well Edward. This is going to be a night you'll always remember.'

* * * * *

Sigbert waited patiently outside the hovel, sitting on one of the logs whilst sharing the warmth of the brazier with Mayda. He knew better than to try his luck with her, for he'd heard other men say that she was not like her sister in her ways any more than she was in her appearance, having a rather hooked and hawk-like nose and very intense piercing green eyes. Her role was simply to serve her sister and deal with the business side of the transaction. Indeed, it was she who had ensured that Edward would be Hild's only visitor that night, a courtesy often shown to nobles, albeit at a significant extra cost. In fact, although Hild's services had been much in demand whilst Alfred's personal guard had been in Wareham, since they'd left there had been few visitors anyway, most of the local men lacking funds for such pleasures and, besides, a lot of them had wives or had established "arrangements" with local women.

Sigbert had assured Mayda that the boy wouldn't need long as it was his first time but they had already been away for much longer than he'd expected. In fact, it was over an hour before Edward emerged, grinning and with his eyes looking as though they were full of wonder.

'Wait here for a moment,' advised Sigbert, slapping Edward on the back as if to congratulate him before going across to settle whatever payment was due with Mayda. When he was told what that amounted to, he could scarce believe it. 'What, for just one time?'

Hild grinned when she overheard that. 'Oh, it was more than that,' she assured him, chuckling to herself. 'Once started, there was no stopping the boy! He had me several times with scarce time between for me to catch my breath! He took to it like a duck to water and had the stamina of a horse. In fact, I swear he would have had me again if I'd let him.'

'Really!' asked Sigbert, hardly able to believe what he was hearing.

'Aye,' laughed Hild. 'He was more than eager once he'd got the way of it and put most men to shame.'

'But he's not much more than a boy,' protested Sigbert.

'Not any more, he's not,' said Hild. 'And what's more, feel free to bring him again if you feel so minded. I like a man who appreciates what I have to offer.'

* * * * *

The priest who had been robbed by Edmund in the forest arrived at the north bridge that same evening but, embarrassed by his predicament, had waited until it was fully dark before entering the settlement. The men on duty at the bridge were at first not sure what they should do with a naked priest but hurriedly offered cloaks or blankets to help him cover himself before one of them escorted him to the Minster, much to the amusement of anyone who happened to see him – including both Sigbert and Mayda as they waited outside for Edward and Hild to finish.

When he heard what had happened, Father Emmett hurriedly went to the Minster himself and provided some spare robes. 'We can't have the members of my flock see you like this,' he ventured, more concerned for the reputation of the Church than for the priest's embarrassment.

The priest was more intent on seeing Governor Osric to complain about what had happened. Once dressed, he was taken to the Vill where he introduced himself as Father Cuthbert. Even though it was late, Osric agreed to see him at once when told of what had happened.

'It's a disgrace that I should be treated thus,' stormed Father Cuthbert. 'Is it not enough that I, a man of God, should be stripped naked and made to ride alone through the forest and that my guard should be slain like a dog? I insist that you round up these rogues at once and bring them to justice!'

'How many men were there?' asked Oswald who, as Garrison Commander, had been called in by his uncle to hear about the matter as well.

'I saw just one but I'm sure there were others hiding in the trees beside the track.'

'Then Father, describe the one you saw,' insisted Oswald.

The priest hesitated. 'Well, he was older than I might have expected and stood taller than most with long fair hair. Also, he had vivid blue eyes, I well remember those and would know him anywhere.' In fact, the priest had hardly dared to so much as look at Edmund and so, in reality, could not have elaborated further on his description even if pressed.

'And the others?' asked Oswald.

'As I said, I didn't see them,' explained the priest. 'They didn't dare to show themselves but they were there right enough, lurking within the trees.'

'So this one man killed your guard, robbed you of your purse then had you strip naked so he could steal your robes as well?' said Oswald, not meaning to query the validity of the priest's report.

'Exactly,' confirmed Father Cuthbert. 'And fine robes they were as well. But the reason they had me strip was that I had more coin concealed in the hem of my outer robe. How could he have known such a thing except that someone had betrayed me?'

'And this purse? How much did it amount to?'

'A dozen coins all told. Although not a huge sum by my own reckoning, it was all intended for the Lord's work.'

'Then all I can say, Father, is that you were a fool to travel so well dressed and with so much coin about your person with the protection of just one man,' said Oswald, as if stating the obvious.

'But is it not your duty to ensure safe passage for all travellers of note?'

'Yes, of course, but only if we know they're coming,' said Oswald. 'We had no word that you would require an escort through the forest or I would have sent a small detachment to meet you.'

The priest was suddenly quiet. 'Even so, what are you going to do to retrieve my property?'

Oswald glanced at his uncle before replying. 'Well,' he said. 'You must first tell me all that was taken.'

'Apart from my coin and all my clothes, he also stole my ring and my gold crucifix. They were of only modest value, unlike the reliquary they stole which contained no less than a bone from the finger of Saint Augustine who, as you well know, is one of our truly revered saints as it was he who first brought the word of God to this then pagan land.'

At that, Governor Osric looked at him somewhat doubtfully. He had seen many "holy" relics over the years, most of which were clearly fakes. 'And why were you carrying this obviously very valuable item?' he asked.

'My Lord, it was the sole purpose for my journey. It was intended as a gift from our Bishop to the Minster here at Wareham.'

'And that's all?'

'Is it not enough? Surely you'll send men to recover it and bring the rogue to justice?'

It was Oswald who answered. 'Given that you were robbed by just one man and that we are still under the threat of an invasion from a large Viking fleet, I cannot spare men to go chasing through the forest to search for him,' he explained. 'You have given us no name and only the vaguest description, so we have very little to go on. When time permits and if my uncle agrees, we will endeavour to find this wretch. If and when we do, he will be brought to account for his crimes, you can be assured of that. Until then, just be thankful that he didn't kill you as well.'

The priest shivered at the very thought of that and hurriedly crossed himself. He made as though intending to leave the Hall but then seemed to think better of it, so turned again. 'I have been humiliated, robbed and insulted by this wretch. My guard has been killed and I am substantially out of pocket. Worse still, a holy relic intended for the benefit of all who reside in this place has been stolen. Therefore my bishop shall hear of this, make no mistake about that.' With that he stormed off.

'Uncle, are you thinking what I'm thinking?' asked Oswald once the priest had gone.

'You mean that it was Edmund who robbed him?' replied Osric. 'That could well be so. The description fits well enough, although there are many others it could apply to as well.'

'Yes, but if it was him, it means he's joined with the robbers in the forest.'

'Exactly,' agreed Osric. 'And if that is the case, then it doesn't bode well, for it means that Edward is still very much at risk.'

'So, would you have me search for him?'

Osric considered the options. 'No, it would be a futile effort. We've searched that forest more times than I care to recall and found neither hide nor hair of the robbers because there are so many places they can hide. We'll continue to keep a close watch on Edward until we can be sure that the Viking threat has abated. Once it has, we can launch a thorough search and thus hopefully put all these matters to rights once and for all.'

Chapter Five

WAREHAM

The next morning, Caelin stood beside Sigbert as together they watched Edward ride Fleet in the pasture.

'He's a very good rider, sir,' remarked the young boy, clearly excited at the prospect of perhaps one day learning how to ride a horse himself. As he had already admitted, he knew very little about horses but found his new role at the stables to be very much to his liking, albeit the work was hard.

'Aye, he is that,' acknowledged Sigbert. 'What's more, he seems to have a way with horses and they seem to trust him. That's a rare gift, to be sure.'

With that Edward returned to them and dismounted. He then petted Fleet as usual and let him nuzzle his hand for a few moments. 'I'd like to ride him some more,' he said. 'But my duties now seem to take up more and more of my time. This morning I've to see Father Emmett who is helping me with my reading and writing and we have a fyrd training session this afternoon.' With that, he stepped back and watched as Sigbert removed Fleet's saddle and blanket then gave the former to Caelin who struggled to carry it back to the stables on his own. As he did so, Edward removed Fleet's bridle to let the horse run free. They both watched Fleet for a few moments then walked back to the stables knowing that the boy would struggle to lift the saddle up onto the stout peg where it was normally kept. In the end, Sigbert had to do that for him as well.

'As I promised, Sigbert has come to see what can be done to make sleeping here more comfortable,' announced Edward.

'Aye,' said Sigbert having quickly looked things over. 'And we can start by erecting a wicker panel close to where you sleep to keep out the worst of the wind and rain.'

'Is that a big job?' asked Edward.

'No, it's one I can manage well enough on my own, although the boy should help so that he'll know how to mend and maintain it himself in the future. It'll take perhaps two days to construct as we'll first need to cut and collect the withies that we'll use to make it. Ideally we would render the panel as well but that will have to wait until we have more time.' He then turned his attention to where the boy slept. It was little more than a heap of straw which, as Edward had suggested, had been piled up in the corner where he used to sleep when he was the stable boy. 'We could form a cot, raised from the ground on legs,' suggested Sigbert. 'That would at least help to keep the rats from crawling into the bed and, if we seal the sides, it should stop them from getting under it as well.'

'Good,' said Edward. 'I'll also arrange for Ida to provide a new blanket as that one has seen better days. Once you have the new one, the old one can be used to keep the horses warm.'

'Thank you, sir,' said the boy meekly. 'It seems I'm lucky to have found a place such as this at which to work.'

Edward laughed. 'I'll remind you of that in a few weeks' time. You now have Father Cuthbert's horse to look after whilst he's here so that will keep you busy enough, but once this threat of an attack by the Viking fleet has abated, we're going to round up at least ten more horses which are needed for the fyrd. We'll see how you manage then!'

'But where will they all be stabled?' asked Caelin. 'Surely there won't be room enough here?'

Edward was impressed that the boy was already thinking about what having more horses would entail. 'Don't worry,' he assured him. 'They'll be used to staying out all weathers so we can simply turn them out into the pasture, but Sigbert will fashion some sort of shelter so they get some respite from the worst of the weather, especially in the winter months. Mind, with so many horses the grass in the pasture will soon be depleted so we'll need to provide more hay and feed, but we can worry about that when the time comes.'

'I think I should also make up some steps which Caelin can use in order to help him reach up high enough to tend to the horses on his own, at least until he grows a bit,' advised Sigbert. 'What do you think?'

'I think it's a good idea. Osric suggested a stool when we discussed that at supper last night, but a step would be better. When can you start all this?'

'Well, if you're with Father Emmett this morning you should be safe enough, so no time like the present.'

*****

WAREHAM FOREST

Having slept on the ground in the open since he'd arrived at the camp, Edmund asked Byram whether he might be allowed to repair and then use one of the abandoned hovels. Byram agreed and suggested that he ask Oswin and the boy, Iden, to help him.

Between them they looked at the buildings, such as they were, then selected the one which needed the least amount of repair.

'The roof timbers look to be sound enough but it needs to be re-thatched,' advised Oswin. With that, he sent Iden to fetch more reeds, a supply of which was kept within the camp for that very purpose.

Whilst he was gone, they set about checking the rest of the structure more thoroughly. The walls basically comprised a series of posts which had been set into the ground, each of them as near vertical as could be managed. Hazel saplings had then been woven between them and any gaps filled with a mixture of mud, straw and animal dung. There were some areas of the render which needed to be repaired and, as he set about doing that, Edmund took the opportunity to speak with Oswin about the boy. 'The lad seems eager to please,' he noted.

'Aye,' said Oswin. 'He fetches and carries for me willingly enough but is regarded by some as being a bit half-witted.'

'It looks to me as though he follows you like a shadow,' observed Edmund. 'I assume you're not related?'

'No, in fact, so far as I know the boy has no kin - or at least none who are still living. We assume his folks were all killed in a raid and he may even have seen them slaughtered.

He won't say much about that. In fact, he says very little about anything, preferring to keep himself to himself.'

''Tis often the way of it, or so I've heard,' agreed Edmund. 'But what about the Viking who calls himself Radnor? Does his presence in the camp not remind the boy of what happened to his kin?'

Oswin shrugged. 'Who can say? I don't think he has even paid him any mind for he sees only what he wants to see – and somehow keeps himself from seeing what he doesn't.'

With that, Iden returned carrying a small bundle of reeds under one arm.

'Surely there's a better way for him to carry the reeds than that?' suggested Edmund. 'If he manages so few each time he'll be going back and forth all day.'

'Let him be,' said Oswin. 'He has his own way of doing things and if you try to change that he'll only become riled.'

Edmund accepted that. 'So, what else can we be doing whilst he fetches more reeds?' he asked.

'If I were you I'd start by removing all the old straw from inside and replacing it with some which is clean and fresh,' advised Oswin. 'What's there is likely to be infested with vermin. Also, if you look over there where that deer skin has been stretched out on a frame, you'll find some more pelts on the ground beside it which have all been tanned and softened. Select one to put over the entrance as that will then keep out flies and other insects, especially at night.'

'And what do I do for warmth?'

Oswin smiled. 'Well, assuming you can't find a woman to keep you warm, you'll need to buy yourself a blanket. Or maybe steal one. Either way, you'll likely need something sooner or later, for Cedric, who is a forester and knows about these things, has warned that we have some very cold nights to look forward to.'

*****

WAREHAM

Caelin went off to replenish the horses' water trough in the pasture. To carry the water, he placed a yoke over his frail shoulders with a pail set at each end. Because they were too heavy for him to manage, each pail was only part filled even though that meant that more trips were needed. Whilst he was away, Sigbert mentioned the events of the night before. 'So, what did you make of it all?' he asked.

Edward grinned broadly. 'Can we not go there again tonight?'

'Lord no, once in a while is enough, even for you!' he teased. 'Besides, from what I hear of it, poor Hild is now in need of a rest!'

'Tomorrow then?' said Edward.

'You'll not find them there tomorrow. Like I told you, they have other places they visit. They stay here for three or four days in every week and then go elsewhere to ply their trade.'

'But why?' questioned Edward.

'Because they can't earn enough from a settlement such as this, particularly now that Alfred's personal guard have left. They must therefore look more widely for their trade. We can go again next weekend but I'll first need to ask

Oswald for more coin - you spent all he gave us on your very first visit!'

*****

Edward arrived late for his lessons with Father Emmett. He found him and Father Cuthbert praying together, both looking somewhat displeased at having been kept waiting.

'I've told you before, you should look to your studies more readily,' chided Father Emmett. 'There's much you can learn from the Bible; things which every man should know.'

Edward apologised as he took his seat at a small table then opened the large volume which Father Emmett had placed there for him to read. It was a heavy tome with richly decorated pages and a lavish cover inset with jewels and precious stones.

'You look so like the rogue who robbed me,' observed Father Cuthbert. 'He was a lot older than you but the likeness is uncanny. He could easily pass as your brother or your father perhaps.'

'Or your uncle more like,' suggested Father Emmett. 'Although I fancy he's fled far from here by now.'

'Even so, the resemblance struck me in an instant...' With that he returned his attention to Edward's schooling. 'So, do you find learning to read and write to be difficult?' he asked.

'In truth I do, Father. Perhaps because my heart isn't in it.'

'That's true enough,' scolded Father Emmett sourly. 'Your heart is in riding that stallion of yours or walking with Odelia beside the river. You must learn that there are more important things you need to consider. For a start, you must look to your future and, whilst doing so, also have due regard for your immortal soul.'

'My future will be as a warrior,' boasted Edmund. 'Like my father and his brother, Lord Edwin.'

Father Emmett considered that for a moment. 'As we discussed last time, before your father became an accomplished warrior, he first served the Church. No doubt whilst doing so he learned compassion and charity. So, if you would emulate him you should start by studying the Bible.'

'But I find these lessons so hard,' complained Edward. 'Learning how to wield a sword comes more naturally to me.'

'No doubt. But I understand your fortune is such that you will one day have a large estate to administer. A sword will serve you well if you're obliged to defend it, but the quill will serve you better if your lands and holdings are to prosper.'

*****

That afternoon, all the members of the fyrd and most of the permanent guard were summoned to the area beside the north gate which was used for training. Sigbert and Edward both attended although, strictly speaking, as a nobleman Edward could have excused himself, as indeed could Sigbert given his special duties as Edward's protector. Oswald's elite squad was down to just those who had survived the battle, so they took turns to ride the two remaining horses whilst the rest of the fyrd underwent further practice for the shield wall. After that, with the threat of invasion still hanging over them, Oswald addressed the men, anxious to ensure that they all knew what would be expected of them if and when the Vikings did attack, particularly if that resulted in a siege.

'If the Viking fleet is sighted by any of the watch towers along the coast, the beacons will be lit and we can then expect everyone from the outlying settlements and farmsteads to come into Wareham seeking protection. When they do, the fyrd will be at near full strength – 1500 men all told if you include the permanent guard and all of you who are resident here. The settlement will then be crowded fit to burst so we'll need to deploy everyone as best we can if we are to ensure that we offer a credible defence. For that you will all be assigned to one of three groups, each comprising 500 men. The groups will each take turns to be on duty so that one is available at all times to keep watch and to provide an immediate defence.' He paused there to ensure there were no questions. When no one spoke up, he continued. 'Whilst your group is on duty you must ensure that the vantage points along the entire length of the fortifications are manned at all times, day and night. Additional men must be stationed at the west gates, the north bridge, the quay and at the entrance to the path at Bell's Orchard. Once the attack is confirmed, bowmen will also be positioned along the banks of both rivers to slow the Vikings' advance. You'll be allocated your duties at the time, but even if not actually assigned to a specific post, whilst rostered you must remain armed and ready to be deployed at a moment's notice.'

'Sir, are we then expecting a siege?' asked one man.

Knowing that everyone dreaded the prospect of a siege, Oswald hesitated before he answered. 'We have no idea what to expect from such a large force but a siege would be their most likely form of attack, hence we're preparing for that. However, they may also try to probe our defences looking for any weak spots.'

'How long would we have to hold out if it is a siege?' queried another man.

'Only until such time as Alfred can reach us with reinforcements,' said Oswald. 'Ealdorman Aelfric may also come to our aid with other fyrds from within the shire and we can expect support from the other burhs. Either way, our defences are sound and we'll be well prepared in terms of supplies and provisions.'

'And what about the quay, sir? Should we not be building a stockade fence there as it's an obvious weak spot?'

'No, the quay must be kept open at all times. We shall of course have additional men mustered there just in case but, once raised, the chains across the rivers will make it difficult for the Vikings to reach us this far upstream. Thus they're more likely to come ashore in the harbour or elsewhere and try to make their way across land. To that extent the terrain and the rivers will serve to delay them, but if they do manage to reach us and breach the fortifications, we'll fall back to the quay and make our stand there. That means it will come down to a shield wall and hand-to-hand fighting.'

'But if that happens, there could be as many as 1500 men plus their wives and families all crammed into the area around the quay,' countered the man who had initially raised the issue. 'Surely that will result in chaos?'

'Exactly, so let's pray that the fortifications suffice so it doesn't happen,' said Oswald. 'But if it does, the people will need to be marshalled properly and kept as safe as we can manage. It won't be easy, but we'll do what we can and hope that Alfred quickly arrives to support us.'

There were the usual mumblings before a man at the back also spoke up. Like others, he could well recall Oswald's failings at the battle near Twynham and whilst none spoke of it openly, the question of his competence to lead them was at the forefront of everyone's mind. 'So, who then will be in overall command?' he asked pointedly.

Oswald knew exactly why he was asking. 'Myself, Governor Osric and Wulfric will take turns to command in rotation,' he announced. 'One of us will be on duty at any one time.'

'Then what about the wounded?' asked another man. 'How will you deal with them?'

'Initially the women will be charged to carry them back to the nunnery where they'll be tended by the good sisters there. The women will also bring food, water and more arrows to those on duty defending the fortifications.'

All in all, what Oswald was outlining was hardly a new strategy and was one they'd practised many times before. Nonetheless, everyone remained uneasy given that the prospect of an attack suddenly seemed very real indeed.

When there were no more questions, the men were ordered to disperse to practise general combat skills under Wulfric's supervision whilst Edward and Sigbert were taken aside and given swords to try.

'Edward,' said Oswald. 'As a nobleman your place is now to stand behind the shield wall from where you must relay any orders given by whoever is in overall command at that time, be it Governor Osric, Wulfric or myself. Remember, that may come down to whichever one of us is still alive, but either way your job will be to keep them fully advised of how the battle progresses and call for reinforcements where needed. You'll have messengers on hand for that but it's something we'll need to practise. For now, I would have you and Sigbert learn how to handle a sword.'

‘Sir, am I to learn as well?’ asked Sigbert.

‘You are,’ explained Oswald. ‘As it’s now your place to protect Edward, it would seem wise to teach you how to wield a sword for it’s likely to become a skill you’ll surely need.’

Sigbert was delighted, for he much preferred the thought of fighting with a sword rather than with his customary spear or bow even though he had no experience of doing so. As he didn’t have a sword of his own, he was allowed to borrow one that had been newly repaired whilst Edward was given Oswald’s to try.

Having already had some basic training in swordcraft, Edward progressed well whilst Sigbert who, although a well-trained warrior, struggled to get the hang of things. Oswald watched them intently and offered advice where he could.

‘Don’t grip the sword too tightly,’ he reminded them both. ‘You need to hold it firmly but also to let your wrist flex and twist. To help with that, try extending your thumb along the side of the blade as that will allow your hand more freedom to move.’

They both tried that but, at one point, the swords came together so hard that Oswald was anxious lest they’d been damaged. ‘Nicks and suchlike can be mended,’ he assured them as he inspected both blades. ‘But a sword is very valuable and should never be wilfully mistreated. So, unless deflecting a blow, avoid clashing the blades together like that if you can, for it’ll do nothing save to spoil them. Instead, use your shield and learn to duck and weave to avoid your opponent’s blows.’

‘But surely we must strike with conviction?’ queried Sigbert.

'Of course, but only when the chance arises. Patience is the key – many warriors seek to strike too soon and, in so doing, leave themselves exposed.'

The lesson continued until both Edward and Sigbert were allowed to take a much-needed rest.

'Swords are a brutally effective weapon but wielding one is heavy work for those not used to it. Always remember, once you tire you become an easy target for your opponent who won't hesitate to take advantage of that. You must also learn how to match your sword against other weapons you'll surely come up against in battle – particularly axes and spears.' As they took a breather, Oswald called one of the other men over to assist him. 'I want you to come at me with your spear,' he ordered.

The man looked doubtful.

'Don't worry, I simply want to demonstrate how easy it is to deal with assaults such as that.'

The man stepped back and half-heartedly jabbed with the spear. Oswald immediately knocked it aside then turned inwards so as to get in close enough to lay his blade across the man's still-extended forearm. 'You see!' he said. 'You could easily sever his arm thus and thereby leave him defenceless and in a great deal of pain. If there's time, you can then finish him or spare him as you see fit. If not, leave him to bleed out and move on, for he'll not be a threat to anyone once so severely maimed.'

*****

After the fyrd training, Edward went to see Odelia. He was worried lest she would somehow know that he'd visited a whore the previous evening, and decided that if she did he couldn't deny it. As he waited for her at the Vill, Governor Osric himself came out to see him.

'So, how did your practice with the sword go?' asked Osric.

'It went well enough, my Lord. But I still have much to learn.'

'It takes time,' mused Osric. 'But it's a skill you'll surely need to master, so remember what I taught you and listen to all that Oswald has to say, for he's a man who surely knows the way of it.'

'Don't worry,' said Oswald, who then joined them. 'We'll make a warrior of him yet.'

Osric smiled to himself recalling that his nephew had once said that the boy would never manage that. It seemed that much had changed in such a short time. 'I regret that may well prove necessary sooner than we would like,' he said, looking at Edward. 'For we've reason to believe that your uncle has now joined with the robbers in Wareham Forest and is thus close enough to cause concern.'

Edward didn't answer at first. 'If I could but speak with him, my Lord, I'm sure our differences could be resolved,' he managed at last.

'It's too late for that, for it seems probable that he's already killed again. This time the guard who escorted Father Cuthbert here.'

'Do you think that was Edmund?' asked Edward.

'It seems likely given the description we have.'

'The good father remarked that I reminded him of the man who robbed him,' admitted Edward.'

'Which suggests it may well have been your uncle and you must therefore remain vigilant for, once he learns that his assassin failed to kill you, he's almost bound to make another attempt on your life.'

With that, Osric took his leave of them.

'So, I gather you visited Hild last night,' said Oswald with no trace of disapproval in his voice. 'And by all accounts you did us proud!'

Edward was not sure what to say so just grinned.

'Just remember what we discussed. Whatever you did with Hild is not what you may do with any lady of quality, and certainly not my daughter,' he warned. 'Whores are only good for one thing. You've managed that well enough from what I hear of it, so you'd be wise not to visit her again.'

'Why not?' asked Edward, trying not to sound disappointed.

'Such women are dirty and often diseased. It's the punishment God inflicts upon them for their sinful and wanton ways. You'd not want to make a habit of visiting low life like that.' Even as he spoke, he remembered that Edward's mother had been a whore. 'Well, some of them are at any rate,' he added, hurriedly trying to redeem what he'd said.

Edward had not missed the obvious connotation. He blushed and was about to say something in his mother's defence, perhaps reminding Oswald that she had been forced to become a whore on the orders of no less than the King himself. As it was, he had no time to say it as, at that moment, Odelia appeared.

'Remember to heed what I said,' whispered Oswald as an aside to ensure that Odelia didn't hear him.

With that, Edward and Odelia walked together, hand in hand, towards the river.

'You were very quiet at supper last evening,' she said.

'Was I?' asked Edward. 'I didn't mean to be. It's just that I'm still not used to eating with others at a table like that. And certainly not in such important company.'

She seemed to accept that. 'Well, you'll have to get used to it. For you're a nobleman now.'

'Not yet I'm not. Alfred has yet to decide which estates and what rank I shall be awarded.'

'Well, everyone now thinks of you as a nobleman, so you must learn how to conduct yourself as such.'

'I'm making some progress in learning how to read and write and am being taught how to wield a sword.'

'All of which I'm sure will serve you well,' she assured him, then kissed him lightly on the cheek.

Edward hesitated for a moment. 'Well then, as a nobleman, I think I can do better than that,' he teased, then put his arms around her and kissed her properly.

*****

WAREHAM FOREST

All at the robbers' camp waited patiently for the two girls to arrive. Byram sent Oswin to meet them so he could escort them back to the camp via a path they used which was virtually unknown to others. He also helped them carry the few belongings they usually brought with them.

Once there, Hild and Mayda both greeted their mother, Winifrid, who warned them they were likely to find themselves very busy as the men were waiting to enjoy Hild's favours, all of them with coin to spend.

As usual when they visited the camp, a bed of clean straw had been prepared in the shelter for Hild to use, with a drape of animal pelts hastily arranged to offer some degree of privacy. Whilst Mayda took coin from each man in order to pay for her sister's services, Hild wasted no time in getting down to work.

Byram exercised his privilege to be the first to lay with Hild, followed by Brother Linton who, having done so, took himself apart from the others where he stripped himself naked then knelt as he thrashed his own back with birch twigs, weeping and begging for forgiveness between each stroke.

After that, the men drew straws in order to decide what order they would visit Hild and she greeted each and every one of them, mostly by name. Her appetite for bedding them was so voracious that she barely allowed any time between them and didn't even trouble to wash herself before or after each visit.

It was beginning to get dark by the time all had taken their turn and Hild at last went to the stream to wash. Having done so, she returned to the others where she and Mayda were offered food. They both seemed happy enough at having earned well for what amounted to little more than an afternoon's work.

'It's now getting late so I would suggest that you stay the night,' offered Byram as they all ate together around the table.

'Why, what have we to fear from the forest at night?' queried Hild. 'Or are you saying you're not the only robbers who now frequent these parts?'

Mayda laughed. 'Ha! Perhaps he's worried lest we find another band who might also welcome a visit. One which might offer even more for your services.'

'There are no others hereabouts,' Byram assured them firmly. 'And even if there were, we'd ensure they would be no risk to you. But remember, there are wolves in the forest you need to be wary of and besides, we don't want you getting lost in the dark.'

Grateful for that, Hild thanked him and agreed it would be wiser to stay. With that, she turned her attention to Edmund. 'You did well to get away from Wareham having killed that assassin,' she said. 'They searched for you high and low.'

Edmund realised at once that, having recognised him, she could easily give him away. 'He got what he deserved,' he said trying to make light of the matter. 'He killed my nephew, young Edward, so I settled matters between us then left as hurriedly as I could.'

'What do you mean he killed young Edward?' queried Hild. 'The boy is as lively as anyone here. In fact, more so than most! I can surely testify to that!'

'What are you saying?'

'I'm saying that he came to visit me. I've cause enough to remember that, for he was certainly intent on getting his money's worth!'

Everyone except Edmund laughed.

'That can't be right,' he insisted. 'The boy's dead, I'm sure of it.'

'Ah,' said Hild. 'Then someone should tell him, for he clearly doesn't yet know it!'

Again the others laughed.

'Are you're sure it was him?' asked Edmund, clearly worried.

'Of course I am. You might not wish to know it, but I recall every man I've lain with – and what his "preferences" are,' she teased. 'Even those who, like you, don't seem to have it in them to linger long in my bed!'

Most of the others enjoyed her jest but Edmund was far too concerned by what she'd said about Edward being alive. 'How can you be so certain it was him?' he pressed.

'He came with old Sigbert who told me the boy's name, that's how. Not that he had much to do with it. He just waited outside, standing guard the whole time.'

It was Byram who then spoke. 'If the boy is indeed still alive then is your plan not thwarted?' he asked, looking at Edmund anxiously. 'For if he lives, you'll stand no chance of getting your inheritance, which means that we shall not get the share of it you've promised us!' Even as he spoke, he glanced at Cedric who immediately caught his drift and was on his feet in a moment.

Producing a knife, Cedric stepped in behind Edmund and laid the blade against his throat. 'So why the hell are we feeding and protecting you?' he demanded. 'We should just hand you over to Governor Osric and be done with it. That way we could claim whatever price has been placed upon your head, for if what Hild has said is true, that's the only way we'll earn anything from your miserable hide.'

By then, several of the others were on their feet as well, all of them fearing they'd been duped.

Edmund had to think fast. 'Much good would that do you. Not only could I lead them to this camp but I also now know your names.' He regretted the words almost as soon as he'd said them, realising there was an obvious alternative they might well decide upon.

'That's easily resolved,' sneered Cedric. 'You might not be worth as much to us once killed, but if I slit your throat that will at least quieten your tongue sufficient to ensure that you can't betray us.' With that, he pressed a little harder with the knife.

'Wait!' pleaded Edmund. 'There's a better way to resolve this which will mean I can still claim my inheritance.'

'What inheritance?' demanded Byram. 'There'll be none if that boy still lives, for he'll be entitled to it all!'

'Exactly,' said Edmund sounding desperate. 'So, all we have to do is kill him and all will be put to rights.'

The others thought about that but none of them seemed convinced.

'And how would we manage that?' challenged Byram. 'After all, you tried to kill him before and it seems you failed. You'll not get a second chance, that's for certain.'

Edmund was thinking fast. 'There is a way whereby I could, but I would need your help,' he said, looking directly at Hild.

'In what way?' she asked curiously.

'Just a simple task. And, if you do as I ask, I'll pay you enough to make honest women of you and your sister. In fact, I'll pay enough to make you both very wealthy indeed.'

'With what?' she sneered. 'You barely have the clothes you stand up in!'

'Actually, that might not be so,' explained Byram, realising that neither Hild nor Mayda knew anything about the extent of Edmund's inheritance. 'If what he's told us is true, he has the prospect of coming into a vast fortune which he's promised to share with us once he's secured it. What worries us is that if his nephew, Edward, is still alive, he now stands in the way. It would thus be in all our interests if the little runt was no longer living.'

Hild and Mayda seemed to consider the matter without so much as a word being said between them. 'So, what would you have us do to earn a share of this vast fortune?' asked Hild, clearly far from convinced.

'Just what you normally do,' said Edmund. 'Use your charms to draw the young fool back and then keep him distracted.'

'Distracted? Distracted from what?' she demanded.

'Distracted from what the man who'll slit his throat is about to do. I'm sure you can find some rogue within the settlement who would manage that if the price is right.'

'Oh no!' she said firmly. 'I'll have no part in that, for they'll hang me if they even suspect I'm involved. Besides, he has old Sigbert to look out for him and he's not a man to be taken lightly.'

'Anyway, that's far too obvious,' added Byram. 'They'll think it was one of us, so that would put us all at risk. If you're going to kill him it has to look like an accident.' With that, he reached across and snatched the crucifix he had given Edmund as a reward for robbing the priest. 'I think you're beyond any help you're likely to get from this, so I'll have it back,' he said, then looked at Oswin. 'Tie this rogue to that tree over there in case he tries to make a run for it,' he ordered. 'He now knows far too much about us to let him escape. We'll discuss this again in the morning – that is unless the wolves get to him whilst we're all sleeping and thereby save us the trouble of dealing with him.'

*****

That night as Hild and Mayda slept together in the open shelter, they heard the sound of someone creeping about close by.

'Oh no, surely they've all had enough by now,' moaned Hild. 'They should be sleeping like babies after all their exertions.' With that, she slid her hand from her sister's breast. 'Tell them to return in the morning - I'm too tired to see them now.'

Mayda threw back the blanket which they'd used to cover themselves only to see their mother, Winifrid, peering in at them, using a lighted taper to see inside more clearly. She was shocked when she found the girls abed together, both of them naked.

'What's this?' she demanded, all but lost for words.

Neither girl answered as they hurriedly pulled the blanket across to cover themselves.

'You know well enough that such unions are forbidden!' scolded Winifrid, almost spitting out the words. 'Is it not enough that one of my daughters is a whore never mind that I should now discover that you lay together as well! It's unnatural and against the laws of God that you should behave as such. As your mother, my lips are sealed but, for the good of your souls, you must desist this unholy practice!'

It was Hild who found the courage to respond. 'Given what I do to feed us both, is not my soul already tainted?' she said.

Winifrid had no answer to that. 'Have you no shame that you willingly share the same bed for… for whatever it is you would do together?'

'Do you imagine that I enjoy being mauled and groped by the men who pay to abuse me?' continued Hild. 'Do you think I enjoy having them fill me with their filthy seed? I do what I do to pay our dues and to put food in our bellies, nothing more. What Mayda and I do here is my only consolation for enduring all that and is for our pleasure alone, whether it be sinful or not.'

Winifrid said nothing. Still shocked, she just stared at them both. 'I came here to warn you against doing whatever it is Byram asks of you tomorrow, for no good will come of it, you mark my words. He may seem an affable fellow but he's more treacherous than any man I've ever known. He's also a callous bastard and you know the way of these things as well as I do. You'll get nowhere near your fair share of whatever's earned, but will hang the same as the others if you're caught.'

'It won't be up to Byram,' said Mayda. 'It's Edmund who is offering to pay us.'

Winifrid scoffed at the very mention of his name. 'You'll fare no better with him,' she warned. 'He's a noble, or at least he claims to be. His sort do as they please and leave the likes of us to take the blame. That's the way of it and always has been.'

'Perhaps,' agreed Mayda. 'But what have we to lose? If he pays only part of what he's offered it'll be enough for us to escape this miserable life and live together as we would wish.'

Winifrid just stared at them both then shook her head. 'Have it your own way,' she said. 'But don't blame me if you pay for your sins, for you'll deserve what follows, whether it be in this world or the next.'

Chapter Six

WAREHAM FOREST

Sleeping in the open was nothing new to Edmund. In fact, since arriving at the camp he'd spent every night like that and, whilst doing so, had often heard the wolves Byram had warned Hild and Mayda about. He'd never actually seen them, but the prospect of the pack venturing into the camp was not something to be taken lightly and, as a precaution, he'd always slept close beside the fire and kept the spear Byram had given him close at hand. However, as he was now a prisoner bound to a tree with his hands tied behind his back, he knew he would be utterly helpless to defend himself if they did appear. Even the thought of what would happen then was more than enough to deter him from sleeping, for he had only to close his eyes to imagine their vicious fangs ripping open first his throat and then his belly to gorge themselves on his entrails.

Despite those macabre thoughts, he must have slept at some point because he was woken abruptly the next morning as others in the camp began to stir themselves. As they did so, he was offered neither food nor water and was ignored until Byram at last saw fit to send for him, at which point he was untied by Oswin and dragged to stand before them all.

'Well,' said Byram, chewing on the remains of whatever had been part of his breakfast. 'I trust you slept well?'

'You could at least have allowed me some way in which I could defend myself against the wolves,' chided Edmund bitterly.

'Why would we do that?' asked Byram. 'If the wolves chose to feast on your treacherous hide our problems would be solved at a stroke. At least we could then claim that we'd found your half-eaten remains somewhere in the forest and thereby claim whatever reward has been placed upon your head without having to explain ourselves.'

'Bastards!' cursed Edmund.

Byram shrugged. 'The wolves have to eat as does every other creature in this forest,' he reasoned. 'Surely that's the way of it?'

Edmund said nothing, knowing that he could expect little in the way of mercy from anyone, least of all Byram. It seemed ironic given that he had at last made some headway in befriending the others in the camp and had only just finished repairing one of the hovels for his own use.

'So,' continued Byram, 'having slept so well, you've no doubt come up with a better ploy by which we can secure all that which you've so generously promised to share with us – or shall we just kill you now and be done with it? I fancy most of us here would prefer the latter as it's a much safer option for us even though the rewards will be less.'

Edmund had no particular plan beyond the rudiments of an idea which had come to him at some point during the night. 'Does the boy still ride that big black stallion?' he asked.

Hild confirmed that he did. 'In fact, I'm told he rides it first thing almost every day. So, what of it?'

'Well, it's a powerful beast,' said Edmund. 'One fall from that should serve to snap his neck like a twig.'

Hild just laughed. 'Have you not seen him ride? He's no more likely to fall than he is to fly.'

'No, but supposing his saddle was to slip? No rider, however skilled, could stay mounted then.'

'Are you suggesting that could be arranged?' asked Byram curiously.

'These things can be "helped" to happen,' noted Edmund. 'Whilst he's saddling the horse, one of these two good ladies could distract him. I'm sure they could manage that given what Hild has told us already about the boy's "natural" appetites. Having once tasted the fruit, he'll be all to easily tempted to sample some more if offered a "reminder" of what he enjoyed when he lay with her the other night.'

'How would that help us?' asked Byram.

'Whilst thus distracted by Hild, Mayda could slip away and slice through the girth strap to his saddle.'

Suddenly Byram was all ears. He looked first at Hild and then at Mayda, anxious to gauge their reaction.

'Oh, no!' said Mayda dismissively. 'I don't even know what a girth strap is!'

'It's the one which passes under the horse's belly to hold the saddle in place,' explained Edmund. 'It'll be easy enough to sever, but don't cut it all the way through as he'd be bound to notice that if you did. Instead, leave enough of it intact to ensure that it'll break once the horse has gone far enough for you to get away from the stables. If you're not there when the accident happens you can't be blamed.'

Hild laughed. 'Aye, that should do it right enough. But you'll need to cut the strap yourself. We'll have no hand in it.'

It was Byram who then spoke, clearly impressed with Edmund's plan. 'Hild, we all of us have much to gain from this boy's death, both you and Mayda included – not to mention your mother. At least listen to what he has to say if only for her sake as it's in all our interests that you help in this.'

Hild still looked very uncertain. 'But what if we're caught? What if somebody sees us?' she pleaded.

'Make sure they don't,' snapped Edmund.

Byram could see that both women were far from being at ease with the proposal. 'We wouldn't ask you to take any unwarranted risk,' he promised. 'But, once back at Wareham, why not at least visit the stables and see how things are set?'

Hild looked at him then at Mayda. 'And that's all we'd have to do?' she said. 'Cut the girth strap and then let matters take their course?'

'Exactly,' confirmed Byram. 'And if you do as Edmund has suggested there would be no one for them to blame, least of all you or indeed anyone from here. Surely that's little enough to ask given what's at stake for us all?'

*****

WAREHAM

The people who resided in Wareham awoke that morning to find their settlement in chaos. During the night the watch beacons all along the coast to the west had been lit, heralding that the much-feared invasion could well be imminent. Already people had begun flocking into the burh, some of them bringing their livestock and such possessions as they could carry with them. Ulrich was frantically trying to sort out accommodation in the form of shelters and tents for as many as possible in the main pasture adjoining the farm when he received a message saying that he was needed at the Vill.

He left them to sort things out for themselves and went straight to join Osric, Oswald and Edward in the Hall.

'So, are you coping well enough?' asked Governor Osric as soon as he arrived.

'Lord only knows,' sighed Ulrich. 'No doubt we'll manage but already all the shelters are taken and most of the tents as well. If any more people arrive they'll need to share or sleep in the open. Are we certain the invasion is underway, my Lord?'

It was Oswald who answered. 'The initial reports are that a fleet has been sighted, but we don't yet know exactly where or how many vessels are involved.'

Ulrich, who was not normally a religious man, crossed himself. 'Then God help us, that's all I can say, for we're still far from ready.'

'Yes, God help us all,' agreed Osric. 'But we must first help ourselves. The watchmen who man the beacons at the headland south-east of here have lit both, which means they fear it is the invasion, but we'll send riders to determine that for ourselves. It's one place where there's a clear view of almost all the sea approaches.'

Ulrich shook his head despairingly. 'That's to the good, my Lord, but, in the meantime, people are pouring into Wareham and it's proving hard to keep track of them.'

'We've prepared for this!' insisted Osric firmly. 'There's space enough within the fortifications for everyone and room to spare, especially if we use the training area as well. Now, what about their livestock. Are most bringing theirs with them?'

'Some are my Lord, but not as many as you might wish as most preferred to leave theirs behind rather than risk it being requisitioned. I've cordoned off a small section of the main pasture adjoining the farm for them to use but I'm worried that the grazing there won't last for long. By my reckoning, we've not yet stored anywhere near enough hay and feed for the livestock to survive a siege.'

'Then we'll need to get more. If necessary, once we've ascertained the extent of the threat there may be time for small groups of armed men to go back to the farmsteads to fetch what's been left behind. So where is the feed we have being stored?'

'I've been using some of the warehouses at the quay to stockpile provisions for both us and the livestock,' confirmed Ulrich.

'Good. Then Oswald, I need you to organise men from the permanent guard to keep watch there and others to keep matters under control within the settlement itself. With so many people coming here we can't afford for panic to set in.'

'My Lord, shall I then send word to Lord Alfred?' asked Ulrich.

Osric thought about that for a few moments before he answered. 'No, let's wait until we know more,' he decided. 'The Vikings are canny bastards and this may be a ruse to draw him away from where he'll be needed most. Alfred will have seen the beacons anyway, but we should send word to Ealdorman Aelfric.'

'Then I'll attend to that, my Lord,' offered Ulrich.

'Good, but wait until we know more.' Osric then turned to address his nephew. 'So, who will you send to speak to the watchmen on the headland?'

'I'll go myself,' said Oswald. 'I'd prefer to see what's happening at first hand. Wulfric can organise things here in my absence. The resident fyrd and permanent guard have already been called to arms, so he should be able to manage well enough as it's purely a question of organisation.'

'Best not to go alone,' advised Osric. 'There may be an advance party of Vikings who have already landed elsewhere along the coast with a view to making their way here before the main force arrives.'

'I could go with him,' suggested Edward. 'There's not much I can do here except to get under everyone's feet.'

Osric wasn't quite so sure about that. 'No, it could be dangerous,' he warned.

'That may be so,' agreed Oswald. 'But with so many people coming into Wareham including some who are all but strangers, an assassin could easily hide himself among them. Edward may therefore be safer if we get him away from here until things become more settled or we know what we're up against.'

'Besides,' said Edward. 'We have three horses including Fleet, so Sigbert could come as well. With him and Oswald I should be safe enough.'

Osric carefully considered the idea. 'All right,' he agreed in the end. 'But leave now and report back here as soon as you can. If you see any sign of an advance party, return at once to warn us. In the meantime, Wulfric can organise the fyrd and Ulrich can sort out the accommodation and prepare a rota to distribute supplies when needed. I'll make myself visible to all within the settlement in order to keep everyone calm. What else do we need to do?'

It was Ulrich who answered. 'We need to pray, my Lord,' he said coldly. 'If this is truly the first signs of the invasion, then, even having done everything we can, prayers may yet be our only hope.'

* * * * *

As they left the Hall, Oswald took Edward aside. 'Find Sigbert then go to the stables and prepare the horses. I'll meet you at the garrison store where we can draw weapons. I'll have Ida prepare some food for us.'

'Will we need weapons?' asked Edward.

'Hopefully not, but better safe than sorry.'

With that they both went off to prepare things as quickly as they could. For Edward's part, he found Sigbert down by the quay talking with the many people who were seemingly unsure of what they should do or where they should go. Most were alarmed by all the rumours that had begun to spread within the settlement.

'Lighting two watch beacons suggests only that ships have been sighted,' explained Sigbert who was talking to a group who seemed particularly concerned. 'It might well be nothing more than a few raiders. And even if it is the invasion fleet, it could yet be many miles from here and intending to strike elsewhere along the coast.'

Edward caught his arm and took him aside. 'We've work to do,' he said quietly. 'You and I are to ride out to the headland south-east of here to speak to those on watch.'

'Why there?' asked Sigbert.

'Osric seems to think we'll be able to see whatever ships there are from there. Do you know the way?'

'Yes, it's a little over ten miles from here as the crow flies but it's not an easy journey. If we leave by the west gate there's a track we can follow from there. It's not the most direct route but it avoids areas which are likely to be too wet or sodden. The terrain then becomes very steep in places but presumably we'll take the horses?'

'Exactly. We need to get them ready so we can leave within the hour.'

With that, they went to the stables and Edward told Caelin to help him saddle three horses, including Fleet. Between them they soon had them ready. 'I want you to stay here for the rest of the day keeping an eye on things,' he ordered. 'People may bring cattle or other livestock to graze in this pasture and, if they do, allow only those who have permission from Governor Osric himself. The guard here will back you up if anyone objects and will direct them to the other pasture in the centre of the settlement which they can use if they wish. In the meantime, keep the gate here fastened at all times. We should be back later today.'

'What about Father Cuthbert's horse?' asked Caelin.

'Keep it stabled for now. It may yet be needed.'

From there they both went to the garrison store where Oswald was waiting.

'So, are we expecting trouble on the way, sir?' asked Sigbert when he saw that Oswald was considering which weapons to take with them.

'We don't know what we're expecting,' stressed Oswald. 'There could be an advance party that has already landed and so we have to assume the worst.' He then offered Edward a sword.

Edward looked at the weapon and accepted it, although didn't feel sufficiently comfortable at the prospect of using it.

'You'll wield it well enough if you have to,' Oswald assured him. He then handed Sigbert a bow. 'I haven't yet had time to sort through all the war gear we took from the Vikings, so choose what you will from that pile over there. We'll be riding hard so a leather jerkin is probably better than mail but you should each have a shield and a seax as well.'

Having chosen their equipment, Oswald was anxious to set off without further delay, so they mounted up and rode out through the settlement, parting the crowds as they went. From there they left via the west gates and joined the track which Sigbert had suggested using and followed it as they made their way towards the headland.

*****

Later that morning, having spent the night at the robbers' camp, Hild and Mayda joined the throng of people coming into Wareham and, like them, were made to wait in line as everyone was checked before being allowed to cross the north bridge. Once inside the burh, most people were forced to follow directions given by the guards but, as residents, Hild and Mayda were allowed to go straight to their camp. They hurriedly stowed away all that which they'd taken with them then went inside their hovel and remained there. After all, there was nothing more they could do save to wait for further news, particularly as with so much going on it was unlikely that any of the men would come looking to avail themselves of Hild's favours.

*****

Governor Osric took up a position outside the Vill with a member of his permanent guard on either side of him, more as a show of strength than to afford him protection. A crowd of people quickly assembled around him anxious for news, but he first called for silence and then calmly waited for them to settle before speaking.

'As you will have gathered, there would seem to be the prospect of an imminent attack from the Viking fleet but, at this stage, we have very little information about what that entails. Even now my nephew is riding hard to the headland to find out at first-hand more about what is actually happening and should report back soon. Meanwhile, this is not the time to panic. Everything is in hand. Accommodation is limited but should suffice so make the best of it you can, although some of you will be required to share with others. Be assured that we have ample provisions to withstand a siege until the King arrives with reinforcements. I would have you share that information with others as fear and panic are as much our enemy as is whatever threat there is from the Vikings. I will say more later but, for now, rest assured that once inside these fortifications, we are all of us safe enough.'

'So where is Alfred?' shouted one man.

'Aye, where is the King and his army?' added another.

Osric raised his hand once more for silence. 'The King is but a few days' march from here and will be sent word once we know how serious the threat we now face is likely to be. In the meantime, if you serve in the fyrd you should report to Wulfric for duty without delay. In Oswald's absence, he is organising our defences. Above all, remember that we have made ready for this day and can withstand whatever attack emerges. So, I stress again. There is no need for panic or alarm.'

*****

As they made their way along the track, Edward got to see just how fast Fleet could run. He had often let the horse have its head whilst riding in the pasture but, as that was relatively confined, there was barely enough space for the horse to show what he could really do. He got that chance as they made their way with all possible haste towards the headland.

In fact, Edward was astonished at the pace which Fleet seemed to attain with ease. They left both Oswald and Sigbert trailing some way behind them so that he, anxious not to become separated from the others, had to stop in order for them to catch up. As he did so, he allowed Fleet to drink from a small stream.

'Don't get so far ahead,' warned Oswald when he and Sigbert at last arrived. 'Remember there could be danger around every bend.'

'But as yet we've seen no sign of anyone,' protested Edward.

'No, and you won't. If some of the Vikings have already landed the first you'll see of them is likely to be when one of them plants an arrow in your chest. So stay close, for there's safety in that.'

They gave the other horses a chance to drink as well, then carried on, riding as hard as they could manage.

When they at last reached the headland they were greeted by one of the men who had been posted there. He and others usually took turns to stand watch in pairs as part of their fyrd service but, for once, they were all there at the same time, most of them staring out to sea whilst one was tending to the beacons to ensure they were kept blazing fiercely.

'What news?' demanded Oswald as he dismounted.

'Sir, a fleet of perhaps twenty ships has been sighted, albeit still some way out to sea.'

'Show me,' ordered Oswald as he, Edward and Sigbert walked over to the platform which acted as a viewpoint. From there they could see other beacons further along the coast, all of which were also still burning.

'Sir, can you not see them?' asked the watchman. 'They're moving very slowly eastwards but are hard to spot as their sails are furled. There's no wind today to speak of, so they've probably taken to the oars in order to maintain some sort of progress.'

Neither Oswald nor Edward could see anything at first but Sigbert spotted the ships at once.

'Look, there they are,' he said, pointing out to sea. 'They're just below the horizon.'

'So where are they headed?' asked Oswald.

'It's difficult to say, sir,' said the watchman. 'But I now doubt they're headed for Wareham.'

'Why do you say that?'

'Because rowing is hard work so men, being lazy bastards, tend to take the shortest route to wherever they're going. Their present course would look to be Wight Island. If they were coming here they'd be closer inshore by now and headed straight towards us. Besides, they'll have seen our beacons so will know full well that they've been sighted.'

'How many ships can you see?' queried Edward.

'About twenty so far as we can tell. Although how big and what type is impossible to say for certain.'

'Then where's the rest of the fleet?' asked Oswald. 'We've had warnings of ten times as many ships as that and possibly a good many more besides.'

'Sir, my guess is that the Vikings are holed up somewhere in Francia across the water but, for reasons known only to them, these ships have decided to leave the main fleet. Perhaps the rest will follow in due course but, if so, God knows where they're planning to strike.'

'So, what are the rest waiting for?'

The watchman clearly had no more idea about that than anyone else. 'Sir, perhaps they're waiting on a favourable wind,' he ventured at last.

Oswald considered the theory and quickly decided that it did make sense. 'Then once they've reached Wight Island, where next?' he asked aloud.

'No doubt they'll first need to rest after rowing so far,' suggested the watchman. 'They'll also use the opportunity to take on fresh water, but I doubt they'll then suddenly turn and come back here, if that's what you're thinking.'

It was exactly what Oswald was thinking. 'Keep watching them as you can never be sure what these bastards intend. Do you have any horses here?'

The watchman nodded. 'Aye sir, there's one at a farmstead not far from here we can use.'

'Good. Fetch it then keep it here. It's to remain saddled at all times and if anything changes, you're to use it to get word to us at Wareham at once. In the meantime, we'll get back there and make our report. Thank God the threat seems not to be as serious as we feared.'

*****

By the time Oswald, Edward and Sigbert returned to Wareham it was already late afternoon. Although tired, Oswald and Edward went straight to the Vill to report what they'd seen, leaving Sigbert to return the horses to the stables and help Caelin to attend to them.

'Uncle, there are about twenty ships but they're a long way out to sea,' reported Oswald. 'As there's no wind, they appear to be rowing their way along the coast, so it's unlikely they'll strike here.'

Osric was not so easily convinced. 'Let's hope you're right. But that means the rest of the fleet is still unaccounted for and their whereabouts remains unknown.'

'Exactly,' said Oswald. 'Hence I think we should keep everyone here until we know more about what's actually happening. We should also send word to Alfred so he's aware of what we've seen.'

Osric was pleased to see his nephew responding so well. 'Good. I'll have Ulrich see to that. In the meantime, I'll leave you to check on the defences, although Wulfric has done well on that account. He has already ordered all the chains to be raised to block both rivers, just in case.'

Impressed with the preparations, Oswald could find little to add. 'We should also send word to Twynham and ask them to send men to collect the two captured ships from here,' he suggested. 'They'll be of more use to us there – although the lack of wind means they'll have to row them back.'

Surprisingly, having been so keen to keep the ships in Wareham, Osric now seemed at ease with that suggestion.

'Then if I may, Uncle, as everything seems so well in hand, Edward and I need to get some rest. We've had a long hard ride to get there and back so quickly.'

Osric looked at them both. 'But a worthwhile journey nonetheless,' he ventured. 'If what you've reported is correct, it would seem that the ships have passed us by, so let's hope that's the end of this matter so far as we're concerned, at least for now. We should give thanks to God for that, as certainly the news you've brought could well have been far worse.'

Chapter Seven

WAREHAM

Aldred, the man they'd sent to Twynham to offer them the two captured longships, returned the next day looking very dejected. 'They all but ignored me!' he complained to one of the guards at the Vill as he waited to speak with Osric, Oswald and Edward. 'There was such panic because the Viking fleet has been sighted that hardly anyone had time to even acknowledge me.'

He was then shown through to the Hall where he repeated his concerns.

'Are you saying that they're ill prepared at Twynham?' queried Oswald.

'I regret that's so, sir. Or at least, that's how it seemed to me. Men were running this way and that with nobody taking the time to properly assess their position.'

'But the people have all been admitted into the burh and offered sanctuary?' asked Osric, concerned for their safety.

Aldred chose his words carefully, fearing he had already said more than he should. 'They have, my Lord,' he said. 'But it seems things there are not as well prepared as they are here.'

Oswald looked at his uncle then back at Aldred. 'So, what arrangements are they making to collect the ships?' he asked.

'None, sir,' replied Aldred. 'They said they can't spare the men needed to come here to collect them. At least, not at present.'

Osric sneered. 'They would refuse a gift of two longships both of which have been repaired at my expense?'

'So it would seem, my Lord.'

'But the whole point in offering them was so they could be used to better protect all the settlements along this part of the coast! Surely, that has to be our priority at present?'

'My Lord, I think that what concerns them is that part of the Viking fleet was already moored off Wight Island and has now been joined by the twenty or so ships we've seen. From there it's close enough to strike at any one of several coastal settlements, including their own.'

'How many ships are there?' asked Oswald, fearing the worst.

'Sir, they claim that it now numbers at least eighty vessels all told.'

'Presumably the others somehow managed to slip past us or perhaps they kept far enough out to sea not to be seen,' suggested Oswald. 'But at least we now know where they are.'

Governor Osric wasn't quite so sure about that. 'Yes, but it still leaves the rest of the fleet unaccounted for,' he pointed out. 'Don't forget, if it does now include the ships that were raiding along the north coast of Devon, it could mean there are at least another hundred ships lurking somewhere along this coast ready to strike at will.'

'Exactly,' said Oswald. 'Or they could just as easily double back to strike here hoping to catch us unawares - or perhaps even attack in two places at once! That would surely cause Alfred some serious problems.'

'Did you speak to the Garrison Commander whilst at Twynham?' asked Osric, returning his attention to Aldred.

'I did eventually, my Lord,' he replied. 'He said to tell you that he's keeping a close watch on the fleet but thinks the invasion will most likely be at Southampton as they can strike there more readily. Also, like here, it offers tactical benefits for then moving inland via the rivers once the burh there has been taken.'

Osric nodded as if to acknowledge the sense of that. 'You've done well,' he said at last. 'Thank you for reporting so promptly. Please say nothing of what you've told us to anyone outside this Hall as we need to avoid causing unnecessary panic. Our defences are well set and we're equipped to withstand an attack if it comes, so there's nothing more we can do for now but wait.'

Aldred bowed and left Osric, Oswald and Edward to consider what he'd told them.

'Uncle, what you said is true, we're as well set as could be expected, although admittedly far from ready. It's a pity they declined the offer of the longships as I'm certain they could have been put to better use than being pulled up onto the quay here and left to rot.'

'Who was the man who sailed them back here after the battle?' asked Osric.

'He's a trader called Edgar,' said Oswald. 'He seemed to know well enough what he was about.'

At that point Edward mentioned what Sigbert had said about the incident in which both vessels had been damaged whilst being sailed back to Wareham after the battle. 'Perhaps he was not quite as skilled as you think,' he implied.

'Do you mean because of the collision that occurred after they entered the harbour?' suggested Oswald. 'If so, don't forget that I was among the wounded on board at the time.'

'So, what actually happened?' asked Osric.

'All I know is that Edgar was commanding the front vessel but was very short handed so struggled to keep control. I don't know who was commanding the other ship but it collided with ours, striking our side with its prow. The damage was not great, but could have been much worse.'

'Then is Edgar an able commander or not?' pressed Osric.

Oswald thought about that. 'Yes, I would describe him as such.'

'Then have him attend us. I would hear his account of what happened and, if then satisfied as to his competence, would see whether he can suggest ways in which we can put both these vessels to better use.'

*****

Following the meeting with Osric and Oswald, Edward went straight to the stables intending to check on Fleet who he had left to Caelin and Sigbert to unsaddle the night before despite having ridden the stallion so hard. It was just as well as, when he got there, he found Caelin struggling with the other horses, including Father Cuthbert's. He'd managed to get them out of the stables but, whilst he was tethering one, the other two had wandered off into the pasture where they roamed seemingly at will. Edward helped him to round up the strays and held them until Caelin was ready to deal with them.

'What are they all needed for?' he asked as the boy returned from fetching one of the saddles which, as usual, he struggled to carry.

'They're needed to collect more hay and feed, sir,' replied Caelin. 'Ulrich says we won't have enough and must therefore get what we can from some of the now deserted farmsteads.'

'They use carts for that so you'll need to fit the horses with harnesses, not saddles,' explained Edward. 'Do you know which carts they're intending to use?'

Caelin looked flustered. 'I think there are two at the Vill's farm,' he said. 'We also have the one here which belongs to the priest.'

'Are there no others in the settlement at present?' he asked.

'I'm not sure, sir. I was just told to prepare the horses and they'd come to collect them shortly.'

'Well, the priest's cart is too small for carrying hay but I suppose it might suffice for a few sacks of feed if there's nothing better. I suggest we get the horses ready but leave it to the men from the farm to sort out the harnesses as they'll know what's needed. When they get here, I want you to go with the horses to look after them. Give them a small feed to start with and make sure they're given something more later. Also, remind whoever's driving them to ensure they're rested and watered regularly. These are not farm horses who are bred for toil so they'll find the work hard.'

'Sir, I thought I was to stay here and stop people grazing livestock in the pasture,' said Caelin.

'I'll have the guard watch over things whilst you're away. You're the stable boy so your job is to look after these horses and not let them be abused. If they are, warn whoever is involved that you'll report them to me.'

Having given his instructions, Edward went to fetch Fleet, allowing the horse to walk beside him towards the pasture. With that, Odelia arrived but stopped first to say a few words to Caelin.

'How are you getting on?' she asked the boy.

Caelin was slow to answer. 'There's much to be done, my lady, and I find the work hard,' he complained. 'Perhaps because I'm not used to it. Also, I sometimes get confused about what needs to be done first.'

'Don't worry, you'll soon get the way of it,' Edward assured him having overheard what he'd said. 'Whilst you're away, I'll let Fleet run free in the pasture. When the horses have finished their labours, let them loose for a while as well. We'll groom them all later.'

'Are you planning to ride Fleet this morning?' asked Odelia.

'Why? Had you something else in mind?'

'I was going to suggest we go for a walk,' she said, shyly.

Edward missed her point completely. 'I'd like that, but I think it's too dangerous at present. I must stay close to the Vill. Besides, even though Fleet was ridden hard yesterday, he misses it if I don't take him out for even a short gallop. Do you mind?'

Odelia smiled. 'No, I love to watch you ride. Perhaps we can walk together afterwards? If we go to the river we won't be far from the Vill so should be safe enough.'

Edward was pleased at the prospect of that and so promised that he wouldn't be long.

*****

WAREHAM FOREST

The monk, Brother Linton, went across to join Edmund who was still bound to the tree with his hands tied behind his back.

'It would seem you have few friends here,' observed Brother Linton.

'I don't seem to have any friends here,' corrected Edmund.

'We all of us have a friend in God,' the monk assured him, taking his place beside Edmund on the ground. 'By the way, I'm known to all as Brother Linton.'

'I know who you are well enough,' said Edmund. 'What I don't understand is why you'd want to speak with me. All the others would prefer to see me dead.'

'I gathered that to be so,' said Brother Linton. 'But you must understand that most of those here have something to hide and are afraid that you'll betray them. You shouldn't have threatened to do that if you want to befriend them.'

'And what about you? Are you not afraid that I'll betray you as well?'

Brother Linton smiled knowingly. 'I have nothing to fear from the law. If caught, I shall simply tell them the truth. That I'm here doing what I should be doing, administering to the needs of my flock.'

'You're a monk, not a priest,' scoffed Edmund.

'We all do God's work as best we may,' replied Brother Linton.

'Which is more than I can say for the rest of these bastards. Having seemingly abandoned any hope of getting a share of my fortune, most are now only interested in collecting whatever price has been set upon my head. What's more, they don't seem overly bothered whether I'm alive or dead when they claim it. In fact, I almost think they'd prefer the latter.'

'You can hardly blame them for that. If it worries you, then having come here seeking their protection you should not have murdered the priest's guard in cold blood. They warned you that it was not their way to kill those they rob lest it bring the authorities down upon them. They all of them have a lot to lose if caught.'

'What else was I supposed to do?' sneered Edmund. 'That guard would have killed me soon enough, for I'm no match for anyone using a spear. Besides, what are they so worried about? If taken, they'll all be hanged anyway for the crimes they've already committed, so my killing the guard won't make much difference one way or the other.'

'There's a big difference between robbing a man and killing him, if not in law then at least in the eyes of God.'

'Did you then know the wretch I killed? Is that why my crime troubles you?'

'I didn't see him but it's unlikely I'd have known him even if I had. And my concern is for your immortal soul because killing is never the answer and is against one of our Lord's commandments.'

'Easy for you to say,' said Edmund. 'You've lived a sheltered life within the sanctuary of the Church. They clothe you and feed you – and for what? Just so you can mutter a few prayers and then charge people for doing so?'

'Not so,' said Brother Linton. 'As you rightly said, I'm a monk, not a priest. Besides, the Church and I don't see eye to eye on many matters.'

'Such as?' asked Edmund.

'For one thing, they've strayed far from the strictures of our calling by venerating dubious relics.'

'That's a brave stand for a monk!' observed Edmund. 'Isn't that what they call biting the hand that feeds you?'

'Having left my order, I'm obliged to look to my own efforts for whatever I need in this world and receive little or no support from the Church. It's a hard road to travel, that much is certain, but it would be harder still for a man of conscience such as myself to ignore something which I know to be wrong.'

'Even though that makes you a heretic?' said Edmund.

'I'm not a heretic,' protested the monk. 'I'm just a man with a troubled soul. I willingly devoted my life to God and to the Church thinking they are one and the same, although quickly found that wasn't so. I therefore remain true to my beliefs and convictions and live as I do with an easy conscience. I draw what comfort I can from that.'

'Ha! That's easy for you to say. I never set out to be a robber, a murderer nor even a slave yet have somehow been obliged to become all three.'

'Then the only comfort I can offer is that which you'll find in the parable of the prodigal son.'

That surprised Edmund. Having been raised in a deeply religious family, he knew the parable well enough but failed to see its relevance. 'What the hell has that to do with anything?' he asked. 'It's been a good many years since I read the scriptures but, as I recall, the prodigal son is about a man who left his home and squandered his inheritance. When he had nothing left, he returned to his father and begged to be allowed home.'

'Not exactly,' explained Brother Linton. 'It's true that in the story the youngest son went off to a foreign land and frittered his share of his inheritance on worldly pleasures and sinful ways. There was then a famine and he realised that even his father's servants were eating better than he was. He therefore returned home and begged his father to forgive him. Of course, like any parent, his father was delighted to see his son come home so gave him clothes and food, then killed the fatted calf to celebrate his return.'

'I recall there was something about his older brother being jealous. After all, he didn't squander his inheritance, but dutifully stayed on to help his father instead.'

'Exactly, but the parable is not about jealousy. I believe it teaches us that the father was so pleased to see his wayward son return that he was prepared to overlook his many failings. In that respect he is like God, our father in Heaven, who rejoices for every truly repentant sinner who returns to grace.'

'So, what has that to do with me?' queried Edmund. 'I didn't go off and fritter anything. I was taken to a foreign land against my will and held as a wretched slave!'

'Yes, but like the prodigal son, you found your way home in the end. Yet instead of giving thanks for that, you set about murdering those who it seemed had usurped you. Your greed for material wealth and for regaining your old status seems to have possessed you. If you would now return to righteousness, there is but one path for you to follow. You must truly repent and atone for all your sins. If you do that, then God will surely forgive you and welcome you back to his fold. Remember, what the parable says – '*There will be rejoicing in the presence of the angels of God over one sinner who repents.*'

'But surely I'm entitled to reclaim what was rightfully mine?' pleaded Edmund.

The monk just smiled. 'We are none of us "entitled" to anything as of right, not even the breath in our bodies nor the blood in our veins. All we have and all we hold ourselves to be is a gift from a merciful and bountiful God and, like any father, he would want to see you return.'

At that, Brother Linton got up and started to walk away.

'So what are you then saying I should do?' called out Edmund.

The good monk stopped before turning to answer. 'I'm saying that if you would redeem your soul you must forget about your inheritance and earthly things. Why not give it all to the good people here that they can then amend their ways as well? Thereby you may repent and do penance for your crimes. If you do that, you'll find redemption not just in this life, but also in the one hereafter.'

*****

WAREHAM

Odelia had remained at the stables talking to Caelin as Edward carefully checked Fleet's saddle before riding, albeit it was by then much later than usual. With so many people milling about the settlement and in particular the quay, no one paid much mind to Hild and Mayda as they wandered into the stabling area of the Vill on the pretext of admiring Fleet. The guard on duty there recognised them both so merely acknowledged them.

'I think Edward normally rides earlier than this,' noted Hild.

'How does that help us?' asked Mayda.

'It doesn't. But it does mean that if we are to do this we'll have to get here before him and then bide our time. With all that's going on, he'll likely come only when he can.'

'So, are you now thinking that we should go through with it?' said Mayda, clearly worried.

'Why not? It looks simple enough. The good thing is that he's much distracted at present as that new stable boy hardly knows what he's about and can barely manage the work he's given. We can take advantage of that. But let's see how he greets us.'

The two women went over to Edward on the pretext of petting Fleet. At first he seemed pleased to see them.

'So, when will you visit me again?' cooed Hild. 'I've told Mayda about all that we did together.'

'Yes,' said Mayda. 'She said that you were like this stallion of yours and so would dearly love for you to come again.'

Edward was flattered and said he would but, in reality, he had no intention of doing so. Oswald's comments about whores had troubled him greatly given that his mother had been one. He had never before thought much about what that really entailed but now, having visited a whore, he felt he had somehow betrayed her. At that, he mounted up and both women waved as he rode off.

Odelia had seen the two women and whilst she didn't know who they were, she instinctively knew what they were. She was not best pleased and said as much to Sigbert when he arrived. 'Are they now the sort of women he prefers to consort with?' she said angrily. 'If so, then tell him I've better things to do with my time.' With that, she turned and stalked off.

When Edward returned, Sigbert repeated what Odelia had said.

'But I was only talking to them,' he reasoned.

'Sometimes that's all it takes,' explained Sigbert. 'You'll need to be careful or you'll lose her, that much is certain.'

'Then what can I do?' asked Edward.

'If it was me, I'd ask for her hand in marriage and be done with it.'

'I've done that. Or at least, I think it's understood between us that we'll wed.'

'Not the same thing,' said Sigbert firmly. 'A formal proposal is what's needed and the sooner the better. You could do a lot worse for yourself than marry such a pretty and well-placed young woman. In fact, you'd be hard pressed to do any better, despite all you have to offer.'

'We're you ever married?' asked Edward.

'What has that to do with anything?' queried Sigbert, seeming reluctant to answer.

'It's just that I noticed that you didn't seem inclined to visit Hild yourself the other night.'

Sigbert laughed. 'I was there on duty to make sure you remained safe whilst with her. But in answer to your question, yes, I was once married to a woman who was worth more to me than life itself.'

'So, what happened?'

'She died giving birth to our son, who didn't live much longer than she did. He would have been about your age by now – well, perhaps a little younger – but the loss of them both hurt me greatly.'

'Hence the prospect of laying with Hild didn't much interest you?'

'I wouldn't say that's true as I've as much interest in laying with a woman as any man. After all, we all of us have our needs in that respect, but I'm not well disposed to visiting whores. Besides, at my age, few things matter more than a warm bed, good ale and food in my belly.'

*****

Having returned to their hovel, Hild and Mayda discussed what they should do.

'What do you think?' asked Mayda.

'I think we could manage it easily enough,' said Hild.

'But is it worth the risk, that's what worries me? We're promised a share of a great fortune but promises are easily broken. Besides, he's a noble, so how could the likes of us ever hold him to the bargain?'

'That's a risk we'll have to take. The greater risk is that we do nothing as I'll soon be too old to ply my trade, which would mean we're both then likely to starve. Remember, the life of a whore is brief and filled with peril. This could be our one chance to find a better way to live if we can but summon the courage to see it through.'

Mayda still seemed to have her doubts. 'So how would we do it?'

'That's easy, we'll go to the stables again tomorrow and do just as Edmund suggested.'

'But why so soon?' queried Mayda, still unconvinced. 'I thought we agreed to assess the situation first.'

'I think we should act before we lose our nerve,' explained Hild. 'Also, we shouldn't be seen around the stables too often lest we arouse suspicion. If we go there again tomorrow, I can distract the guard easily enough. As I do so, you steal his knife and, once you have it, use it to cut the girth strap. If you keep the horse between you and the stables, nobody will see what you're about.'

'What about the guard?' said Mayda. 'He's bound to know it was us.'

'Not if once it's done, you leave his knife on the ground nearby so that when they find it he'll be blamed. And don't worry, he's a vicious bastard who once beat me for not doing as he wished in order to satisfy his filthy wants and desires, so it'll serve him right. Besides, he'll soon convince them of his innocence and with the settlement now so crowded, they won't know who else to blame. They'll most likely assume it's the handiwork of another assassin who came in with the hordes of other people seeking shelter here.'

Although Mayda remained doubtful about the plan, they seemed to have agreed that they should go ahead with it.

'That haughty little lady from the Vill didn't seem very keen to see us,' noted Mayda.

'That's true,' agreed Hild. 'She's happy enough for me to teach the boy what's what and will benefit from that when he gets around to bedding her, though he won't be much use to her or to anyone once he's killed. Mind, I wouldn't want to see him maimed or left to linger like a cripple,' she added. 'That would be a waste.'

'You're too soft,' chided Mayda. 'But don't worry, you've seen the way he rides. If he takes a fall at his usual reckless pace he'll likely break every bone in his body. No one could possibly survive that.'

* * * * *

Odelia returned to the Vill where she found her mother, a lady by the name of Eanflead, busily hiding their valuables in case the Vill should be taken by the Vikings if and when the attack came. She was a tall and somewhat serene woman who many felt had adopted airs above her station considering she was married to a mere Garrison Commander, even if he was the nephew of the Governor himself.

'What's wrong?' she asked, seeing at once that Odelia was upset.

'It's nothing,' Odelia assured her, not wishing to say anything more.

'Is it Edward?' she pressed, knowing it almost certainly was. 'What's he done to upset you so?'

'Nothing, except that when I went to the stables I found him talking to two harlots. Who knows what he gets up to when my back is turned? And something happened the other night. I'm not sure what it was as he wouldn't say but…'

Eanflead put her hand on her daughter's shoulder. 'You'll have to get used to how men behave,' she said consolingly. 'They are often thoughtless and sometimes cruel even though they don't mean to be. It's just that they're so easily tempted by the prospect of what might be on offer elsewhere. They usually regret it afterwards and beg for forgiveness if found out, but it won't stop them doing it again.'

Odelia looked at her mother who she had not expected to be so wise in such matters.

'It's just the way they are,' continued Eanflead. 'You'll not change them. But you must make it clear from the outset that you'll not tolerate the situation either.'

'How do I do that?' she asked.

'I think you already know. In fact, I think that in walking away from him the message will be plain enough, even to a man.'

*****

On Sigbert's advice, Edward left it until later before going to make his peace with Odelia, thereby giving her time to calm down. Even so, he got a cool reception.

'If you've a mind to consort with harlots, then I'll have nothing more to do with you,' she warned.

Edward could see she'd been crying and moved to embrace her, but she shrugged him off.

'I was only talking to them,' he tried.

'Really? And you expect me to believe as much?'

'It's true,' he pleaded, conveniently ignoring all he'd previously done with Hild. 'But if it upsets you so, I'll not so much as speak to them again.'

'Nor go to see them,' insisted Odelia. 'I don't know if you have visited them and I don't want to, but you must promise to have no truck with them ever again.'

'I promise,' said Edward willingly. 'Now, can we at least walk together? Just to show we're still friends.'

She hesitated at first but then agreed. 'Very well. But I'm still angry.' As if to make her point, she kept herself a little way apart from him and didn't even put her arm in his as she usually did. They made their way along the riverbank until they reached their usual spot beside the willow tree where Edward immediately leaned across and tried to kiss her.

'We're not alone,' she insisted, pushing him aside.

When Edward looked, he could see a man wading in the river, close to the far bank. Alarmed in case he was an assassin, he pulled Odelia aside so they could keep the tree between them and the stranger. The man saw them and waved then tactlessly carried on with what he was doing.

'Do you then know him?' asked Edward.

'His daughter and I used to play together and sometimes we would help him,' she said.

'Help him do what?'

'He catches eels,' she explained as they watched him lift a basket from the river and, having released a bung at one end of it, tipped an eel out into a sack tied to his belt.

'How did he mange to catch that?' asked Edward.

'The baskets are a trap. They're made from willow and are divided into two chambers by a very narrow neck. He places rotted meat at one end and then lays them in the river for the eels to swim into when they smell the bait. To reach it, they have to go through the neck and, once they have, they can't then find their way out again and are thereby caught.'

'Are the eels really so easily fooled?' said Edward.

Odelia laughed. 'You wouldn't believe how stupid they are. It seems they love to explore dark holes and suchlike and sometimes swim into a basket even when there is no bait. In fact, you sometimes get more than one eel in each trap!'

The man then caught another eel which he also tipped out into his sack before placing the trap back in the river.

'How many will he take?' queried Edward, not so much out of interest, more because he dearly wanted the man to leave.

'He has to give half of what he catches to my great uncle Osric in return for the rights to take eels from the river. He therefore needs to catch a goodly few to make it worth his while.'

By then the man had worked his way further downstream and Odelia seemed more inclined to resume what they'd gone there for. They both sat beside the tree and, being of one mind, embraced, albeit a little awkwardly at first. They then lay down together trying to make sure they couldn't be seen. Edward held her for a moment then leaned across to kiss her. As he did so, his hand strayed towards her breast, something he'd learned about from Hild. He was immediately rebuffed.

'If that's how you would have things between us there's something you need to ask me first,' scolded Odelia.

Unsure what she meant, Edward looked at her.

'Something which you will need to speak to my father about. And probably Governor Osric as well as he's head of our family.'

Still Edward wasn't sure what she meant.

'And I fancy that, given your new station in life, Alfred's consent will also be needed before I can give you an answer…'

At that he realised what she was saying. 'You mean if we're to wed?'

She smiled. 'Only if that's what you want. Or perhaps you'd rather take your pleasure with those two harlots?'

'Do you?' asked Edward. 'Want to marry me, I mean.'

'I don't know. You haven't asked me yet.'

Edward hurriedly got up onto one knee. 'Odelia, will you marry me?' he asked as intently as he could manage having not rehearsed what he wanted to say.

She smiled. 'Do you promise that there'll be no more communing with whores and harlots, even after we've wed?'

'Of course,' said Edward.

'Then swear it,' she pressed.

'I do,' said Edward. 'I swear that I shall never consort with their like again.'

'Then you may ask me again once you've spoken to my father and to Governor Osric. Until both they and Alfred have agreed I cannot offer my commitment, for if one of them were to refuse, my reputation would be tainted.'

'Why would it be tainted?' he asked, mystified by what she'd said.

'You really don't know much about the way of these things, do you?'

Edward shook his head.

'Once pledged to each other, it's accepted that a lady may be tempted to allow small "favours" – as a sort of taste of things to come. If the consent of her family was then withheld for some reason, she might come to be regarded by others as being "unsuitable".'

Edward was still not quite sure what she was saying. 'Then I will speak to your father and to Osric. If they agree, I'll then ride to Winchester and seek Lord Alfred's blessing as well. As you say, I can do nothing unless he agrees.'

* * * * *

It was later that day that Father Cuthbert requested an audience with Governor Osric. Given how much was going on at that time and how much Osric had to do, he was not best pleased at having to make time for what he was sure would be some trivial request or, more likely, a complaint.

'Father, what can I do for you?' he asked when he at last found time to speak with the priest.

'My Lord, it is most urgent that I return to my parish. I've already stayed away longer than I intended and there's much there which now demands my attention.'

Osric leaned back in his chair. 'Would this have anything to do with the prospect of an imminent Viking attack?' he asked.

Father Cuthbert knew at once what he was implying. 'Well, not directly, my Lord,' he replied. 'I'm concerned for my life as are we all, but my flock will be as afraid of what's to come as are the good people here. Obviously, my place is with them where I can provide what comfort I can.'

Osric considered that. 'Perhaps that's so, but if you travel back now I fear your flock will quickly be deprived of your pastoral care as you will doubtless need to pass through Wareham Forest in order to return to them.'

At first, Father Cuthbert was not sure what he meant.

'The robbers will kill you,' warned Osric bluntly. 'Be assured of that. You'll have nothing for them to steal and, besides, you were witness to the crime when they killed your guard. On that basis alone they'd rather murder you than allow you to pass.'

'But surely you'll spare a small contingent to protect me at least as far as Winchester?'

'I can't spare so much as a single guard at present, much less a small contingent to travel so far. Does your bishop not have his own guards he can send to escort you?'

'I fear his men are, like yours, already committed elsewhere.'

'In that case, if you feel compelled to return to your duties, I regret that you must do so alone and unguarded.'

'But my Lord, I'm sure Lord Alfred would not approve of you leaving me to fend for myself. Particularly after what happened to me whilst travelling here.'

'Then I suggest that you send word to Lord Alfred and ask him to send men to protect you. I'm sure that with the whole of Wessex likely to come under attack at any time he will have nothing more important on his mind than your welfare – and nothing better for his men to do than to come here then travel with you all the way to Winchester.'

Chapter Eight

Even if Edward's proposal of marriage had seemed somewhat weak and ill-prepared, it at least showed that he was thinking in those terms, which left Odelia feeling very excited. Nonetheless, with so many people whose permission would be needed before the betrothal could be confirmed, she decided not to say anything to anyone at that point, not even her mother. She also decided not to go to the stables the next morning to watch Edward ride lest she let something slip whilst she was there.

For his part, Edward was disappointed not to see her but found plenty to do. Both he and Sigbert helped Caelin to put out feed and water for the horses, all of which had been worked hard the previous day pulling the carts that were being used to carry the supplies needed to feed all the additional livestock which had been brought into the burh for protection. Governor Osric had granted permission for a few additional horses to be grazed in the pasture at the Vill, but the rest of the livestock had been confined to the one that adjoined the Vill's farm. As such, it was close to where so many people were temporarily camped, which seemed logical as it remained the responsibility of each man to attend to whatever animals he'd brought with him.

Having finished helping Caelin, Edward noticed that Hild and Mayda had returned and were talking with the guard who was stationed there, a man named Algar.

'So, why have you not been to see us lately?' teased Hild as she and her sister flirted with Algar. 'It must be weeks since last you came to visit me.'

'We're all too busy,' he explained somewhat weakly. 'Our duties have been extended because of this threat from the Viking fleet. We lost many men in the recent battle and have to cover their duties as well.'

'Well, I've missed seeing you,' purred Hild as she moved much closer towards him before pressing herself up against him. 'You must have missed us.'

'I've missed these,' he said, grinning as he tentatively began feeling her breasts, worried lest she might slap him and thereby reveal to others what he was doing. Being distracted whilst on duty was an offence for which he could be severely punished, possibly even flogged, particularly given that the settlement remained on full alert.

Mayda then moved closer as well. 'What about mine?' she insisted, feigning jealousy. 'Are they not good enough for you?'

Algar could scarce believe his luck. None of the men had ever lain with Mayda and yet here he was, seemingly being invited to do so. 'Let me compare them,' he said as he set about fondling first one woman's breasts then the other's. As Hild moved her hand towards his groin, he didn't notice as Mayda deftly slipped his knife from the sheath he wore attached to his belt. As soon as she had it, she turned away from him. 'Nope. You've made your choice so that's it so far as I'm concerned,' she said firmly.

Hild took her cue from that and also turned away. 'And you've had all the free samples you're going to get from me,' she pouted. 'If you want any more, you'll have to come and see me properly. But don't leave it too long. A woman can get tired of waiting, you know.'

Hild then joined Mayda and together they walked away. 'Did you get it?' she whispered.

Mayda looked back coquettishly and nodded. 'Men are such fools,' she laughed. 'How could they be so easily beguiled? It's like stealing things from a sleeping baby.'

*****

Edgar, the man who had been responsible for sailing one of the two captured longships back to Wareham after the battle, stood outside the Hall and waited to see Governor Osric. Although he resided some way along the coast, he still served in the local fyrd and, like others, had come into the settlement when the watch beacons were lit. When he was at last ushered through to the Hall, he found Osric and Oswald both seated, although Edward was not present as he had matters to attend to at the stables.

'I'm assured that you are one of the most experienced men in these parts when it comes to matters of ships and suchlike?' said Osric.

Edgar was a proud man who stood tall and straight but even he was unsettled at being interviewed by Governor Osric in person. He wanted to answer by saying that there were few men in all Wessex with as much sailing experience as himself but, instead, confined his answer to merely confirming the point. 'That's true enough, my Lord,' he answered modestly.

'As a trader, I have a small craft of my own and have spent some time at sea, sailing all along this coast and even venturing across to Francia on some occasions.'

'Yet despite all that experience, I gather there was an unfortunate incident whilst sailing the two captured longships back here which resulted in damage to them both.'

Edgar stiffened himself, almost aching to defend his reputation. 'That's so, my Lord, although what transpired was through no fault of mine. Both vessels were woefully undermanned and those we did have to help sail them were all weary from the battle. With wounded on board, we were obliged to enter the harbour without delay, regardless of the tide, and thus found ourselves confronting a turbulent sea. The conditions were such that they would have tested even a complete and experienced crew. Also, the man who captained the second ship admitted from the outset that it was beyond his ability to manage it in those conditions but it was considered imperative that we get the wounded back to Wareham with all possible haste. Hence we felt obliged to continue even against our better judgement.'

Osric was surprised to hear all that as it suggested there was more to the issue than he'd been led to believe. 'You will appreciate that these are both very valuable ships so I would know how this damage was sustained,' he pressed.

'My Lord, as the more experienced helm, I led the way, but with so few men at the oars my ship was turned sideways soon after we entered the harbour. I'll warrant this was caused by a strong and quickly ebbing tide. The second ship was making good headway but was following closely to enable the helm to copy what I was doing. Thus he had no time to avoid us and his prow struck the side of our hull a glancing blow. It was not enough to hole either ship and both completed the journey without further collision or undue delay.'

Osric settled back to consider what he regarded as a frank and detailed summary from a man who clearly knew what he was about. 'Thank you for such a clear account,' he said. 'I'm satisfied with what you say so would now seek your advice regarding another matter.'

'Of course, my Lord.'

'You may know that we had intended for both ships to be taken to Twynham where it was felt they could serve some more useful purpose. Unfortunately, that's not now the case and I would hear your views on how they might be better deployed from here.'

Edgar was surprised. He'd assumed he would be required to form a crew and sail them to Twynham, a task he was both ready and willing to undertake. What Osric was now asking was a different matter altogether. 'Have they yet been repaired, my Lord?' he inquired.

'They have,' advised Oswald. 'Although the sails and rigging have yet to be checked.'

'No matter,' said Edgar. 'One option would be to deploy them within the harbour where using the sails for long is unlikely to be viable given it's such a confined area.'

'You would deploy them within the harbour?' said Oswald, clearly surprised at that.

'Aye, my Lords. May I ask whether either of you have any experience of battles at sea?'

Both men were silent, thereby answering the question.

'That's hardly surprising, my Lords, because the Vikings are wont to avoid such conflicts if they can for the simple reason that if their ships are badly damaged, they could find themselves stranded here and unable to sail home. Therefore, if confronted at sea they tend to sail away but, if unable to do so and are forced to fight, they have their own way of doing so.'

'And what way is that?' asked Osric.

'Their favoured method is to lash their ships together to form a floating platform. For that, they take down or furl the sails and, if they have the time, even un-step the masts and rely solely upon the oars in order to manoeuvre without being dependent on the wind. They then fight in much the same way as they would on land, with a shield wall followed by boarding and fierce hand-to-hand fighting.'

Neither Osric nor Oswald were surprised by that and had heard as much before. 'Have you ever been in such a battle?' inquired Osric.

'I have, my Lord, albeit some years ago. As a member of the crew on board one of three ships sailing together, we chanced upon a small fleet of Viking raiders which had been deployed in the way I've described and were blocking the entrance to a harbour we needed to access. I can only say that what followed was every bit as bloody as a battle on land but with the added fear of knowing that if things did not go well, there was no option except to swim, drown or be taken.'

'Were you then successful?' asked Oswald.

Edgar was quiet for a moment. 'We lost one ship and many men before our captain was obliged to break off and sail away. So no, I cannot claim that we had any success in that encounter.'

'Yet are you now suggesting that we deploy these ships in much the same way?' continued Oswald.

'I am my Lords,' said Edgar firmly. 'And for good reason. As you are aware, the entrance to the harbour is narrow and, at times, very difficult to navigate. The Vikings will only come through in small groups but, once within the harbour, will either reform as a fleet or, more likely, attempt to enter the rivers. That would be the logical way for them to attack this settlement and you could make it very difficult for them by mooring the rafted ships off the small island at the mouth of the River Frome. With a shield wall of, say, twenty men on board for protection, a dozen bowmen could wreak havoc with fire arrows as the Viking ships are forced to run the gauntlet past them, particularly whilst restricted to the main channel.'

Osric immediately liked the idea. 'That way we could account for several ships at least before they even reach us here!' he noted, finding the prospect of what was being proposed very interesting, particularly as he'd wanted to keep the ships at Wareham in the first place.

'It seems like a good idea,' mused Oswald. 'But why do we need the ships for that? Could we not just station some men on the island anyway?'

It was Osric who answered. 'Because it's not much more than a mud flat and is under water at some stages of the tide. The men could all too easily become stranded there and thus be lost for very little advantage.'

'Then would it not be the same for your rafted ships?' asked Oswald.

Edgar smiled knowingly. 'No, sir. If it looked as though the ships would be overrun by the Vikings there is a very simple solution. They could be separated, abandoned and then set afire. With the mooring lines cut, provided they were afloat and the tide was not actually rising, the outflow of the river would likely carry the burning ships into the midst of the Viking fleet thereby wreaking havoc.'

'And if the tide was not ideal? What then?'

Edgar shrugged. 'Then it would be better to scuttle the ships rather than risk them falling into Viking hands.'

That surprised both men but it was Osric who raised the obvious concern. 'But what about the men? How would they escape if the ships were scuttled or destroyed?'

'We could use smaller boats to get them off, my Lord,' suggested Edgar. 'I assume you will have a contingent fighting a rear-guard action, loosing arrows as they retreat along the banks of whichever river the Vikings use? If so, the men from the ships could join them. As for the Vikings, being committed to their oars whilst having to negotiate the chains would ensure that they suffer very heavy losses indeed.'

Both Osric and Oswald were impressed. 'This improves our chances no end,' enthused Oswald. 'In fact, could we not dispense with the shield wall completely and provide protection for the bowmen in the form of wicker panels on board both ships? That would release more men to defend the settlement itself.'

'That could work,' agreed Edgar having hurriedly considered the matter. 'Certainly the shield wall would serve no purpose on board other than to provide protection for the bowmen and that could easily be achieved by wicker panels.'

'Good,' said Osric. 'Then that's settled. And what's more, I think we now have the man to command this aspect of our defence. Wulfric will advise you as to which bowmen are best suited for this, but we must exclude Sigbert. Even though he's one of our best bowmen, he's needed to protect Edward at all times.'

'My Lord, I had not intended to put myself forward...'

'Nonsense. I can think of no better man for the job,' decided Osric. 'You will report direct to Oswald as Garrison Commander but with authority to deploy the ships and those aboard them as you see fit.'

*****

Having finished saddling Fleet, Edward checked the girth strap as usual to make sure it was secure. It was then that he noticed the two women were still there and, knowing Odelia would object if she decided to join him after all, went over to them and asked them to leave. 'You shouldn't be here,' he stated firmly. 'We've all got work to do.'

'But you haven't come to see me again,' pouted Hild. 'Am I no longer good enough for you? Or is it just that you're now getting it for free? Is that the way of it?'

'No!' he stormed. 'That's not it at all. It's just that I've now promised and…' he stopped himself from saying more.

Mayda moved towards him, swaying her hips invitingly. 'Perhaps you just need to try some different fruit,' she teased.

'He doesn't need to try anything different,' scolded Hild. 'He knows what he likes well enough, for he made that plain enough the other evening.'

Edward protested but she was having none of it. 'I can teach you things your new lady will thank you for,' she whispered, drawing close to him. 'Things that will make her squeal with delight.'

As Hild distracted Edward, Mayda slipped away on the pretext of having taken offence at his rejection of her. She went across and began to pet Fleet, carefully keeping the horse between her and the stables, just as Hild had suggested.

Having looked around to check that no one was looking, she produced the knife which she'd stolen from the guard then reached down to below the horse's belly and cut the girth strap almost all the way through.

'Leave the horse alone!' shouted Edward, roughly shaking himself free from Hild who was trying to embrace him, then stepping away from her.

'But he's such a beautiful beast,' said Mayda. Then, having discretely dropped the knife, she went back to join her sister.

'I don't think we're very welcome here,' said Hild.

Mayda frowned. 'That's a pity. I know you were hoping that we might persuade this young man to visit you again.'

With that they hurriedly walked away without daring to so much as glance back at either Edward or the horse.

*****

Whilst constructing the panel to make the stables more comfortable for Caelin, Sigbert had seen the two women and was glad to note that Edward had sent them away. He then watched as Edward led Fleet out into the pasture and mounted up. He also noticed that Fleet seemed reluctant to move at first, shying away as if resisting Edward's command.

'Come on boy,' urged Edward. 'What's ailing you this morning?'

Still the horse seemed ill inclined to respond regardless of whatever Edward did to encourage him. It was almost as though he knew something was wrong. Edward thought that was strange as usually the problem was holding Fleet back. He began to worry lest the horse was unwell or was perhaps unsettled by one of the new horses which had been allowed to share the pasture and was just thinking that he should return him to the stables when the horse suddenly responded. Even so, it was not in his normal manner. He held his head up much higher than usual and although he was moving forward, he was stepping sideways at the same time. With Edward's encouragement, he at last broke into a canter, although not into his customary gallop. It was that which made Edward realise that something was indeed troubling Fleet, so decided that if he didn't settle down after the first few laps of the pasture, he'd return him to the stables and try to ascertain what was wrong. As it turned out, he was barely able to complete even one lap before the girth strap broke.

All Sigbert could see was Edward suddenly slip sideways then fall to the ground, landing on his shoulder. At first, he was dragged behind the horse by his foot which had become entangled in something but then the saddle came off as well and Edward rolled away to remain motionless on the ground.

Sigbert knew at once that Edward was badly harmed and rushed across to where he lay.

*****

Fleet reached Edward long before Sigbert. As soon as he realised that he'd lost his rider he returned to where the boy lay and stood over him, gently nudging him with his nose as if trying to help him up.

'Easy boy,' urged Sigbert when he got there, sensing that Fleet had been unsettled by what had happened. Meanwhile, Edward was laying very still, face down on the ground with one arm twisted back at an awkward angle and blood smearing the side of his face. As he bent down to tend to the boy, he was relieved to find that Edward was still breathing. 'Don't try to move,' he insisted. 'Your back may have been harmed in the fall.'

Edward seemed not to hear his advice and tried to turn over. He quickly found that he couldn't manage it unaided as he could barely move his arm without that it pained him dreadfully. Also, he was so dazed that he seemed not to know what had happened or even where he was. In the end, Sigbert persuaded him to remain still. 'I think you may have broken your shoulder,' he said as he examined him. 'It's the one you hurt when Knave fell from under you during the battle, so don't try to move it. We'll need to get help.'

The stable boy then arrived as well. 'Is he alright?' he asked, sounding fearful.

'I'm not yet sure. Go to fetch help and tell them to bring a litter as I doubt Edward will manage to walk by himself.'

The boy hesitated, unsure of where he was supposed to go.

'Hurry,' urged Sigbert. 'Tell that guard over there to send word to the Vill and also to the nunnery.' He then returned his attention to Edward. 'Does it hurt anywhere else?' he asked.

At first, Edward struggled to answer, then seemed to forget what he'd intended to say.

'Alright, don't try to speak,' urged Sigbert. 'I'll get you back to the stables where we can then see what damage has been done.'

*****

Two men arrived with a litter and, between them, gently helped Edward onto it before carrying him back to the stables. Once there, they laid it down on the straw whilst they waited for one of the nuns to arrive. When she did, she hurriedly checked Edward over.

'I don't think his shoulder is broken,' she announced sounding relieved. 'It's simply become misplaced.'

'Can you push it back?' asked Sigbert.

She looked at him then shook her head. 'It's the sort of thing that Ingrid used to do but she never showed me how.'

'Then have you something for his pain?'

'I'll fetch a potion we make from the bark of the willow, although whether it will be enough to help him I cannot say for certain.'

'Do it,' said Sigbert. 'And please hurry. He's obviously in a great deal of pain.'

Osric arrived shortly after that having received word at the Vill. He was accompanied by Algar and another guard. 'What happened?' he demanded, clearly worried.

'My Lord, he fell from his horse,' explained Sigbert.

Osric looked incredulous. 'Edward fell from his horse? I can't believe such a thing! Have you not seen how well he rides?'

'I think it was an accident, my Lord. The girth strap broke and the saddle came off, taking him with it.'

'Has one of the nuns looked at him?'

'Yes, she's gone to fetch something for his pain. She doesn't think his shoulder is broken; more likely it's been displaced.'

'And can she reset it?'

'No, my Lord,' said Sigbert. 'I think she knows what to do but has never done it on her own. Ingrid used to manage injuries such as that when needed.'

'Well, I've done it often enough to men injured on the battlefield,' said Osric. 'But he'll need something for the pain first. Has he complained of any other injuries?'

Sigbert shook his head. 'He's hardly said a word, my Lord, and certainly nothing which makes much sense. My fear is that he struck his head on a stone or something when he fell and is still partly stunned.'

Even as he spoke the nun returned with a small phial from which she made Edward drink. She then bathed his head and seemed satisfied that the bleeding had stopped. 'His head will surely ache for a while but at least that wound seems not to be serious,' she announced.

'Right, we'll give your potion time to work before we try to reset his shoulder,' said Osric. 'Where's the saddle now?'

Sigbert pointed to the pasture where it had been left where it fell.

'Send someone to fetch it and bring it here,' ordered Osric. 'What about Fleet?'

The horse had remained beside the gate, anxiously watching as his master was being attended to.

Sigbert turned to the Caelin. 'Can you remove his bridle on your own?' he asked.

Caelin said that he could by using the steps which Sigbert had made for him, so went across to do so.

'Take Edward back to the Vill, he'll be more comfortable there,' ordered Osric.

The two men who had brought the litter immediately took it up once more and carried Edward back to his lodge as gently as they could. The nun went with them whilst Osric and Sigbert inspected the saddle which Algar had collected from the pasture. It was Sigbert who noticed that the girth strap had been partly severed before it broke.

'It's as I feared,' mused Osric. 'This suggests foul play. Who else was here at the time?'

Sigbert thought for a moment. 'There was myself and Caelin but we were in the stables together. Edward saddled the horse himself. I saw the two whores come down, but Edward sent them packing. Algar, you were also here on duty, were you not?'

Algar confirmed that he was.

'The two whores you say?' mused Osric.

'Aye, my Lord,' said Sigbert. 'They were making a nuisance of themselves yesterday and came again today, but Edward went over and insisted they leave. As I recall, they did so at once.'

As Caelin returned with Fleet's bridle, Sigbert noticed that the boy had a knife tucked into his belt, one he'd not seen before. 'Where did you get that?' he asked, trying not to sound as if he was accusing the boy of anything.

Caelin looked worried. 'Sir, I found it just now,' he managed.

Osric caught Sigbert's drift. 'Found it? Where did you find it, boy?'

Caelin pointed to where Fleet had been tethered. 'Just over there, my Lord. It was on the ground so I picked it up. I was going to hand it in, my Lord, but haven't yet had time.'

Osric took the knife from the boy's belt and showed it to Algar. 'This is yours, is it not?' he demanded.

Algar looked puzzled and then patted the empty sheath in which he normally carried it. 'Why, so it is my Lord. I must have lost it.'

'Lost it when?' he inquired. 'Whilst you were cutting through the girth strap to this saddle perhaps?'

'No, my Lord,' said Algar looking incredulous. 'Why would I do such a thing?'

'The same reason rogues like you do anything. For coin or possibly a favour.'

'No, my Lord,' he insisted. 'That's not true. Besides, I've not been near the horse nor the saddle!'

'We've only your word for that. So, when did you first notice that the knife was missing?'

'I didn't. Not until you mentioned it, my Lord.'

'I think you've got a lot to answer for,' he said, then turned to the other guard. 'Take him to the Vill and hold him there. Inform Oswald of what's happened but tell him to do nothing until I get there. We'll then hear what this wretch has to say for himself.'

*****

By the time Osric and Sigbert reached the Vill Edward had settled somewhat, no doubt helped by the potion the nun had given him. He had been laid out on his cot so Osric helped him to sit up then examined first the wound to his head and then his shoulder, feeling to see how much the joint had been displaced. 'Do you know where you are?' he asked Edward.

Edward nodded, but seemed too drowsy to actually answer.

'Good. I need to put your shoulder back into place. It will hurt like hell when I do it but after that it should begin to feel better.'

Edward nodded again as if to confirm that he understood, although still looked very distant and confused.

Osric gave Edward a strop to set between his teeth, then had Sigbert and the nun restrain him as he took hold of the injured arm and, when the boy least expected it, firmly but skilfully rotated it until it "clicked" back into place. As it did so, Edward tried to scream but his voice was muted by the strop. Instead, he passed out with the pain.

'It's gone back into place easily enough but will take time to heal,' advised Osric. 'There may be other damage as well, so he must now rest.'

'Aye, and I fancy he'll be sorely bruised for a while as well,' noted Sigbert.

For a time, Edward lay there almost as if he was sleeping. 'What… what happened?' he asked when he eventually came round.

'Your saddle came off when the girth strap failed,' explained Sigbert.

'But… but I checked it,' stammered Edward. 'I always check it!'

'We think someone may have cut it on purpose,' Osric told him.

Edward wasn't sure what to make of that. 'Who… who would do such a thing?' he asked, still confused.

'Don't worry about it for now but we found a knife belonging to the guard who was on duty there. It was on the ground near where you saddled Fleet.'

Edward struggled to think back on the events at that time. 'But how could he manage that? I didn't leave the horse unattended.' Even as he spoke, he then remembered something else. 'Wait, I did leave Fleet when I went to send those two whores away.'

'So, could he have done it then?' asked Sigbert.

Edward was unable to answer at first. 'No,' he managed at last. 'At least, I can't see how. More likely it was one of the two whores. I remember now that one of them went to look at Fleet whilst the other one tried to distract me.'

'That's interesting, but it still makes no sense. I mean, why would they try to kill you?' asked Sigbert.

'I don't know,' said Edward, still struggling to recall all that had happened.

'Well, for now you need to rest,' urged Osric. 'But don't worry, we'll get to the root of this.' He then turned to Sigbert. 'I'll start by interrogating the guard but may need to call upon you to attend at some point as you were there at the time. In the meantime, Edward, you need to rest and I suggest that you remain in your bed for the rest of the day at least. The less you move that shoulder the better.'

* * * * *

Osric and Oswald sat together in the Hall, anxiously discussing all that which had happened at the stables.

'So Uncle, is Edward badly injured?' asked Oswald.

'He'll mend,' said Osric. 'I've reset his shoulder but he's badly bruised and he also hurt his head when he fell. Mind, he was lucky not to break his neck.'

'If one of my guards is responsible, I'll have the bastard flogged,' threatened Oswald angrily.

'No, this is a matter for me as Governor. The charge is one of attempted murder so it falls within my jurisdiction, not yours as Garrison Commander.'

'But he's under my command,' protested Oswald. 'I should therefore deal with him.'

'Let's have him brought in and hear what he has to say for himself. We can then decide between us what's to be done.'

Osric then signalled for Algar to be brought in and, as they waited, he asked Oswald what he knew about the man.

'Very little,' he admitted. 'Although not a member of my elite squad, he is one of the permanent guard and, so far as I know, has always served us well.'

Algar was then dragged before them, loudly protesting his innocence. When Oswald ordered him to be quiet, he meekly fell to his knees and waited. It was Osric who then started the interrogation.

'Do you deny that this knife belongs to you?' he challenged, holding up the weapon which they believed had been used to tamper with the saddle.

'No, my Lord, although as I've said, I don't recall losing it.'

'So, what cause had you to murder Edward?' he asked accusingly. 'As far as I'm aware he never did you any injustice.'

'None, my Lord. In fact, I owe him much for I was one of those whose life he saved at the battle, so had no cause to see him harmed.'

At that point Oswald took up the interrogation. 'Why then did you cut the girth strap to his saddle?' he asked, a little more kindly.

'I didn't, sir. Like I said, I never went anywhere near the horse or even the stables for that matter. I positioned myself a little way off from where I could best see all that was going on. Those were my orders, sir.'

'Yet your knife was found close to where the horse was being saddled,' pressed Oswald. 'Or are you going to claim that you lost it somewhere else and it somehow walked there of its own accord?'

'I truly don't know, sir. I fear it may have been stolen and then left there to make it look as though it was me,' he protested.

'And who would do such a thing?'

Algar looked unsure of how best to answer. 'I think it might have been Hild or perhaps Mayda,' he said quietly. 'They distracted me and so could well have taken it.'

'Distracted you?' demanded Oswald. 'In what way did they distract you?'

Still Algar seemed reluctant to answer. 'With their charms, sir. They were all over me, entreating me to visit them again.'

'You allowed them to do that?' said Oswald angrily. 'You let two whores disarm you whilst on duty! You know that you'll be flogged for that alone?'

Algar bowed his head in shame. 'I do, sir. And I regret it. But truly, I played no part in trying to kill Edward. Had I even seen what they were doing or had any inkling of their intent I would have intervened to stop them.'

Osric leaned across to speak to his nephew. 'Given what Edward has already told us, this has the ring of truth about it,' he said quietly.

Oswald agreed. 'But what cause had the two whores to kill Edward?'

'Perhaps they were paid to do it. If the description that priest gave is to be believed, there's every chance that Edmund has now sided with the robbers in the forest. Is it not possible that he sent someone to offer money in return for doing what he couldn't do himself? I wouldn't put it past him.'

'It may be even simpler than that,' suggested Oswald. 'Edward went to visit Hild one evening, albeit under Sigbert's watchful eye. Although we've no proof, I've long suspected that she visits the robbers to ply her sinful trade and, in so doing, may have let slip that Edward is still alive.'

Osric looked shocked. 'Edward went to see one of the whores? Who sanctioned that?'

'I did,' admitted Oswald firmly. 'The boy has his "urges", as do we all, and is of an age where he should know about such matters. Also, I was anxious he should not explore things at the expense of my daughter's reputation. Besides, he needs to know how things are between a man and a woman and has neither father nor friends to explain such matters to him.'

'Even so…' said Osric.

'Uncle, I think we're agreed that this man is guilty of nothing more than the dereliction of his duty. Therefore let me, as Garrison Commander, punish him. We should then call the two whores here and see what they have to say for themselves.'

Osric considered that then agreed.

With that, Oswald pronounced judgement on behalf of them both. 'We have yet to decide what part you played in the attempted murder of Edward,' he said. 'But are both convinced that at the very least you are guilty of a grave dereliction of your duty. To allow yourself to be distracted and disarmed could have left this settlement wide open to attack. It's a heinous crime, particularly at a time like this given the prospect of the Viking invasion. You'll therefore be punished accordingly.'

Still on his knees, Algar looked up at him imploringly. 'My Lord, what man would not be distracted in such circumstances?'

'Perhaps,' admitted Oswald. 'Hence I'm inclined to mercy but cannot let this pass.' He then hesitated as if still trying to decide what punishment would be meted out. 'Three days' continuous duty,' he announced at last. 'If I so much as see you being anything but diligent and committed to your duty, I shall see you flogged. Do I make myself clear?'

'Thank you, sir,' he said gratefully, knowing he had got off lightly. 'You'll not find me wanting, I swear it.'

*****

Odelia went to visit Edward as soon as word of his fall reached her. Given that she was visiting him at his lodgings she was, for the sake of her reputation, accompanied by Ida who had taken an almost motherly liking to the boy. Sigbert was already there having been asked by Osric to remain with Edward at all times as a precaution against any further attempt on his life.

'Are you in much pain?' asked Odelia as Ida set about making Edward more comfortable.

Edward was still sitting up and putting on as brave a face as he could manage. 'I'll be fine, but can barely move my arm without that my shoulder hurts dreadfully,' he complained.

'You should take better care of yourself,' chided Ida. 'You ride that horse as though all the hounds of hell are at your heels.'

'The horse was not to blame,' offered Sigbert. 'In fact, if you recall it was as if he seemed to know there was something amiss and was reluctant to even start out on your usual ride together.'

Edward looked at him, trying to recall what had happened. 'Yes, you're right. I remember that now. I had to almost force him.'

'He also came straight back to see you after the fall and was nudging you as if trying to help you to your feet.'

'I don't remember anything about the fall itself and very little about what happened afterwards until Osric put my shoulder back into place. Even then I passed out with the pain afterwards.'

Ida put her hand on Edward's brow. 'God be praised, there seems to be no fever,' she said sounding relieved. 'But you need to rest. I've made some broth and will bring you a bowl shortly. That should help to restore you.' With that she left.

'I'll wait outside,' said Sigbert tactfully. 'I'm sure there's much you have to say to each other.' As he withdrew, he purposely left the door ajar.

Odelia settled on the edge of Edward's cot and gently leaned across to soothe his brow with her hand. 'They say the guard had been paid to kill you,' she said, sounding worried.

'I doubt it,' said Edward who felt much comforted by her being there. 'More likely it was those two whores.'

'But you promised you wouldn't see them again!' she scolded.

'I didn't. I mean I did, but only because they came to the stables again. I ordered them to leave at once but Sigbert says that one of them went over to pet Fleet. I bet that's when she cut the girth strap. But don't worry, Osric and your father are looking into it.'

Odelia seemed to accept that. 'Which reminds me, have you yet spoken to my father and Governor Osric?'

'About what?' teased Edward beginning to feel better.

'You know perfectly well what about!' she scolded.

'Was it something important?' he asked. 'It's just that my head hurts so and my memory is not so good after the fall. I seem only to remember the things which mattered to me most…'

"Good. Then you won't remember what I said to you, will you?'

He laughed. 'I will speak to them as soon as I can. But I won't be able to ask Lord Alfred for his permission until I am able to see him.'

'Then you'd best hope that whilst you're lying here in your cot feeling sorry for yourself, I don't change my mind and marry someone else. There are plenty of other fish in the sea.'

Chapter Nine

On Osric's orders, Oswald sent two members of the permanent guard to arrest both Hild and Mayda and haul them back to the Vill for interrogation. Having been treated none too gently along the way, the women were then made to remain outside, both of them terrified at the thought of whatever fate awaited them.

As they were eventually led into the Hall, Oswald got up to leave. 'I assume this is no longer a military matter,' he said. 'So if I may, Uncle, I would take my leave of you as there's much which still requires my attention elsewhere.'

Osric raised his hand. 'I'd like you to stay if you will, for there's something I wish to discuss with you afterwards.' He then instructed the guards to remain with them as well but said nothing as the two women knelt before him. Instead, he just stared first at Hild and then at Mayda who both lowered their eyes to avoid his gaze.

He could see why he had never once availed himself of Hild's services. Both she and her sister looked to be dirty and dishevelled, with poor complexions and hair which was worn uncovered and was both lank and unkempt. Given the state of their appearance, it worried him that Oswald had allowed Edward to visit them.

'I have it on good authority that you were both in the stabling area of my Vill just before Edward was thrown from his horse,' he announced at last.

‘That’s true my Lord,’ insisted Hild, speaking for them both. ‘It’s our custom to enjoy a walk after a night spent…’ she stopped herself at that, not wishing to say what they had been doing of a night although guessed correctly that as Governor, Osric knew exactly what that entailed. ‘Anyway, we’ve taken a liking to that big black stallion and often go to see him as he’s such a magnificent horse.’

‘I’m also told that whilst there you distracted my guard and robbed him of his knife. A knife which I suspect you then used to cut the girth strap to Fleet’s saddle. That action resulted in Edward being thrown from the horse and seriously wounded.’

‘Not so, my Lord,’ pleaded Hild. ‘What cause had we to harm him?’

‘Don’t try to protest your innocence! You were seen by several people who were there at the time.’

‘Who are these people you mention, my Lord?’ demanded Hild, unable to hide her concern. ‘There was no one else there except Edward and the guard. Sigbert and the new boy were working in the stables.’

‘Exactly,’ said Osric. ‘We’ve spoken to the guard who told us that you both set about distracting him. We’re convinced of his innocence and Edward would hardly cut the girth strap to his own saddle. So that leaves only you.’

‘Surely it could have simply broken, my Lord?’ suggested Hild. ‘Such things can happen.’

‘It could. But it didn’t. The strap had been partially severed and the knife you stole from the guard is almost certainly that which was used to do it, for it was found on the ground near to where Fleet had been saddled. The evidence is therefore plain enough.’

'But my Lord, why would we do such a thing?' she tried somewhat hopefully.

'That only you can tell us. And you'd do well to confess it now, for you're to be charged with attempted murder. That's a crime for which you'll both be hanged if judged to be guilty.'

Even as he spoke, the words 'attempted murder' struck a chord. 'Is Edward then not killed?' asked Mayda.

'No, but he's seriously wounded,' said Osric. 'And no thanks to you.'

At that, both women seemed to change their tack. They glanced at each other, their faces pale with shock before Hild spoke again, this time seemingly to accept the accusation. 'I am relieved to hear that, my Lord,' she said. 'For we had no quarrel with the boy but when we went to visit the robbers in the forest we found Edmund was there. He could hardly believe it when we told him that Edward was still alive. He said that he stood to inherit a fortune if the boy was killed and would give us a goodly share of it if we helped him to made it look like an accident.'

'So, you admit that you intended to kill Edward purely for money?'

'No, my Lord,' pleaded Hild. 'There's much more to it than that. He offered not just to pay us, but to give us enough so that we could mend our ways and live out our lives where no one would know of our past. I'm not minded to sell my body by choice or by nature and am no more wanton than any other woman in Wareham. I do what I must to feed us both. It's not a life either of us would choose, my Lord, but our predicament is such that we have no hope of ever finding a man who would support us.'

'You do realise that what you've just said is akin to confessing your guilt? If so, I'm minded to pass sentence without hearing anything more.'

Hild brazenly looked up at Osric, this time staring at him directly as she spoke. 'My sister had no hand in this. It was me who stood to gain by agreeing to Edmund's offer and therefore me who cut the strap. If that means I'm to hang then so be it, for I've no fear of dying. In fact, I'd rather die like that than starving when I become too old to attract the interest of the men who come to avail themselves of my body. They're mostly dirty and abusive anyway. They use me and beat me and I must endure it – not just for my sake, but also for that of my dear sister whom I've pledged to look out for. So, death holds no fear for me. In fact, I'd welcome it and would as soon have it over and done with than suffer more of my wretched existence, praying only for better in the life to come.'

Osric was shocked at her outburst and, in truth, more than a little surprised by what she'd said. He guessed at once that Hild was only trying to save her sister by taking all the blame herself, something which suited his purpose as he had yet more to say on the matter. 'There is perhaps a way we might be able to spare you both,' he offered.

Both women looked up at him expectantly.

'Do you know how to find the robbers' camp?' he asked.

'I think so, my Lord,' admitted Hild. 'We go there from time to time. They usually send someone to meet us but we're not blindfolded so I think I can remember the way.'

'How many men live there?' asked Oswald, suddenly realising why his uncle was asking about the camp.

'There are eight in all, my Lord, one of whom is a monk. Plus there's now Edmund who has only recently joined them. All are rogues and wretches and none of them are worthy and...'

'Then tell me who leads them.'

She hesitated, not sure whether it was wise to answer that, but Mayda had no such reservations.

'Their leader is a man who goes by the name of Byram, my Lord,' she said boldly. 'He is perhaps of slightly better standing than the others although is still of a devious nature.'

Oswald immediately recognised the name. 'Byram? Was he not once a member of our permanent guard here at Wareham?'

Mayda shrugged as if implying that she didn't know.

Oswald turned to his uncle and spoke to him quietly so the two women couldn't hear what he said. 'If it is the same man, Uncle, he was a good warrior but was found to be taking bribes from men he should have been detaining. When he was discovered, he deserted his post and fled. No doubt he sought refuge in the forest.'

Osric considered the information, but had no recollection of the incident. 'All the more reason to bring him to account,' he said.

'But Uncle, how will you do that?'

'There is a way, but it requires that these two women help us,' he said, this time loud enough for both Hild and Mayda to hear. 'If they do, they may both escape the noose.'

'How so, my Lord?' asked Oswald.

'If they were to show us the way to the robbers' camp then, in return, I might be persuaded to spare them and perhaps even offer a small part of whatever loot is recovered as a reward. Enough at least for them to then support themselves as honest women.'

Hild and Mayda looked at each other, hardly able to believe their luck.

'So, what do you say?' asked Osric. 'Will you show us the way or not? Or is your loyalty to these rogues such that it's worth paying for with your lives?'

Both women readily agreed to his proposal. 'There is one thing, my Lord,' said Hild. 'Our mother lives in the camp but plays no part in the robberies. We would not see her harmed, for her life has been even harder than our own.'

'Very well,' agreed Osric. 'I'll do all I can to ensure that her life is spared. But I'll have no tricks, do you hear me? You'll take us to the camp then return here where I'll ensure you receive your due.' He next turned to the guards. 'Take these two unfortunates away. They are to be detained here in case they decide to warn the robbers of our coming but are not to be ill-treated. Any man caught abusing them will answer to me.'

They thanked him as the guards hauled them both to their feet then led them away, albeit this time more gently.

'Uncle, do you really intend to let them off so lightly?' asked Oswald once both women had gone.

'I do. They are not treacherous by nature and I can think of many people who would have done as they did to escape such a wretched existence. Besides, I've no mind to see two women hanged. To capture Edmund and have him brought here to justice is a far better prize as it would remove whatever threat he poses to young Edward. Even better if, at the same time, we can at last have done with these robbers who prey on good honest travellers coming to or from Wareham. That would be of benefit to us all.'

'Then do you propose to attack the robbers' camp?'

'That's exactly what I mean to do. Or rather, it's what I mean to have you do on our behalf provided that wound to your leg has healed sufficiently.'

'It has,' Oswald assured him.

'Good. Then how soon could you be ready to leave? I fear they have many informants who might guess what we have in mind and will send word to warn them of our coming if we delay too long.'

Oswald thought about that for a few moments. 'I could have a contingent ready within a matter of hours but it would need at least twenty men. Can we afford to have so many away from here with the threat of invasion still hanging over us?'

'That's what I wanted to discuss with you and why I asked you to stay. I'm minded to think that the threat has abated somewhat. I received a message earlier to say that Lord Ethelnorth and his men moved to meet the Vikings they were pursuing and trapped them at a place called Buttington. There he barricaded them inside their camp so securely that they were forced to eat their horses rather than starve. Desperate and hungry, they then attempted to break out but were soundly beaten, albeit with heavy losses on both sides including, I regret to say, Lord Ethelnorth himself who was among those slain in the battle.'

Oswald looked aghast. 'Lord Ethelnorth has been slain?'

'I fear so. His death will be a great loss to the Saxon cause. I'll arrange for Ulrich to send word of our condolences to Alfred.'

'So, where are the Vikings now? Surely not all were killed?'

'No, the survivors are fleeing to Essex where they'll no doubt reinforce others from East Anglia and Northumbria.

Apparently, even the fleet moored at Wight Island has now set sail to join them and presumably the remainder will do so as well.'

'Then does that mean the danger has passed?' asked Oswald.

'Hopefully so. There may yet be some raids from those who seek to replenish their supplies and take on fresh water as they make their way to join the others, but a full-scale invasion here at Wareham seems unlikely, at least for now.'

'Then God be praised for his mercy,' said Oswald, unable to hide his relief.

'God be praised indeed,' agreed Osric. 'However, we should not overreact to this news for you know how cunning these Vikings can be. I therefore intend to say nothing at this stage and thereby detain everyone here for a day or two longer – at least until we can be certain of what's transpiring.'

'Then can we at least begin to relax our guard…?'

'Not yet,' advised Osric. 'Alfred is even now returning to Winchester. He'll then co-ordinate matters from there and contend with whatever threat is posed by the combined forces. That leaves us still exposed as not all the fleet is as yet accounted for.'

'But we can spare enough men to attack the robbers?'

'I believe so. Whilst in the forest you'll not be far away and can thus be summoned back if needed but it's the best chance we shall get. Once taken, we can then make an example of all the robbers and have done with them.'

'Then there's no time like the present. I would suggest that I roster enough men and that we leave tonight.'

'Do so. But I must insist that you take the time to prepare a proper plan. I'm bound to remind you that the last time you took command of a detachment of this kind things did not go well.'

Oswald resented the insinuation. 'Uncle, the battle near Twynham worked out well enough in the end and I took what decisions I could with the information I had at the time. The outcome was even better than we could have hoped for and fully justified my actions. You now have the two captured longships as proof of that.'

'It's true that the matter ended better than expected but you have the quick thinking and courage of a stable boy to thank for that. As a commander, you must learn not to prejudice your decisions with hopes of personal glory. Learn to listen to the advice of those who go with you, particularly those who have more military experience than you, whatever their rank.'

*****

Whilst Sigbert waited outside, Odelia, accompanied by Ida, went to see Edward again, lugging a heavy volume of the Bible with her. 'I thought we could read this together when you feel well enough. It's a good chance for you to improve your learning.'

The expression on Edward's face betrayed the fact that he wasn't especially pleased at the thought of reading.

'Alfred greatly admires learning,' explained Odelia. 'He'll be impressed by what you've accomplished when you see him so will hopefully look well upon what you have to speak to him about.'

Put like that, Edward was inclined to agree. 'Perhaps when I'm better we can go down and sit beside the river and do our reading there,' he suggested hopefully.

'I don't think we'll get much reading done there!' she said, knowingly. 'In a day or so we could go to the Minster and work there. Father Emmett's presence will ensure that you keep your mind on your studies and at least there won't be any horses to distract you – nor any wanton harlots for that matter either!'

Edward went to protest the last point but then realised she was teasing him.

*****

No sooner had Odelia and Ida left than the nun who had attended Edward after the fall returned to see him. She was accompanied by the abbess, who felt it was her duty to at least visit Edward but merely watched as the nun examined him. She started by looking at the wound to Edward's head then, satisfied with that, placed a small phial of her potion on a table beside his cot in case he needed it for the pain, then warned him to rest. 'It could be several weeks at least before your shoulder is fully healed but, if you abuse it, it will take even longer,' she chided.

'But when will I be able to get up?' he asked.

'Only when the pain has subsided and you feel strong enough, but the longer you rest the better.'

With that, she tied a sling around Edward's shoulders. 'If you really mean to get up, keep this on at all times,' she advised. 'It will help your shoulder to heal and, more importantly, will stop you from trying to use it.'

Edward thanked her and asked whether he would soon be able to ride.

She shook her head almost despairingly. 'That's up to you,' she said. 'But if you were to have another fall the damage to your shoulder could easily become permanent, so I'd certainly advise against it. Besides, most men would be grateful if they could still manage to walk after a fall like that, never mind ride a horse.'

'Thank you both for coming and for seeing to me so well,' said Edward.

'You just be careful and mind what you're about,' scolded the abbess. 'If the good Lord wills it, the body will heal itself. But remember, the devil is always there to tempt you into doing that which is best avoided.'

*****

Osric and Oswald were the next to visit Edward and went as soon as they'd finished interrogating the two whores and discussing Oswald's plans for the attack on the robbers' camp.

'Ah!' said Osric warmly. 'It's good to see you're still resting.'

'I would much rather be up and about,' moaned Edward. 'I find it hard to remain abed when there's yet so much that needs to be done, but the nun who so kindly attended to me has advised against it, at least for now.'

'She's right,' agreed Osric. 'You need to fully rest your shoulder for a day or two at least, and even after that you'll need to take things easy for several weeks.'

'Odelia has suggested that I start by meeting her at the Minster so that she and Father Emmett can help me with my studies.'

'That's also a good idea,' noted Osric. 'In the meantime, there is some other news which I think will please you. Things have improved dramatically and the threat of invasion seems to have abated, at least for the time being. Also, we are now certain that Edmund was behind the plot to kill you. That's not surprising in itself but it seems he enlisted the help of those two whores. One of them has confessed to cutting the girth strap to Fleet's saddle.'

'What will you do with them?' asked Edward.

'Nothing,' replied Osric. 'I've detained them here. They'll be spared if they show us the way to the robber's camp, for we've searched the forest many times before but never once managed to find it. Also, to reach the forest we must first cross part of the open heath, which affords them ample opportunity to see us coming. This time, given that we shall know exactly where they are, we can attack under the cover of night. We'll hopefully bring Edmund to justice. Either that or we'll kill him.'

'What of the other robbers, my Lord?'

'I expect they'll try to fight their way out and thus most of them will be slain. Those that aren't will be brought back here to be hanged like the common criminals they are.'

'And you can spare the men to find them?' asked Edward.

'I believe so. They won't be far away if things suddenly change for the worse, so it seems prudent to take the chance to settle things with the robbers once and for all – or at least until others come to take their place.'

'Can I not go with them?' asked Edward.

'Absolutely not!' insisted Osric. 'It'll doubtless come to a fray and you're in no fit state to defend yourself.'

Edward was disappointed but could see the sense of that. 'Then what about rounding up the horses? Whilst I've been abed, I've thought some more about how we might manage that.'

'I think that will also have to wait at least until you're better. But how would you do it?'

'I'd need twenty men, more if you can spare them. We'd build two pens on the moors with a gate between them, one big enough for at least thirty horses, the other large enough for the ten or so we need. We'd then use the horses we have to drive the wild ones into the larger pen and close it off behind them. I'd then pick out the ones best suited to our needs and have the men work in pairs to rope them and drive them into the smaller pen. We'd then release the others.'

'How long would all this take?' asked Osric.

'We'd need to stay on the moors for at least a week so we have time to calm the horses enough to lead them here. I'd then help the men to break them in and train them.'

Both Osric and Oswald looked a little surprised.

'That's a lot of work,' noted Oswald.

'Well, it won't be easy. The horses will be wild and no doubt very frightened, but at least you won't have to buy them.'

'There is that,' acknowledged Osric, laughing. 'It's a good plan but I dare not spare that many men for over a week at present and anyway, you are yet in no fit state to organise things.'

Edward was disappointed but had expected as much. 'Well, there is something else I would like to speak to you about, if I may.'

'Of course. What is it?' asked Osric.

Edward looked to Sigbert who, having been told previously what Edward was intending to ask, tactfully made his excuses and left the lodge. Once he'd gone, Edward decided to come straight out with it.

'I think you both know that Odelia and I have become very close. I would therefore like to ask for her hand in marriage.' Out of respect, he then looked directly at Oswald. 'Sir, as her father, I would first seek your consent.' He then turned to Osric. 'My Lord, I also recognise that, as head of her family, I need your permission as well.'

Oswald was positively beaming with delight and seemed ready to agree at once whereas Osric was a little more circumspect.

'It would be a good match and one which I'm sure we would both welcome,' said Osric. 'Your prospects are much improved and I need hardly say that we have both come to respect and admire you.'

'Thank you, my Lord.'

'However, you have only been courting for a very short while. Are you sure this is what you want?'

'I am, my Lord.'

'Then I must first ask whether you have yet spoken to Odelia?'

'I have and have every reason to believe that she will consent to be my wife, although she would not say as much until I have the blessing of you both.'

Osric was impressed with that. 'That's to the good,' he said. 'But there is another issue as well which must be addressed.'

'My Lord?' queried Edward.

'Given your new status and your bloodline, Alfred will need to give his permission for the match as well.'

'My Lord, I have already considered that. If you are both minded to give your consent I will go to see him as soon as I'm able to ride.'

'Good. He's now returning to Winchester but I'm sure he'll be delighted to see you. But you will also need to think about where and how you will live once wed, although we have time enough to decide such things.'

'Then may I take it that I have your permission to formally propose to her?' asked Edward hopefully.

Osric smiled broadly. 'More than that, you have my blessing as well. Your father would also have been greatly pleased to see our two families united in this way and so, for my part, I'd welcome you to our family with open arms. It would surely be a match made in Heaven.'

Edward realised that Oswald had said very little. He looked at him as if to prompt him. Realising Edward was still waiting, he got up and went across to stand beside the cot and put his hand on the boy's shoulder, carefully avoiding the one that was injured. 'I see in you the son I never had,' he said, seeming almost tearful. 'I therefore welcome this news with all my heart.'

*****

Even though there was much he needed to arrange for the attack on the robbers' camp, Oswald was so excited by Edward's request to marry his daughter that he went first to find his wife, Eanflead, to tell her the news. Surprisingly, she seemed less taken with the prospect of her daughter marrying.

'She's said nothing to me about this,' she complained. 'As her mother is it right that I should be the last to know?'

'She hasn't yet accepted his proposal. Quite rightly, she's insisted that he seek the consent of my uncle as head of our family. And, of course, mine as her father. Are you not pleased with the news?'

'She's too young to marry for love,' she said sourly. 'Should it not be for us to choose a suitable match for her? After all, with all her grace and beauty she could find a husband who is far above our station in life.'

Oswald was hardly able to believe what he was hearing. 'I think our daughter has managed that well enough for herself,' he said. 'Edward's bloodline is one of the most noble in the whole of Wessex, second perhaps only to that of the King. He is also wealthy – or at least he will be. How could we hope for a better match than that?'

Eanflead was still not convinced. 'Edward was but a stable boy only a short while ago and was born as a bastard. He has a good heart and I grant you that his prospects have greatly improved, but he is still uncouth and lacks refinement. Had he even suggested marrying your daughter when he first came here you would have taken a staff and thrashed the very thought from his head. You even complained to Osric when you felt she was paying too much attention to the boy after he'd been beaten by that wretch, Coenred.'

'You voiced no objection when he first suggested courtship,' Oswald reminded her.

'That was because she needed to mix with those of her own age and there are so few in this settlement who would be suitable company.'

'But a stable boy was good enough for that, is that how you saw it?'

'A stable boy who we could keep a close eye on and dismiss if and when we saw fit to do so. I thought of him as a distraction, nothing more, and certainly not as a suitor for her hand in marriage. Besides, I was certain it was nothing serious. What surprised me was that you agreed to it at the time.'

'That was then,' argued Oswald. 'Things have now changed. He's learning your courtly ways and, in this matter, has behaved impeccably. More importantly, he's proving to be an asset to this settlement and the people have him taken to their hearts. Believe me, he'll go far in this world and is the perfect match for our daughter.'

'Has your uncle agreed?' she asked.

'Willingly,' said Oswald. 'Of course, given Edward's status, Alfred's permission will be needed as well.'

'And will he give it?'

'Of course he will! Alfred will see it as the joining of two great Saxon families, so will welcome the prospect. In fact, I'll be surprised if he isn't already expecting it.'

Chapter Ten

Oswald summoned all the members of the permanent guard who were not already on duty elsewhere and ordered them to attend him. Once they'd assembled, he asked for volunteers to go with him to attack and hopefully arrest the robbers in Wareham Forest and, more importantly, bring Edmund to justice. Following his uncle's lead, he omitted to mention the good news regarding the Viking fleet lest word got out and people took it upon themselves to then leave the safety of the burh too soon.

Almost all the members of the guard would normally have been only too willing to go on a mission such as the one he proposed but, being the first they'd undertaken since the battle near Twynham, some still had concerns about Oswald's competence to lead them. Nothing was said openly but those who could made an excuse or asked instead to be left with the contingent needed to protect the settlement whilst the party was away.

Despite that, he managed to recruit a detachment of twenty men albeit they were, for the most part, those who were all too often spoiling for a fight. He regarded that as an advantage given the sort of ruffians they would be up against, but he also recruited a man named Garulf who, being a forester by trade, had specialist skills they might need. Whilst not a member of the permanent guard, Garulf served in the fyrd and was said to know the paths and tracks through Wareham Forest better than anyone.

Wulfric, as Oswald's second in command, was ordered to remain at Wareham to organise things there. 'You can call upon the rest of the fyrd if you're short-handed,' ordered Oswald. 'Or you can send word by way of a messenger if you need support as we're likely to be but a few hours' march from here.'

'By rights we should be going with them,' mused Edward when he and Sigbert spoke about the mission.

'Not a chance,' said Sigbert firmly. 'I'd rather stay here. Anyway, why bother? Twenty trained men should be able to deal with a few robbers easily enough, with or without our help.'

*****

Anxious to ensure they wouldn't be seen as they crossed the open heath, Oswald had deliberately delayed their departure until dusk. Then, as the small party assembled at the Vill prior to setting off, he addressed them all. 'We march out as soon as it gets dark,' he informed them. 'Bring anything you think you'll need given that it's likely we'll be out all night and probably most of tomorrow as well. In particular, come fully armed with either a spear or a bow as I don't expect these robbers to give up without a fight.'

After the battle at Twynham, all the members of the permanent guard had been allowed to utilise whatever they needed from the war gear which had been stripped from the dead Vikings, hence most of them were reasonably well equipped. Once all had fetched their weapons, Oswald had both Hild and Mayda led out and explained that Hild would lead them directly to the robbers' camp as she knew the way. 'Mayda will be detained here under guard as surety for her sister's full co-operation,' he told them. 'If Hild then betrays our coming, Mayda will be hanged on our return for her part in harming Edward.' At that, he noticed the two women exchange a worried glance which seemed to suggest that whatever scheme they'd come up with between them had thereby been thwarted. Confident of that, he continued. 'We can't risk Hild trying to run off once in the forest, so retie her hands – but in front, not behind her back as the path may be difficult and she'll find it easier to manage that way, especially in the dark,' he ordered. 'We don't yet know the layout of the camp but I intend to strike at first light tomorrow, hoping to catch them off guard. If any try to make a run for it they're to be cut down with arrows. I don't care what happens to them, but we have good reason to believe that the traitor Edmund will be there as well. If so, I want him taken alive. Also, there's a woman there who's to be spared. It doesn't matter if she gets away, let her go and concentrate on the robbers. Likewise with Hild; once she's led us to the camp she's free to go if she wishes, but I'd prefer to bring her back with us if we can.'

As they prepared to set off, Father Cuthbert and Father Emmett both came to bless their mission and offer prayers for their safe return. That done, the small group set off in single file, crossing the north bridge then following the road to Winchester across the heath until they reached the edge of the forest itself. Once there, Hild was told to lead the way but she remained bound and was closely escorted. At first, she kept to the main track but told them they would need to branch off onto a much narrower path at some point which might be difficult to find in the dark.

'Shall we then light the torches, sir?' asked one of the men.

'No, torches may give us away, which is probably what she intends,' decided Oswald. 'There's a bright moon tonight so we should be able to see our way clearly enough and besides, your eyes will soon get used to the dark. So, stay close and keep as quiet as you can. Remember, the forest has eyes and ears and I intend to take these bastards by surprise.'

They travelled through the forest for over an hour before Hild led them off the main track and had them follow a hidden path which even Garulf had to admit he didn't know existed. It seemed to wind its way between the trees and went on for much longer than anyone expected, so much so that they found the going hard. At last they stopped when Hild indicated that the camp was but a little way ahead of them. Oswald told the men to remain quiet whilst he and Garulf crept forward together so they could assess the position more closely.

They found the camp readily enough and crept as close as they dared whilst being careful to remain hidden within the foliage. Although it was difficult to make out anything clearly, the moon and the light from the robbers' cooking fire made it just about possible to form a reasonable assessment of how things stood. From that they decided that everything looked to be quiet enough as the only people they could see were Edmund, who was tied to a tree, and a man who was tending the fire.

'This should be simple enough,' announced Oswald as he and Garulf rejoined the others. 'They have Edmund right enough but it's not as we thought. He's obviously being treated as their prisoner and looks to be securely bound so we'll leave him till last. As far as we know there are no more than eight in the camp, including a monk, so we should be able to take them with ease, particularly if we have the element of surprise. Now, form up into two groups, each of which should include some skilled bowmen. One group can work their way around to the other side of the camp to close off any chance of the robbers getting away. Once in position, remain quiet and wait for my signal to attack. When I give it, we strike hard and fast from both sides at once, bursting from cover and creating as much noise and confusion as we can. But stay within your group, targeting the hovels as and when you reach them. If any of the robbers try to remain inside, break in and haul them out. Kill any who resist but remember, the woman who lives with them is to be spared and I want Edmund taken alive. And be wary, these men are desperate and have nothing to lose. Given even half a chance, they will put up a fight if we let them.'

'What about the man we saw tending the fire, sir?' asked Garulf.

'I'll leave him to you. He looks to be half asleep anyway so shouldn't give you much trouble. A single arrow should suffice to put him down.'

The forester seemed happy enough with that. 'It'll be a pity to wake him so abruptly,' he joked. 'The only thing is, sir, if we're now where I think we are, there's another path yonder, albeit it's also one which is seldom used.'

'Why is that important?' demanded Oswald.

'I just wondered why, if the camp is over there, we haven't seen any sign of a guard. Surely they'll have posted someone to keep watch?'

'Well, if they have, we've seen no sign of him,' said Oswald.

'Sir, that's not surprising given that Hild has led us here via a secret route. But there may yet be a guard posted on the other path – presumably that's the one they normally use to come and go from the camp.'

It was a fair point but Oswald dismissed it. 'There's nothing we can do about a guard we can't see so just keep your eyes open and remain vigilant,' he advised. 'If any alarm is sounded, take that as your signal to attack. We need to catch them when they're weakest and not give them time to muster even a rudimentary defence. And remember, there's no point in being merciful; any we take alive will likely be hanged anyway.'

*****

Edmund was once again wide awake, anxiously watching for any sign of the wolves in case they dared to venture into the camp, perhaps being drawn to it by the scent of the game which was being stored in the makeshift shelter. As sleep eluded him, he had several times fancied that he saw things moving in the shadows close to the barricade which surrounded the camp, but realised it was probably just his mind playing tricks on him.

Then, when he heard the unmistakeable sound of something scurrying about in the undergrowth, his fear got the better of him.

'Didn't you hear that?' he shouted to Godwin, the one-eyed man who was tending the fire.

Godwin just laughed. 'Be quiet you fool. If that was wolves you wouldn't have heard a thing. They'd come upon you so quietly that the first you'll know of it is when they sink their fangs into your throat!'

'You're not only half blind, you're also deaf as well!' accused Edmund. 'Or are you going to tell me that was nothing but the wind?'

'Most likely it was a deer or maybe a badger. Anyway, why should I care either way? If it was wolves they won't bother me for they'll not come near to the fire. Besides, I'll have plenty of time to get away whilst they're busy chewing on your worthless bones!' He seemed to find that amusing and chuckled away to himself but stoked the fire again, just in case.

Edmund realised there was nothing he could do except to press himself back hard against the tree where he hoped he wouldn't be seen. Of course, it was a futile effort and he knew it. Wolves have eyes which can see in the dark and if that should fail them, they can sense their prey at some distance even when they can't see it.

*****

Leaving Oswald, Garulf, Hild and ten men where they were, the other half of the small Saxon contingent, under the command of a man named Eadric, moved off as slowly and as quietly as they could. It took a little while for them to reach their position on the far side of the camp but, once there, they settled down to wait for Oswald's signal to attack which, all being well, they knew wouldn't be given until just before dawn.

For his part, Oswald cursed when he heard the exchange between Edmund and the man beside the fire, knowing that it meant both were wide awake. All his men heard it as well but were not unduly concerned until a horn was sounded somewhere beyond the camp, proving that Garulf had been right – a guard had indeed been set and had now alerted everyone in the camp. Having lost the element of surprise, all Oswald could do was to urge his men to attack at once. 'Go now!' he screamed as loudly as he could. All then reacted as one.

His men surged forward but, in such poor light, they failed to see the barricade of thorns and brambles. As they stumbled into it, several of them cried out as they struggled to force their way through. One of them drew a seax and tried to cut a gap but it was all too late; the delay had cost them vital minutes which was all the time the robbers needed.

Godwin, the man tending the fire, was on his feet almost at once but was immediately felled by Garulf's arrow which took him full in the chest. Even as he fell, the rest of the robbers began spilling out of their hovels. Although none were prepared for the onslaught they encountered, several managed to let fly an arrow, aimed at the shadowy figures desperately trying to free themselves from the vicious thorns. Oswin, the gentle giant among them, did even better than that. Being one of the first to emerge, he didn't bother with a weapon. Taking up a position beside the fire so he could see more clearly, he grabbed the first man to reach him, roaring his defiance as he threw him to the ground. He then waited for the next one to come at him but found himself confronting not one but three guards who quickly had him surrounded. Whilst he was prepared to make a fight of it, they all rushed him at once and, despite his size, gave him no chance to prevail. As he battled with one, another grabbed him and, with the help of the third man, tried to pull him down. Still he struggled against them but was then struck hard from behind and, clutching his head, slumped to the ground like an ox stunned for slaughter. The three guards hurriedly restrained him with a rope and left him there, still dazed and quite unable to put up anything more by way of a fight.

Byram was also quick to join the fray. He realised at once what they were up against and, as an experienced warrior, knew they were lost. 'Make a run for it!' he ordered, shouting to make himself heard. 'Get away from here if you can.' With that, he caught sight of Hild and, as he did so, turned to look at Winifrid and scowled. He wrongly assumed that she had betrayed them, so simply killed her on the spot, driving his seax deep into her belly. As she fell, he turned again and found himself confronting Oswald. Even in such poor light, the two men recognised each other but wasted no time on words. Instead, they set about exchanging blows. Byram spotted that Oswald was favouring the wound to his leg and sought to exploit that, although what followed could hardly be described as a fair fight – his seax against Oswald's sword. Within a few strokes, Byram was taken by a slashing strike across his stomach. As he reeled away from that and fell, Oswald left him for dead and set about rallying his own men. Although he didn't know it then, two of them had been killed in the initial attack, but the rest seemed to be doing well enough.

One of Oswald's men found Brother Linton who had remained in his hovel and was on his knees with his hands calmly raised in prayer. Unwilling to kill a monk, especially one who was unarmed, he left him to his devotions. In the meantime, the Viking, Radnor, was struck by a shield driven hard into his chest. He reeled away and fell to the ground, winded and struggling for breath. Two of Oswald's men roughly seized him and turned him over before tying his hands behind his back. There was something in the way Radnor had been taken that reminded the boy, Iden, of all the terror he'd witnessed during the attack on his home and family. Screaming like a fiend, he ran unarmed at one of the guards who would surely have killed him had Duncan not pushed him aside. Even as he did so, an arrow meant for the boy killed him instead. Realising what had happened, Iden was suddenly terrified and all thoughts of fighting had gone out of him. Instead, he simply raised his hands and allowed himself to be taken prisoner. That left only Edmund for them to deal with. As he was still tied to the tree, he looked to be an easy target so, with their blood lust roused, the men formed up around him, their spears poised.

'Wait!' he pleaded. 'I'm not one of them! Can't you see that I'm a bloody prisoner here!'

Hearing that, Oswald stepped in. 'Leave him, you fools!' he ordered. 'I told you, I want him alive!'

As they stepped back, Oswald went to Edmund and, towering over him, glared down at him triumphantly. 'So, it would seem that you're not just a traitor and a murderer, you're a miserable coward as well!' he accused. 'You kill men readily enough but don't have the guts to die yourself when your turn comes around!' He continued to stare at Edmund for a few moments more, then spat at the ground. 'You'll soon wish you'd taken what was coming to you and died here.' He then turned to two of his men. 'Tighten his bonds, I don't want him to be too comfortable,' he ordered. 'And treat him as you will, just make sure he lives long enough to feel the noose around his neck in the morning.'

With that, Oswald wiped the blood from his sword and sheathed it, then surveyed the carnage. Having failed to notice the barricade, two of his men had been killed by arrows whilst trying to scramble through it. Apart from that their casualties were light, with several men being wounded in the fray but none seriously so. He ordered the bonds securing Hild's hands to be cut so she could tend to her mother's body, even though Winifrid was far beyond any help she could offer. 'Light the torches so we can see what the hell we're doing here,' he shouted. 'Tend to our wounded and secure the prisoners. The rest of you check the hovels to be sure we have them all - by my reckoning there's still one of them at large.'

'Sir,' said Garulf. 'The one who's missing is probably the one who sounded the alarm. He presumably had more sense than to return here just to die with the others.'

'That's as maybe,' agreed Oswald. 'But we've also yet to find Byram's body. I didn't see exactly where he fell but I'm sure I killed him. It's over there somewhere so find it and we'll take it back to Wareham and have it strung up as a reminder to all of how we deal with thieves.'

All the men set about following his orders, although some were more interested in hurriedly searching the bodies of the dead robbers in the hope of finding coin or at least some small items of loot which they could take for themselves.

It seemed that apart from Edmund and Brother Linton, only three robbers had survived the fray alive and one of those was not much more than a boy. Oswald turned his attention to them. 'Ask them to name the ones we've slain,' he said to one of his men.

In the meantime, one of the guards returned to say that they'd still not managed to find Byram's body. 'Sir, are you sure you killed him?'

Oswald shook his head. 'I can't be certain, but I struck him well enough and felt my blade scythe across his belly. I can't believe he could have survived that but even if by some miracle he did, he must be bleeding freely and so won't have crawled far. We'll no doubt find his body in the morning.'

Oswald then had Brother Linton hauled to his feet and dragged over to stand before him. 'So, what are we to do with you?' he asked.

'I think that's hardly for you to decide,' said Brother Linton, clearly unconcerned at whatever fate awaited him.

'What do you mean?'

'I mean that I was doing God's work here. All these men are sinners in your eyes but not all are beyond redemption. The Good Lord called me here to do what I could in that respect.'

'So are you claiming that you did no more than tend to their spiritual needs? If so, does that mean that you played no part in their crimes?'

'I'm a man of God and will not answer to you for whatever sins I've committed on this Earth,' he replied firmly. 'Nor will I submit to be judged by you or your betters.'

Oswald was actually quite impressed by his courage. 'What, not even to men acting on orders from your King? Would you have me hang you along with the others without hearing what you have to say for yourself?'

'You'll do as you will. It's all part of God's great plan and thereby beyond whatever you or I deign to make of it.'

'Will you not even plead for your life?'

Brother Linton shook his head. 'What's death to me? I look forward to meeting my maker and have nothing to fear from dying beyond the pain. Even that I shall endure and regard it as being a test of my faith.'

'Well, if you played no part in the crimes which were committed here, at least name those who did.'

'Their names are known to God and are thus no business of yours,' said the monk. 'As to my own actions, I've readily confessed all my many sins and have done nothing since which I need to repent. All I would ask is that you let me say a few words on behalf of those who have died when you bury them. After that you may do with me as you will.'

'That's easy enough as I'm not going to bury them; you are,' scoffed Oswald. 'Aided by the other prisoners over there, you can scratch out a grave big enough for them all in the morning. They were happy enough to rob and thieve together so will no doubt enjoy each other's company on their way to hell.' He next turned his attention to Hild. 'So, where have these rogues hidden their hoard?' he demanded, knowing she wouldn't tell him even if she knew. More likely she would attempt to recover it for herself at some point. In fact, he rather hoped she would.

'Very well,' said Oswald when she remained silent. 'My instructions were to give a share of it to you and your sister but, if it can't be found, there's nothing more I can do.' With that he left her and walked over to where Edmund was being held. 'So what pretty story will you come up with to excuse what you did whilst in Wareham?'

'I killed the man who tried to kill my nephew,' said Edmund. 'Is that not what Saxon justice allows?'

Oswald laughed. 'It might suffice, except that you paid him to do it in the first place.'

'You've no proof of that,' he protested.

'Then it's as well he failed and that Edward still lives. Be that as it may, we have a reliable witness who will testify that you also killed a guard who was accompanying a priest through this very forest. On that basis alone, it's the noose for you, my friend. How's that for Saxon justice?'

'I'll not hang,' said Edmund boldly. 'I'm a nobleman by birth so will opt for the sword, as is my right.'

'We'll see what Governor Osric has to say about that,' sneered Oswald. 'Although if left to me you wouldn't even live long enough to stand before him.'

*****

Having had his men search the camp as thoroughly as they could using torches, Oswald realised there was little hope of finding where the robbers had stashed their hoard of loot until the morning. 'It'll be light in a few hours,' he said. 'We can search more thoroughly then. In the meantime, secure the prisoners and put them over there with Edmund. You can take it in turns to watch them through the night.' Even as he spoke, another thought occurred to him. He called one of the younger men over. 'Can you find your way back to Wareham from here?' he asked.

The man said that he was certain he could.

'Right, I want you to return there tonight and tell my uncle that we're safe and have the prisoner secure. Tell him we have two men killed and some casualties but will stay here tonight and search for the robber's spoil in the morning. We'll return tomorrow bringing Edmund with us and hopefully Byram's body as well.'

'That's not a good idea, sir,' warned Garulf, overhearing him. 'He'll struggle to find his way back through this forest in the dark, even with a torch. He's almost bound to get lost. Or more likely be eaten by wolves.'

Oswald realised Garulf was right so selected another man to go with him as well. 'Stay together,' he ordered. 'Both of you take a bow and keep moving. You should fare well enough.'

'What about Hild?' asked one of the other men.

'I don't much care what she does,' he said. 'But keep an eye on her in case she decides to recover the hoard for herself. She's bound to know where it's hidden.'

*****

Elsewhere in the forest, Byram had managed to crawl away from the camp and had taken cover behind a large tree. He was lucky that Cedric, who had been the one on lookout and who had sounded the alarm, had seen him fall and half carried him to the glade – the small clearing they used as a place to meet up again in the event that they had to scatter if the fyrd was getting too close. Once there, he laid Byram down and covered him with his cloak to stop him shivering. He would have liked to light a fire to warm them both but knew it would likely be seen if he did, so had to make do without one.

Once Byram was settled, Cedric fetched some water from a stream and tore off a few strips of cloth from the cloak but could do little more than push them into the wound like a wad to staunch the flow of blood. He made no attempt to look at the wound more closely as there seemed little point for, as he'd already surmised, Byram was unlikely to survive the night.

*****

As most of the men slept, Oswald called two of them who seemed to be wide awake to speak with him. 'I think Hild will try to escape,' he told them. 'I'm not concerned about that, which is why I haven't had her hands retied, but I reckon she'll know where their spoil is hidden and will go there to retrieve it. Follow her if she does and bring it back here.'

'How the hell will she escape?' asked one of them.

Oswald pointed to the men who had been posted to watch the prisoners. Tired from the fray and having been up for most of the night, one of them was already sleeping and the other was barely awake. 'That's how,' he said. 'But don't disturb them, the other prisoners are all restrained so are secure enough. Therefore let her go if she will. In fact, I'm hoping she'll do just that as it's our best chance of finding the spoil. Just follow her and bring back whatever it amounts to as quickly as you can.'

The two men turned away.

'And make sure you don't get tempted to take it for yourselves,' he warned.

They looked back at him, at first not sure what he meant, then seemed to realise that he was worried the temptation of what it included would prove too much for them to resist.

Sure enough, just as it was getting light, Hild took her chance and began edging her way towards the barricade. Both men watched as she found a gap then followed her as she made her way between the trees. She quickly found what she was looking for - an old hollow tree stump only a short distance from the edge of the camp. It stood near head height but was withered and all but devoid of branches. After hurriedly looking about her in case she'd been followed, she delved inside the tree and pulled out a large sack. Even as she did so, one of the men raised his bow and took careful aim.

'What the hell are you doing?' demanded the other one, his voice not much more than a whisper.

'That sack could contain more wealth than you've ever dreamed of getting your hands on. And she's nothing but a whore so no one will miss her.'

'But you can't just kill her!'

'Oh can't I?' he said and, with that, loosed an arrow which struck Hild between her shoulders. She let out a groan of pain as she dropped to the ground then reached back with her hand, desperately trying to pull the arrow free. She lay there, moaning and writhing in pain for several moments but was then finally still.

'You fool, you've done for her! They'll hang us both when they find her!'

'They won't find her. They won't even bother to come looking for her. We'll hide her body in the undergrowth over there and tell Oswald that she ran off. I'll say that I loosed an arrow to stop her but can't be sure whether or not it found its mark. Now, let's go to see what's in that sack. We'll then hide that as well and come back for it later.'

When they retrieved the sack they were both disappointed with what it contained. There was no coin or silver, just three items which comprised the reliquary which had been taken from Father Cuthbert, a small brooch in the shape of a bird and, most valuable of all, a beautiful ring of woven gold with a large green stone.

'Surely there should be some coin at least?' remarked the other guard hopefully.

The one who had killed Hild realised at once what had happened. 'They've already divided everything up between themselves, having sold anything of smaller value for what they could get,' he said.

'Then why didn't they sell these things as well?'

'Because they're not so easily divided. Besides, who would buy them? That brooch is pretty enough but it's neither silver nor gold, just base metal, and the reliquary is the one promised to the Minster at Wareham. No one would want to buy something which has been stolen from the Church.'

'Then what about the ring? That alone would be worth enough to feed us both for many winters to come!'

'Aye, but who could afford to buy it? Only a nobleman would have the wherewithal and as like as not they'd recognise it or know who it had belonged to. Try to sell that and you'll pretty soon find yourself swinging from the end of a rope.'

The other man realised he was right. 'So what do we do?'

'We hide the whore's body then take this sack back to Oswald as we were supposed to. We tell him that Hild retrieved the sack then, when she realised she'd been followed, she tried to make off with it but dropped it when I hit her with an arrow. We searched but couldn't find her body. There's no one can prove otherwise.'

'So we'll have nothing to show for our trouble and you killed her for no good cause?'

'Pah! What does that matter? She was nothing but a whore and is probably better off dead anyway.'

*****

Once back at the robbers' camp, the two guards went straight to report to Oswald and gave him the sack. As he peered inside it, he was also surprised by how little it contained. 'So was there no coin?' he asked pointedly. 'Nor any hack silver and suchlike?'

'No sir. Just the items you see, although I'll warrant that even they're worth a goodly sum all told.'

Oswald realised at once that what they'd recovered was either of no value or near impossible to sell, but he still eyed both men suspiciously in case they had already removed some items and hidden them for themselves. It worried him that they'd killed Hild, the only person other than the prisoners who might know what they'd taken and could therefore give them away, but he decided not to levy any accusations at that stage. 'So Hild is dead?' he asked.

'Yes sir,' admitted the man who had killed her. 'At least, I believe so. She ran off so I loosed an arrow and we heard her cry out. I'm thus certain that I at least hit her.'

'But you didn't actually find her body?' challenged Oswald suspiciously.

'No, sir.'

'You're telling me that you managed to find this sack but not her body? What did she do, toss it back to you then disappear?'

'Sir, we did look for her,' lied the other man. 'But we could find no trace of her and assumed she was wounded and had crawled off somewhere to die. You said it didn't matter if she got away so, as we had the loot, we didn't waste any more time and came straight back here as ordered.'

Oswald acknowledged the point and decided to let the matter drop as searching them would achieve nothing except to stir up resentment. Besides, if they had stolen any part of the loot they would have hidden it to recover later. He therefore resolved to keep an eye on them for the next few days and, if they left the settlement, he'd have them followed.

'Right, stir yourselves,' he said loud enough to wake all who were still sleeping. 'It's light enough now and high time we were gone from here.'

'Shall we first burn their hovels?' asked one of the men.

'No, destroy them but we dare not risk a large fire lest we set the whole forest ablaze. Fashion some litters so we can take our own dead back with us but set the monk and the prisoners to burying their dead. They can all rot here for all I care.'

By midday the camp had been ransacked and destroyed, the dead robbers had been laid to rest in a makeshift grave and the prisoners' bonds had been retied.

'What about the monk?' asked one of the men.

'Leave him to mutter a few words over the dead then let him go where he will. So far as I'm concerned, we've achieved our objective and I've no stomach for hanging a man of God any more than would my uncle. Now gather up anything we can use, particularly their store of food, and let's be gone. We've been here long enough already.'

* * * * *

In the glade, Cedric looked across at Byram who had passed a very restless night and was clearly in a great deal of pain. He fetched some more fresh water from the stream and decided he had to risk examining the wound, although he had very little experience of dealing with injuries. He gingerly started to remove the wadding he'd applied during the night, all of which was caked in blood. When he eventually dared to expose the wound itself, he winced at what he saw. Oswald's sword had scythed deep into the flesh and had almost certainly cut through several organs as well. As the wound was still bleeding, Cedric tried pressing the edges of it together, then reapplied some fresh strips of cloth, also torn from his own cloak, even though he knew it was a futile effort.

He rinsed the blood from his hands in the stream then sat back and wondered what he should do next. As he listened to Byram's laboured breathing, he pulled out his own knife thinking that perhaps he should spare him more pain and suffering, but then held off. Instead, he decided to wait and see what happened, although doubted that it would achieve more than to prolong Byram's pain.

It was not so much that he was afraid of mercifully killing Byram, it was more that he knew that sometimes men survived wounds, even ones as bad and as deeply set as that.

Chapter Eleven

WAREHAM

The two messengers Oswald had sent back to Wareham during the night had both arrived safely with the news of his success in finding the robber's camp and in capturing Edmund. As the main party returned later that day, the people who resided in the settlement gathered at the Vill in order to see Edmund being brought to justice, jeering and taunting him as he was made to wait outside the Vill whilst Oswald made his report to Governor Osric.

In truth, Edmund didn't look much like the treacherous murderer they all expected. Instead, he arrived looking ragged and dejected, with his hands bound and his head hung low as he contemplated his fate. Several people commented on some heavy bruising to his face which suggested he'd been beaten, but one of the guards assured them that was not the case as Oswald had ordered that none of the prisoners were to be ill-treated. Instead, he insisted that any injuries were those Edmund had received whilst being held as a prisoner of the robbers. Not surprisingly, few believed that to be true.

'Uncle, we've brought back Edmund together with three other prisoners, all of them members of the gang who frequented the forest. The rest were killed but their lookout escaped and Byram's body could not be found. I personally inflicted a deep wound to his belly but it seems that despite that, he managed to slip away – or more likely crawl, probably to die elsewhere. I was certain he couldn't survive the wound for long so didn't waste any more time looking for him.'

'And were there no others present in the camp?' queried Osric.

'The whores' mother was there as we expected but Byram killed her as we attacked. I assume he thought it was she who had betrayed them. There was also a monk but I spared him as he insisted he'd been there solely to administer to their spiritual needs and had played no part in their crimes.'

'And you believed him?'

Oswald was surprised at the question. 'I did. Would you have had me arrest him as well?'

'Who's to say?' suggested Osric. 'But what concerns me is that once again you nearly managed to turn what should have been a relatively straightforward arrest into a debacle.'

'What do you mean?' demanded Oswald, astonished by the accusation. 'I successfully defeated the robbers and brought Edmund back for trial. What more should I have done?'

'You had those at the camp outnumbered by over two to one, yet two of your men were killed and several more were wounded! Not only that, but you can't even be certain as to whether their leader was killed or is still at large. That hardly rates as a triumph!'

'Uncle, the two men who died were killed by arrows as they tried to scramble over a vicious barricade of thorns which we couldn't see in the dark!' explained Oswald angrily.

'Then you should have checked more carefully to ensure there was no such barrier before you advanced. That's the role of a commander, to assess any danger *before* proceeding.'

'I did!' stressed Oswald. 'I personally went forward with Garulf to inspect the camp but we neither of us noted anything untoward.'

'Then you should have waited and attacked at first light, as we planned. If you had, it's likely you'd have seen the danger and still taken the robbers by surprise.'

'That was the plan but the alarm was raised when some of the men were spotted. I therefore had no choice but to attack at once.'

Having made his point, Osric changed tack. 'And what of the loot they'd managed to accrue?'

Oswald produced the sack and removed the three items it contained, setting them down on the table, one by one. 'This was all we were able to recover,' he said. 'They were in this sack which was hidden in a hollow tree. Hild went to fetch it, presumably intending to take it for herself, but I had two men follow her. They think they struck her with an arrow as she tried to run off with it and, although they couldn't find her body, both are certain she was killed.'

Osric looked at him, his expression one of obvious doubt. 'Was there no coin or hack silver?'

'Only what you see, Uncle. And I know what you're thinking. Did the men who recovered it steal the lesser items for themselves?'

'And what do you say to that?'

Oswald didn't answer at first. 'I'm not sure,' he admitted at last. 'I'll have them watched and if they leave the settlement within the next few days they'll be followed by men I trust.'

'They're both members of your permanent guard so should be above suspicion in the first place,' grumbled Osric.

'Yes Uncle, but no one is above temptation,' replied Oswald defensively.

Osric turned his attention to the items on the table, first picking up the reliquary to examine it more closely. 'This is surely the one which Father Cuthbert described. I'll have him look at it and, if it is the same one, it was intended as a gift to the Minster here so at least we can ensure that it now reaches its rightful home. Was there no sign of the coins they stole from him, or his crucifix and ring?'

Oswald shook his head. 'I can only assume the coins were distributed between the robbers who each then hid their share – or spent some of it on the whores when they went to visit the camp.'

'Well, either way we can have little hope of recovering any of it now.'

'What of these other items?' asked Oswald.

'The brooch is of little value,' pronounced Osric, who then picked up the ring and examined it very closely indeed. 'As to this, I already know who owned it, and it certainly wasn't Father Cuthbert,' he announced.

'How can you be so sure of that?' queried Oswald.

'Because I've seen it many times before, although admittedly not for many years. It was a ring given by Lord Alfred himself to my friend, Lord Edwulf, of whom you've heard me speak often enough. It's also the one which that wretch Edmund remembered and described to Alfred when questioned.'

'Then how the hell did it get here?'

Osric shrugged. 'Who can say, but I'm sure that it is the very same one. We'll display it and see whether Edmund recognises it. Either way, it must be returned to Alfred who I suspect will want young Edward to have it as it was first given as a gift to his grandfather.'

Oswald saw the sense of that. 'Where shall I display the items?' he asked.

'We'll doubtless need to hang the prisoners, so erect a scaffold just beyond the west gates. Set up a trestle beside it and display all these items there but ensure they're well guarded. Someone may come forward to claim the brooch, but only a person who has previously reported its loss will be able to do so.'

'And what of Mayda?' asked Osric.

'I'll deal with her later. For now, have the rogue Edmund brought in, for I am anxious to hear what he has to say for himself.'

Oswald motioned to the guards who half dragged, half pushed Edmund into the Hall and forced him to his knees. The guards then remained on either side of him, their spears poised in case he caused any trouble.

'So, you're to face justice at last?' mused Osric.

'You've no right to detain me thus,' protested Edmund sourly. 'I've committed no crime for which I must answer to you.'

Osric looked across at Oswald who had also remained in the Hall. 'In fact, that is partly true,' he admitted. 'Your most heinous crime is against your King and against the Saxon people, but you also stand accused of two murders and several counts of conspiring to have your nephew killed. Those crimes were all committed here and are thus within my jurisdiction.'

'I'm no more guilty of murder than you are!' he protested. 'Look at how your guards brutally killed the members of the robbers' band. Twenty or more trained warriors against eight ordinary men only recently roused from sleep? That was nothing short of murder, particularly as their number included a young boy, a monk and a man who was half blind, not to mention another who had but one hand! Or do you have another name by which to call it?'

Osric decided not to rise to the bait. 'Well, none of that diminishes or excuses their crimes so I, for one, would call it justice, although I grant you it was harsh. But it was their choice whether or not to resist arrest so they got only what they deserved. Besides, every one of them would have been hanged for the crimes they've committed. As for your role in this, you were seen to murder Father Cuthbert's guard and also that assassin you employed to kill Edward. Then, when you learned that Edward had survived, you persuaded two whores to cut through the girth strap to his saddle with intent to see him killed in that way instead.'

'Who accuses me of these crimes?'

'Sigbert, who is much trusted and well-respected in this settlement saw you kill the assassin. And the good Father Cuthbert was present when you robbed him and killed his guard. No doubt they'll both identify you beyond any doubt.'

'So what if they do? I'm of noble birth and will claim the right to be tried by my equals.'

'Your equals?' queried Osric. 'I wonder who in Wareham might be considered your equal?' I rate you even lower than the beggars and wastrels who frequent the darker corners of this settlement.'

'Ha! You should choose your words more carefully! Just remember that my bloodline is nobler than yours, so if I'm no better than the worthless wretches you speak of, what does that say about your own lineage?'

Osric found that amusing, even though the point was well made. 'All I can say is that I'm glad it won't be left to me to try you. If it were, there'd be no need for a trial for I'd judge you guilty just on what I already know to be true. In fact, I'd be tempted to kill you myself but fear you would die too quickly if I did.'

Edmund looked at him, hardly daring to ask the obvious question. 'If I'm not to be tried by you, what's then to be my fate?' he managed.

'You'll be taken from here to Winchester where Lord Alfred himself will decide how best to deal with you. But I warn you, whilst merciful and just, he's unlikely to show much compassion for the likes of you.'

Edmund decided to say nothing more given that his fate now rested with the King rather than Osric.

'Take him away,' ordered Osric when he realised that Edmund was done. 'Tell the guards they can do with him as they will. I've no wish to set eyes on him again, although I want him alive to face his fate in Winchester.'

*****

Edward was feeling much stronger and, with Sigbert's help, managed to get out of bed and dress. 'I need to see Odelia in private, if you don't mind. Could you send word and ask her to meet me at the Minster?'

'Of course. But are you sure you're yet well enough?'

Edward nodded. 'I am. I also need to see Fleet so will go there first.'

'I'm not sure you've got your priorities quite right in that,' laughed Sigbert. 'But I'd best come with you. I can leave word for Odelia on the way.'

Once at the stables, they found that Fleet was loose in the pasture. When Edward whistled the horse looked up and, seeing who it was, trotted over to greet him. 'There boy. You see, I'm not badly harmed,' said Edward, petting the horse as usual. 'I'm unable to ride you for a while but will try to come every day to see you.'

Caelin came across, anxious to speak to Edward. 'Are you then recovered, sir?' he asked.

'I'm much improved, thank you. And you seem to have managed well enough without me.'

Caelin looked pleased at that. 'I've done what I can, sir. The steps Sigbert made for me have meant that I can now reach high enough to groom the horses. I still find much of the heavier work to be hard but others have been kind enough to help me where needed. All of them said they were happy to do so as a mark of their respect for you.'

Edward hardly knew what to say. 'Then please thank them all for me,' he said, then changed the subject. 'Now that I'm up and about, let's see how Sigbert is getting on with the improvements to your sleeping arrangements here in the stables.'

'You'll not find much to marvel at,' admitted Sigbert. 'I've made a start but had to stop in order to help out with a malingerer who managed to fall from his horse!'

'Ha!' said Edward, enjoying the joke. 'Then you'll have time enough to get on with it over the next few days as I'm intending to use them to improve my learning.'

Edward petted Fleet one more time then turned to leave. As he did so, Fleet whinnied pitifully as if pleading with him to stay longer. Edward could not resist going back to stroke him again. 'Don't worry, my fall was no fault of yours. And I know now that you even tried to warn me.'

With that he left and made his way to the Minster where Odelia was indeed waiting. Father Emmet seemed not to approve when they embraced but allowed them to do so although, for the sake of Odelia's reputation, he didn't leave them alone together. Edward was pleased to note that Father Cuthbert was not there as he would doubtless have disapproved and would have said as much without hesitation.

'Are you truly feeling better?' she asked. 'I would have come to see you again but my mother forbade me as you needed to rest.'

'I am, thank you. And what's more, I have managed to speak with your father and with Governor Osric.'

'Then what news?' she asked anxiously.

'Well, it seems my lot is sealed,' he sighed. 'Everyone thinks it's a good idea that we should wed, so all I have to do is go to Winchester to see Alfred and then that's it.'

'Not quite,' teased Odelia. 'I've not yet given you my answer.'

Edward looked worried. 'I thought…'

'You might have thought a lot of things, but if I recall I said I'd answer only once you'd spoken to my father and my great uncle.'

'Ah,' said Edward. 'That's true enough. So are you now going to keep me waiting until I've seen Alfred as well?'

She smiled broadly. 'No, I wouldn't be that mean. My answer will be "yes", but only if the King also agrees. And I shall still expect a formal proposal even once he has.'

'But what if he doesn't?'

'Then all I can say is that I hope your shoulder soon improves,' she said.

'Why would that matter?' asked Edward.

'Because,' she said, still smiling, 'you can hardly expect me to carry my own baggage when we elope.'

*****

It was also left to Osric to inform Mayda that both her mother and her sister were dead. For that she was taken to the Hall where he and Oswald waited.

'It grieves me to inform you that Byram suspected that your mother had betrayed them so killed her as the camp was raided,' explained Osric. 'It's a pity for I hold her to have played no part in the crimes committed by the others.'

'For what it's worth,' added Oswald, 'she died quickly enough and without suffering. I witnessed it myself.'

Whilst Mayda listened carefully, she showed little emotion given that she and her mother had never been especially close. 'Then what about Hild?' she asked anxiously. 'Why has she not returned with you?'

'Your sister ran off and tried to seize the robbers' booty for herself,' said Oswald. 'I hadn't intended for her to be killed but she died because of her greed.'

On hearing that, Mayda seemed barely able to take it in. 'Are you then saying that my sister is dead as well?'

Oswald confirmed that to be the case.

Mayda stood in stunned silence for a moment, then started to weep. Her whole body seemed to shake as the tears fell, so much so that she had to steady herself against the table.

Neither Osric nor Oswald spoke, thereby giving her time to compose herself.

'What of her body?' asked Mayda at last.

'I regret that it was never found,' said Oswald, surprised at the extent of her grief. 'The men who killed her searched for it but had orders to return to the camp as soon as possible.'

That clearly concerned Mayda, but she said nothing.

It was Osric who then spoke, although he showed no pity or compassion for the girl either. 'I said I would be merciful if you and your sister helped us to find the robbers' camp and even promised you a share of whatever was recovered. I will keep my word even though we found but three items in their hoard, all of them stored in a sack and hidden in a hollow tree.' Osric then waited to see whether she would protest that the robbers had more loot than that, but she said nothing. With that, he gave her a few coins instead. 'There, that's all you'll get from me,' he said sternly. 'So far as I'm concerned, you may now go free but must first witness the execution of the others from the camp in the hope that by doing so you will learn the error of your ways. Thereafter you're banished from Wareham. You should by rights be branded as a whore but I'll spare you that as I'm assured that you never sold your own body for coin, merely aided your sister in selling hers. However, if I see you again in this settlement you'll be executed like the others for your part in trying to kill Edward. Hopefully you'll now find the means to make your way in this world and thereby in the next one as well.'

Mayda knew better than to argue. She was well aware that she could have faced severe punishment on several counts and was therefore getting off lightly. Besides, with her sister dead she was unlikely to stay in Wareham anyway. She therefore merely acknowledged the ruling.

Once Mayda had been taken away, the three other prisoners were led in for their turn to stand before Governor Osric. As they did so, he looked at each of them in turn. They were certainly a ragged bunch but, as there were none there he recognised, he insisted they each state their name and say how and why they came to be among Byram's treacherous band.

The first man dropped to his knees and said that he was known to all as Oswin, but had been Christened as Albrecht. Osric was impressed that despite his great size, he had not given the guards any trouble beyond initially trying to resist arrest. 'My Lord, I was a labourer by trade but fell on hard times so joined with Byram rather than starve.'

The next man refused to kneel or to even speak. Instead, he stood with his head held high so that two guards had to step forward and roughly force him to his knees in homage.

'My Lord, if I may,' said Oswin. 'This man is known to us as Radnor and whilst he understands our tongue, I've never once heard him speak it.'

Osric realised at once that Radnor was a Viking. 'So how did he come to be with you?' he asked.

'My Lord, we believe he was left behind following a raid in which he suffered many wounds from which he was not expected to recover. But the good Lord saw fit to spare him.'

'Well, I'll not spare him now,' mused Osric.

Radnor sneered but was otherwise silent.

The last of the three prisoners was the young boy who muttered that his name was Iden. He seemed unsure of what he should do but, in the end, knelt beside Oswin with his head bowed.

'What age have you?' demanded Osric.

Iden said that he didn't know but then Oswin spoke for him as well. 'My Lord, if I may, he has but ten or perhaps eleven years of age. We believe he was made an orphan when his family were all killed in a raid. We found him quite by chance, wandering lost and alone in the forest and took pity on him, although he never once played any part in what took place beyond the camp except to act as a lookout. I took it upon myself to watch out for him, having him fetch and carry for me and for others. He's a good boy, my Lord. Honest and hard working.'

Osric acknowledged the information and then sat back as if to consider what best to do. 'You are all of you members of a gang which has troubled us for longer than I care to recall. You have robbed and threatened innocent travellers and have poached deer and game which rightfully belongs to me and to Ealdorman Aelfric. There can be no doubt about your guilt and I suspect that you each played a part in the crimes of which you stand accused, although no doubt some are more guilty than others. As such you deserve no mercy and I therefore sentence you all to be hanged. However, execution of the boy will be stayed. Instead, he will be indentured to me and found work in my stables. We have need of a new boy there.'

The boy looked up, then glanced first at Oswin then at Governor Osric. 'Thank you, my Lord,' was all he said.

'You may not thank me when you're set to work, for you'll earn my mercy with sweat – and I warn you, if you fail me or try to run away, the sentence will be revised and you'll be hanged as surely as these other two wretches. Now take them away.'

As the prisoners were led back to their cells, Oswald remained. 'I would that we could hang Edmund as well,' he said.

'Given that his main crime is one of treason, that privilege belongs to Alfred alone, but I think Edmund should be made to watch as the members of Byram's gang dangle from the rope. It may serve to weaken his resolve and thereby encourage him to acknowledge his sins before dying. At least that way he may yet be able to redeem himself in the life hereafter.'

* * * * *

It was later that day that Edward asked to see Osric in private. He had already heard from others that Edmund was to be taken to Winchester to be tried by none other than Lord Alfred in person.

'Ah, young Edward. How are you faring? Are you sure it's not too soon for you to be up and about?'

'My Lord, I cannot lie idle any longer and seem to manage well enough, although I must wear this sling at all times.'

'Then be sure to do so. In the meantime, you'll have no doubt heard that Edmund has been brought to justice at last?'

'I have, my Lord. That's indeed very welcome news.'

'It is,' agreed Osric. 'For it means that the risk to you is now significantly reduced, although I would advise that you remain wary.'

'I will, my Lord. And am grateful to those who captured him. As you know, I need to seek Alfred's consent and his blessing to wed Odelia. To that end, I wonder if I might go with the men who are to escort Edmund to Winchester? I can then ask for Alfred's consent and also discuss many other things which I need to raise with him, particularly regarding my future. There's much which needs to be decided if I'm to take a wife.'

Osric saw the sense of that at once. 'But are you up to travelling?' he asked.

'I think so,' said Edward.'

Osric knew the boy couldn't possibly have recovered so soon, but didn't say as much. He had often seen men who, having suffered severe wounds in battle, had no option but to march the next day, something he regarded as a cross which all warriors had to bear. 'I'm minded to say that you should wait in order to give your shoulder a chance to properly heal,' he advised.

'But my Lord, this is the perfect opportunity for me to see Alfred. Besides, was it not you who once told me that a warrior must learn to carry on despite his wounds?'

Osric couldn't resist a smile. 'Well, if you're certain you can manage and insist on going with them, I shall give you command of the escort as that befits your new station and will be good practice for you. Sigbert can also go with you as he'll be needed to give evidence at Edmund's trial, as will Father Cuthbert, so you should be safe enough with them.'

'Thank you, my Lord.'

'I would suggest that in order not to risk further harm to your shoulder you travel with the priest in his cart as you're not yet fit to ride,' added Osric.

Edward didn't much like the idea of travelling in the cart. 'My Lord, if the rest of the party are to travel on foot, I'm sure I can ride Fleet and still keep up with them.'

Osric wasn't convinced but acknowledged that if it was him, he would also have preferred to ride rather than travel in the back of a cart along such rough and uneven tracks. 'Are you sure you'll be able to ride with one arm in a sling?'

'I'll likely need help mounting Fleet but, apart from that, should manage well enough,' replied Edward.

'Very well,' agreed Osric. 'But rest when you need to and don't push on too hard. Edmund's execution can wait. I'll have Oswald select six good men from the permanent guard to go with you and ask him to ensure they're all well armed. The prisoner can walk between them but must remain bound at all times. Travelling like that you should be safe enough and the journey there should take no longer than three days, less if the weather is kind.'

As he considered that, Edward made a strange request. 'Given how long we shall be on the road together, might I then speak with Edmund before we leave?' he asked. 'I feel a need to at least have made my peace with him.'

'I'm not sure that's wise,' said Osric.

'But he's the only other living member of my bloodline,' explained Edward. 'There's much he could tell me before he dies, things I should like to know.'

At first Osric seemed reluctant to agree but, in the end, seemed to see the sense of it. 'Then you must first let Sigbert speak with him and prepare the way, for Edmund has shown himself to be a violent and vindictive man. He can't harm you physically whilst restrained, but may say things which cause you significant hurt nonetheless.'

*****

WAREHAM FOREST

It was later that day that Byram regained his senses enough to at least utter a few words, although it was hard for Cedric to make out what he was trying to say. The only thing he could understand clearly was the word "vengeance", but he wasn't sure what or who he was meant to avenge or why.

'Vengeance?' he queried. 'Vengeance on who and for what?'

'V…vengeance,' repeated Byram, reaching up and intently gripping Cedric's arm whilst staring hard into his eyes. 'V… vengeance!'

'Yes, I hear you. But vengeance on who?' he pressed. 'Tell me what would you have me do.'

Byram didn't answer but raised his arm enough to point to Cedric's bow. 'V…vengeance,' he repeated then fell back exhausted by the effort.

In truth, whilst Cedric could not be entirely certain who Byram was referring to, there were two obvious possibilities. The first was Oswald who had cut him so badly and left him to suffer a lingering death. The second was Edmund whose greed and treachery was responsible for all their misfortunes, including ultimately the death of almost all of Byram's band.

*****

WAREHAM

Sigbert happily agreed to speak with Edmund as Osric had suggested, so he went to the chamber where Edmund was being held under guard. It was actually a former store, a damp and airless place with rats scurrying about freely looking for whatever remnants of grain or other morsels they could find there. Edmund was seated on the floor, manacled and chained to a stout vertical post which formed the main support for the roof. He looked every bit as dejected as he had when he was first brought back to Wareham and had since been stripped so that he wore nothing more than a loincloth. Also, his face and body bore the marks and bruises to show he'd been severely beaten – and probably more than once.

'Not so sure of yourself now?' said Sigbert when he considered the state Edmund was in.

Edmund just looked at him.

'What, are you at last contemplating your fate? Do you begin to feel the noose tight around your throat already?'

'I'll not hang,' Edmund assured him. 'I shall elect to be slain by the sword as is my right.'

Sigbert considered that. 'Well, I'll grant you it's a quicker way to die, although personally I'd prefer to meet my maker with my head still on my shoulders, not tucked beneath my arm. Mind, I suppose the result is much the same in the end.'

'It's for that very reason that nobles can also request not to be beheaded,' said Edmund, referring to an option which allowed for a noble to be killed by having the sword driven down through the shoulder to pierce the heart, although no doubt Edmund preferred not to dwell upon the details of that given it was the fate which most likely awaited him. There was also an option whereby a man who had the favour of a king could have his throat cut, but it was unlikely that Alfred would agree to that given the principal charge was one of treason.

'Even so,' said Sigbert, 'I imagine you'll be rehearsing what you can say to save your soul when you stand outside St Peter's gate and plead to be admitted.'

'I'm hoping I shall fare well enough in that respect, for I'm like the prodigal son,' he said, recalling all that which Brother Linton had told him. 'I'm assured that there will be rejoicing in Heaven when they see that I've repented my sins.'

Sigbert looked at him strangely. 'Have you?' he asked. 'Repented I mean?'

'Yes, I see now that I was wrong. My mind was addled by all that which I'd been forced to endure as a slave and therefore sought only to restore myself. I also realise that had I spoken with young Edward we could have reached an accommodation which might well have better suited us both.'

'Would you then speak with him?'

Edmund looked up expectantly. 'Can that be arranged?' he asked.

'Perhaps,' said Sigbert. 'Although I'd not leave you alone with him, not for his protection but for yours. You've done him great harm whilst he has done nothing to warrant being treated so badly by you.'

'Which is why I would welcome the chance to set things right between us. There are things which should be said before I'm killed.'

'What things?' demanded Sigbert.

Edmund hesitated before replying. 'Things about our family which only I can tell him.'

'Very well,' agreed Sigbert. 'That being so I'll see what I can do.'

*****

Father Cuthbert also went to visit Edmund but his intent was purely to confirm whether or not he was the man who had robbed him. As soon as he saw him he was in no doubt about that but was surprised when Edmund tried to reach up and kiss his hand.

'Father, I would repent my sins,' said Edmund. 'May I attend you at the Minster in order for you to hear my confession in the presence of God?'

Father Cuthbert was immediately pleased at the prospect of saving the soul of such an evil man, particularly one who was about to die. 'Of course, my son. I shall ask Governor Osric, although I suspect he will insist on guards being present. Are you content with that?'

'I am, Father. In fact, I'm minded to freely admit all my sins before God and care not who hears me.'

When he went to report that to Osric, the Governor was less than impressed. 'It's a ruse,' he said without hesitation. 'If he goes to the church he'll no doubt try to claim sanctuary there. If he does that, we'll never get him to face justice, at least not in this world.'

'But surely if his soul is troubled you should not deny him the chance to seek redemption,' said Father Cuthbert.

'As like as not Alfred will put him to the sword and, before being executed, he'll get his chance to make his peace with God. If at that point he truly repents then no doubt the good Lord will be merciful but, so far as I'm concerned, he's a prisoner and will remain as such. But tell me, are you certain he is the man who robbed you?'

Father Cuthbert confirmed that he was.

'Is this then the reliquary he stole from you?' he asked, taking the casket which was still wrapped in the silken cloth and passing it to Father Cuthbert.

As the priest removed the cloth, he recognised the casket at once. He then opened it and lifted out the small fragment of bone. 'I'm so very relieved to see it again,' he said. 'The good

Lord truly moves in mysterious ways for it was intended as a gift to the Minster here at Wareham and now here it is, safe and sound. Is that not a miracle in itself? With your permission, I'll now present it to Father Emmett.'

'Of course,' agreed Osric. 'But I would have you wait until after the hangings tomorrow as I want to display it alongside all the other items we recovered from the robbers.'

'Why?' asked the priest. 'Surely no one will try to claim a reliquary such as this?'

'I'm not interested in someone trying to reclaim it. I want to see if a certain person recognises the ring which we also recovered.'

'A ring?' asked Father Cuthbert hopefully. 'I heard tell that one was found amongst the robber's hoard. Is that not mine as well?'

'No, I regret it's not yours,' Osric assured him. 'Rather it's one which is known to me and is of some significance. It should rightfully be returned to Lord Alfred in person. Unfortunately, neither your crucifix nor your coin were recovered either.'

Father Cuthbert seemed to accept that and thanked Osric for his help.

'Father, there is one thing I would have you do,' said Osric.

'What is it, my Lord?'

'I would have both you and Sigbert travel to Winchester with Edmund so that you may both give witness at first hand to the crimes he has committed.'

'To Winchester?' queried Father Cuthbert. 'As you know, that would suit my purpose very well.'

'Good. Then you can travel comfortably in your cart and will be well protected this time by half a dozen guards. Besides, with Edmund in bonds there's one less rogue to trouble you and all the other robbers have been killed or accounted for.'

'What, all of them, my Lord?'

Osric hesitated. 'Not quite all,' he admitted. 'There could yet be two of them who remain at large.'

Chapter Twelve

As ordered by Osric, a temporary scaffold had been hurriedly erected by Sigbert just beyond the west gates. It was a simple structure comprised of nothing more than a horizontal beam supported by a frame at each end and from which two lengths of rope had been suspended. Positioning the scaffold just outside the fortifications was intended to signify that the people who were to be executed there were not considered to be part of the settlement community, that point being emphasised by the fact that all convicted criminals were regarded as outcasts and therefore denied the right to be buried within the settlement itself. They would instead be allocated an unmarked grave, usually somewhere beside the road.

On hearing rumours that the Viking threat had abated, quite a few of those who had taken shelter within the burh had returned to their homes or farmsteads but there were still a good many people who had remained. Hence a large crowd had gathered to see that justice was at last done to the thieves who had troubled them for so long. With regard to the recovered loot, not surprisingly that attracted little attention given that the reliquary was known to belong to the church and the brooch was of only nominal worth. The ring attracted some curiosity if only because its value was so far beyond the reach of anyone apart from noblemen or perhaps the very wealthiest merchants.

Eventually, Edmund, Mayda and Iden were led out and made to stand directly in front of the scaffold from where they would witness the hangings at very close quarters indeed – a ploy which it was hoped would deter Mayda and Iden from further crime, with Edmund being regarded as beyond salvation. All three of them were in chains and, in order for them to fully contemplate the error of their ways, they had been separated overnight and kept apart not only from each other but also from the two prisoners who were to be hanged. They therefore watched intently as Radnor and Oswin were also led out, both closely guarded and with their hands tied behind their backs. To show their contempt, the crowd began jeering and jostling the prisoners almost as soon as they appeared, although most were probably there simply to view the spectacle as executions always attracted a good deal of macabre interest.

Radnor was the first to be helped up onto a stool which had been placed directly under one of the ropes before having a noose looped around his neck and tightened. Oswin watched this in silence, looking so pale and shaken that he too had to be helped up onto his stool. That done, Governor Osric stepped forward and called for silence before reading out the long list of charges levied against them both. When neither professed their innocence, he rebuked them for their crimes, warning all that what was about to follow would surely be the fate of anyone who resorted to crime or lived outside the law. As Osric took his seat once more, Father Emmett uttered a few well-meaning prayers although it's unlikely that either of the condemned men took much comfort from what he had to say.

Hanging was regarded as being a dreadful way to die, partly because the "drop" from the stool was so short that the poor wretch was usually left kicking and choking for some time before being released by death. Not surprisingly, therefore, Radnor, defiant as ever, preferred not to await that fate but rather to greet death as a Viking should. With a shout of defiance and what sounded like a curse, he forcefully threw himself from the stool hoping thereby to at least break his own neck and be done with it. Unfortunately for him, even that was not enough and he dangled there, his legs twitching as he suffered his final agonies. It actually took some time for him to die with the jeers of the crowd ringing in his ears but no one made any attempt to quicken his end. Once he was finally still, Osric stepped forward and offered Oswin the chance to say a few last words. Even the crowds were by then silent, their appetite for what would follow all but sated.

Oswin looked down at Iden and smiled bravely. 'Learn from what you are about to witness,' he told the boy. 'And be sure not to make the same mistakes as me. Having known your freedom, you'll find your life in bondage that much harder to endure but accept your beatings and whatever ill treatment befalls you. Governor Osric seems to me to be a fair man, so if you are diligent and work hard you should fare well enough. As for me, what I'm about to suffer is only what's due. I now regret all I've done and earnestly repent my many crimes, but I neither expect nor ask for mercy.' He then looked across at the crowd. 'All I would ask is that if I seem to linger, would someone step forward and pull down hard on my legs to ensure that I die more quickly. I would take it as a kindness if you would.'

No one came forward to do as he asked. He was sure that Iden would have obliged if he could but he was in chains and also closely guarded, so Oswin had no choice but to accept his lot.

With that Osric ordered the execution to proceed. A man who had been standing behind Oswin stepped forward, secured the noose around Oswin's neck and then waited for the Governor's signal to proceed. When it came, he quickly kicked away the stool so that Oswin had his turn to dance for the crowd.

Mercifully, being such a large man, Oswin didn't suffer as long as Radnor, his weight ensuring that he died relatively quickly. With both men finally dead, the people began to depart and the three remaining prisoners were led away. Although Mayda looked to be unaffected by all she'd witnessed, Iden was distraught and seemed hardly able to believe what had been done. He kept looking back to where Oswin's body still hung. It was swaying slightly as it turned in the breeze and his face was grotesquely distorted.

As for Edmund, he had nothing to say for himself at that point, at least not until he noticed the ring on the trestle. 'That's mine!' he shouted almost triumphant. 'That's the ring I spoke of!'

Having waited to see if he'd recognise it, Osric calmly walked over to him. 'How can that possibly be so?' he demanded.

'Don't you see?' stormed Edmund. 'It's the ring I described to Alfred. The one he gave to my father! Surely you recognise it as well for you would have seen it often enough on my father's hand?'

Osric calmly picked up the ring as if to examine it for the first time. 'That was all a long time ago. What proof can you offer that it is the very same one?' he asked. 'It could be another just like it.'

'As you know full well, there can be no proof except that you send it with me to Winchester where Alfred may confirm that it is indeed that which he gave to my father all those years ago.'

'We'll see about that. But for now we must leave it here a while longer in case someone else comes forward to claim it.'

'No!' screamed Edmund. 'It was my father's and anyone who claims it now will have stolen it! I demand that it's shown to Alfred in person!'

Osric seemed amused by that. 'You're in no position to demand anything,' he said coldly. 'It's for me to decide what's to become of it.'

With that, Edmund was hustled away by two of the guards, still protesting and shouting. Oswald went across to speak with his uncle. 'So, you were right,' he said quietly. 'It is the same ring. And if so, it's made a very timely appearance. How is that even possible?'

'Who can say?' replied Osric. 'It remains a mystery and I doubt we shall ever know the truth of it.'

'I think Father Emmett and Father Cuthbert would see the hand of God in a coincidence such as this,' said Oswald, half joking.

'Perhaps,' agreed Osric. 'Either way, it proves that he is who he claims to be, but even so I'm pleased it will be left to

Alfred rather than me to be the judge of what that means for his fate.'

Oswald looked at his uncle, not sure why executing Edmund should trouble him.

'Don't forget that like Alfred, I knew his father,' explained Osric. 'Not only that, but Lord Edwulf was a man I much respected and admired. He would turn in his grave if he knew that his eldest son would end his days as a murderer and, worse still, a traitor to the King.'

* * * * *

Knowing that they were leaving at first light the following morning, Edward spent the afternoon at the stables grooming Fleet ready for the journey.

'I swear that horse understands every word you say to him,' said Sigbert when he found him there.

'Perhaps he does,' mused Edward. 'It's not unusual for a bond to be formed betwixt a man and a horse, although the one I have with Fleet seems much stronger than any I've ever heard of before. At least, I hope that's the way of it.'

'Speaking of which, I've been to see Edmund as you asked.'

'So, what did he have to say for himself?'

'He says that he regrets much of what has transpired between you and admits he was at fault.'

'Then is it safe for me to see him before we leave tomorrow?'

'Aye, I think so. And there's no time like the present, but I should go with you. He's a treacherous bastard and I still don't trust him, whatever he says about seeing the error of his ways.'

Edward agreed, so together they returned to where Edmund was being held. As they entered his cell, Edmund got up but seemed lost for words and in no small way affected by the executions he'd witnessed earlier that day.

'Why did you try to have me killed?' asked Edward pointedly. 'I meant you no harm and my inheritance is such that there would have been more than enough for us to share.'

Edmund nodded as if to acknowledge the truth of that. 'I regret that I could see nothing beyond reclaiming what I thought was rightfully mine. I wish we'd spoken before as it seems I've wronged you without good cause, but you must understand how much I suffered when I was forced to watch as my family were slain and our home destroyed. I was then taken away, beaten, enslaved and treated like shit. That was very hard for me to endure given I'd been so high born.'

Sigbert noted that the words fell short of being an apology but said nothing.

Edward, however, seemed prepared to believe what he was being told. 'Then do you regret trying to have me killed?'

Edmund looked at him almost pleadingly. 'I do with all my heart,' he said. 'If I could change things I would, but it's too late for that now. My fate is sealed but I would ask for your forgiveness before I meet my end.'

Although not sure what to say to that, Edward had some sympathy given all Edmund had endured. It was a strange quirk of fate whereby having been lowly born as a bastard and forced to work in a stable before his true lineage was acknowledged, the path of his life was almost the exact opposite to that of his uncle. 'I can forgive you,' he said. 'But only on condition that whilst we journey to Winchester you tell me more about our family and, in particular, about my father who I never knew.'

Edmund looked surprised. 'I will, of course I will. But remember, I only knew your father up until the time he became a monk and took the name of Matthew. Even so, I'll tell you all I can if in return you'll speak for me when I stand before Lord Alfred. I don't expect to be spared, but would rather die the death of a noble than that of a traitor, if only for our family's sake.'

Edward didn't reply to that. Instead, he simply nodded his agreement then turned and left. Afterwards he remarked to Sigbert that Edmund had indeed sounded remorseful.

Sigbert just scoffed. 'I wouldn't pay much mind to any of that crap. He's just telling you what he thinks you want to hear. In truth, he's no more contrite than he is sorry for what he tried to do and doesn't know the meaning of repentance. If you ask me, he'd do it all again given half a chance, so don't waste your pity on him.'

* * * * *

WAREHAM FOREST

After having witnessed the hangings, Mayda hurriedly bundled up her few belongings and made her way from Wareham knowing that having been banished, she could never return. It was a serious punishment which could well mean that she would starve as she'd be unwelcome elsewhere as well, although she was grateful that she had not been unjustly branded as a whore. When she reached the forest, she knew the way to the old camp and went directly there but could scarce believe what she found. All the hovels, such as they were, had been ransacked or levelled and everything which might have been of use either broken or taken. She found the large, freshly dug grave easily enough but could only assume that her mother was among those who were buried there as the simple cross which served as a marker had no names attached to it – not that she could have read an inscription even if one had been provided. Given that she and her mother had never been especially close, she found no tears to express her loss but, instead, stood for a few moments with her thoughts set on anger rather than sadness. After that she left and went next to the hollow tree where Byram had hidden the more precious items his gang had stolen from unwary travellers. She knew the hiding place well enough but was not surprised to find it empty. There was no sign of Hild or her body but, knowing she had been killed somewhere nearby, she searched more closely. After a while she found a small mound of freshly turned earth which she realised at once was probably another grave. If so, it was almost certainly that of her sister, although once again there was no marker which named her. She knelt there for a moment, this time openly weeping as she uttered a few prayers imploring God to receive her sister's soul and asking Him to forgive all she had been obliged to do whilst on Earth. When she'd finished, she picked a small posy of wild flowers and laid them on the grave, then left.

From there, she went next to the glade which was known to all the members of Byram's gang and used as a place of relative safety, expecting to find Byram there, albeit wounded and possibly dying. If he was still alive, she intended to take her revenge not just for having killed her mother but also because she blamed him for most of what had befallen the others, particularly her dear sister. She desperately needed to purge the rage from her soul even though, as a woman on her own, she knew full well that neither justice nor vengeance were an option for the likes of her. Most likely, what she had in mind would cost her not just her freedom but also her life. Even so, she was undeterred. After all, given her plight and with her mother and her sister both dead, she had nothing else to live for anyway.

When she reached the glade, she had sense enough to wait before leaving the cover of the trees. From there she could see that Byram was being carefully tended by Cedric and had been laid out beside the stream and covered over with a cloak. Given that her intent was to kill him, she left it until Cedric went off in search of food before showing herself.

When she did eventually emerge, Byram seemed to recognise her even though he was beyond speaking and perhaps delirious from his wound. Mayda knelt beside him. 'I only hope you can hear me,' she hissed bitterly.

His eyes gave the merest flicker – a response which she took to mean that he could at least understand her even if he couldn't respond.

'Good,' she said, then lifted the cloak to look at his wound. Finding it still raw and bleeding, she winced then laid the cloak back down to cover it. 'That looks to be painful enough but I hope you'll still feel every bit of the agony from what I'm about to do.'

Byram touched her arm with his hand as though trying to stop her.

'No, don't look to me for mercy,' warned Mayda. 'For I'm told that you showed none to my mother. Instead, you butchered her, believing wrongly that she had betrayed you.

But it was you who betrayed us all with your greed for a share of Edmund's fortune. It was you who persuaded Hild and I to assist in trying to kill the boy – and look what became of that. My sister paid for your greed with her life, as did almost all the other members of your band, except Iden, Cedric and myself – and I'll warrant that even we'll get what's coming to us soon enough.'

At that she heard Byram utter what she thought was the name 'Iden'.

'Don't worry, the boy's safe enough for now,' she told him. 'He's the only one who is, although even he will suffer for he's been taken into bondage at the Vill where I imagine they'll work him so hard that there'll be times when he'll wish he was dead. As for me, I'm banished, which means I'll likely starve, but I've no intention of dying like that. I see a much better end for myself, one which will satisfy the thirst for vengeance which has somehow taken hold of my very being.'

With that she picked up a knife that was lying on the ground next to Byram and pressed the blade up tight beneath his chin. He swallowed hard against the pressure of the blade as she held it there and stared into his terrified eyes. She then drew the knife slowly across his throat and watched as the blood welled up behind the blade. Byram gasped and choked as he struggled to breathe, then finally died.

Having killed him, she looked around the camp and quickly found Cedric's bow and a quiver of about a dozen arrows. She nocked one of the arrows into place then sat down beside Byram's body and waited for Cedric to return.

*****

Cedric had managed to catch a small fish from the deeper part of the stream and clearly meant to cook it but, when he returned to the glade, he could see at once what had happened.

'Why?' he asked simply.

'Because that bastard killed my mother,' replied Mayda.

'Why does that so concern you? As I recall, you scarce had a good word to say to each other.'

'Even so, having served you all so well for so long, she deserved better than that. Besides, his greed was in part responsible for the death of my sister as well.'

Cedric remained standing, worried by the fact that she had drawn back the bow and was pointing it towards him. 'That I can understand, for I hear tell that Hild was more than just your sister. In fact, she was more than just a friend. Is that not the way of it?'

Mayda was surprised as she had thought her relationship with Hild was a secret which only they and, more lately, their mother were aware of.

'You do realise that it wasn't Byram who killed her?' said Cedric gently. 'It was two of the guards from Wareham.'

Mayda nodded. 'I know that,' she said. 'But even so, he must carry his share of the blame. Were you the one who took her body?'

'I didn't "take it",' corrected Cedric. 'But I was the one who found her so I buried her as best I could lest the wolves got to it first.'

Mayda seemed satisfied with that. 'How did she die?' she asked.

Cedric looked at her for a moment before he answered. 'When I found her she had an arrow in her back,' he told her.

'Bastards!' said Mayda. 'So they couldn't even look her in the eye when they did it.'

Cedric said nothing for a moment, anxious not to rouse her any further given that she still held the bow. 'What news of the others?' he asked.

'All dead or soon will be. Except Iden who is to be spared but is cast into bondage. The other two were hanged and Edmund will be taken to Winchester to stand before Lord Alfred. There can be no doubt that he's guilty of treason and, as a "nobleman" has already elected to die by the sword. He'll therefore not suffer as much as he deserves.'

'It seems to me that it makes little difference how you die. The result is the same and God only knows we've seen enough of death to know the truth of that.'

'Perhaps that's so,' acknowledged Mayda. 'But having just witnessed both Radnor and Oswin swing from the scaffold I wouldn't be so sure. There has to be a better way to die than that. What became of the monk?' she asked.

'You mean Brother Linton? They spared him as he claimed to be doing God's work and said that he was only serving his flock.'

'Doing God's work!' she protested. 'Is that what you call it? What he did with my sister didn't look much like God's work to me! Is it not strange that these men who are of a religious persuasion seem to have appetites that put ordinary men to shame? Although to be fair, he always repented of it afterwards and even chastised himself.'

'Well, they left him to say a few words over the graves and I assume he has since moved on and will doubtless find other souls to save. So, what's to become of me? Are you planning to use that bow to send me to join the others in whatever hell they're going to? If so, you'd best know how to use it, for at present, unless you favour your left hand, you're holding it the wrong way around.'

Mayda glanced at her grip and realised that was why it felt so awkward to hold. She hurriedly changed her hands over.

'You'll need to do better than that as once the arrow is loosed there'll be no time to shoot another. I'm sure I don't need to tell you what will happen if I then reach you, wounded or not.'

She thought about that. 'I've no reason to kill you unless you crave vengeance for this wretch whose throat I've already slit.'

Cedric shrugged. 'He's nothing to me now nor ever was. I tended him out of loyalty, not love, so if he's dead that's an end to it so far as I'm concerned.'

'Good, then I ask only one thing of you.'

'Which is what?'

'Teach me how to use this bow.'

'Why would you wish to learn that?' he asked, relaxing enough to sit down, albeit still keeping his distance.

'Because I would avenge my sister. There's nothing else for me to live for so will take my revenge where and when I can and suffer what consequences come from that.'

'Then who exactly do you intend to kill?'

'All of them,' said Mayda.'

'By all of them, I take it you mean Byram and Edmund. Well, you've already taken care of Byram, although in so doing, you've probably done him a favour as he was already in a great deal of pain. As for Edmund, he'll get his just desserts when he reaches Winchester, although as you say, as a noble he'll probably get a more merciful death than he deserves.'

Mayda said nothing.

'What, is there someone else you have in mind as well?' pressed Cedric.

'All this stemmed from the greed of just two men,' explained Mayda. 'Both heirs to a family fortune so vast they could have easily shared it and not even noticed the split. Yet they argued over it, squabbling like children over who would get what whilst ordinary people like us paid the price for their quarrel. Hild in particular, not to mention all the others.'

Cedric then realised what she intended. He also recognised that with the death of her sister, she appeared to have lost all sense of reason as well. 'Are you saying that you intend to kill young Edward?' he suggested, shocked at the very thought of it.

Mayda nodded. 'Exactly. For once, he and his kind must pay just like the rest of us.'

'Then good luck with that. You'll not kill him with a bow, of that I'm certain. They'll cut you down long before you can get close enough to even try. But why kill him anyway? He played no part in all of this. Besides, he's not much more than a boy. He's also much loved by everyone in Wareham for the courage he showed in the recent battle. If you kill him, they'll as likely tear you limb from limb if you're caught.'

'I don't care what they do to me. Like I said, I've nothing left to live for anyway. But if they do, all I would ask of you is that you bury me next to Hild. At least then we'll be together again. So, will you teach me how to use this bow or not?'

Cedric shook his head. 'You'll not master the art of shooting a bow in just a few hours,' he warned.

'How long then?' she asked.

'How long have we got?'

'Edward is leading a small group of men who are taking Edmund to Winchester for trial tomorrow. They'll probably leave Wareham at first light.'

'And will he then return from Winchester?'

Hild thought about that. 'Yes, I think he will. He now has a woman in Wareham who he'll want to see again.'

'Then that gives us what, two or three days for them to get there, several days for Edmund's trial and two or three days more for them to return. I can't teach you everything in that time but perhaps I can teach you enough.'

'So how will we do it?' she asked.

He shook his head. 'Oh no,' he insisted. 'There's no "we" about it. I'm not minded to get myself killed, nor would I wish to blacken my soul more than I already have. Sure, I'll take a life readily enough if I have to in order to survive or to protect what's mine, but I'll not commit cold-blooded murder. Not for you or for anyone. However, I will teach you what I can in the time we have but I won't help you beyond that, so by the time you come to shoot the boy, I'll be gone.'

She nodded to confirm that she understood what he was saying.

'If they're headed for Winchester they're almost bound to use the main track through the forest,' advised Cedric. 'That being so, there's a place which may suit your purpose well enough. It's one that we often used when robbing strangers.'

'Then can we go there?' asked Mayda.

Cedric nodded. 'We can. In fact, we should, but only to watch them as they pass on their way to Winchester tomorrow so we can assess how many men will be with him and what you're up against.'

'Good, then let's go there now.'

'No. First, if it's all the same to you, I'll remove the ring which Edmund stole from that priest and you can have his crucifix. He'll have no further use for adornments now and they must be worth something.'

'You can have them both,' insisted Mayda. 'There's nothing I want from this bastard.'

Unable to believe his luck, Cedric took the items for himself. 'I suggest I now bury him,' he said. 'We can then rest here for the night and leave at first light tomorrow to take up a position from where we can watch Edward pass by. But that's not the time for you to make your move, you do realise that? You'll only get one chance so you must be certain that your shot is accurate enough to kill him outright, for there'll be no time for another. What's more, if you miss or fail to kill him there'll be hell to pay and you'll have achieved nothing. And like I say, I don't want any part of that, for if they kill you, they'll likely kill me as well. Either that or we'll both be taken prisoner and hanged.'

*****

WAREHAM

'You will take care whilst you're away?' urged Odelia as she and Edward embraced. It was a warm evening so they had gone together to sit beside the river, feeling it was safe to do so now that Edmund had been captured.

'I've nothing to fear now,' said Edward. 'And anyway, I shall be well protected.'

'Yes, but it's your shoulder which worries me.'

'It'll be fine as I shall be riding Fleet. He'll take good care of me and I'll be home safe and sound before you know it.'

'Is this now your home?' she asked.

Edward had not considered that but realised he had certainly come to regard it as such. 'I shall make my home wherever you would wish to reside,' he said, pulling her closer and gently kissing her forehead.

'I suspect that will be decided for us,' she said. 'But we must wait and see what Alfred has to say about the matter. Do you think he'll agree to us being married?'

'I don't see why not,' said Edward. 'Obviously, I'll be marrying far beneath my true station in life but I'm sure he'll allow that.'

She looked at him then realised he was teasing her. 'Never mind your true station in life,' she said, playfully hitting his chest. 'Just remember that whether Alfred gives us his blessing or not, I've yet to give you my answer.'

'Ah,' said Edward. 'I'd forgotten that. But it cuts both ways, for I've yet to formally propose and can't do so until I return from Winchester.'

'Exactly,' said Odelia. 'All more the reason for you to hurry home. For if you would woo a lady, the first thing you must learn is not to keep her waiting.'

Chapter Thirteen

Edmund was led out early the following morning and made to wait as a rope was tied around his waist and then secured to the rear of Father Cuthbert's cart. His hands were manacled and, for the sake of decency, he had been given a coarse tunic and leggings to wear in place of the loincloth.

The escort detachment comprised six guards all of whom would march on foot. Between them, they had experience enough and could be relied upon to proffer advice if needed but wouldn't otherwise challenge Edward's command. As a group, they presented a formidable sight, each of them wearing a light mail vest which, given they would be visiting the King, had been issued especially for the journey. They also had a simple helmet and were all well armed with a spear, a seax and a shield. Although Edward was offered a mail vest, he felt it would be too restrictive and heavy to wear whilst riding and difficult to get on and off given that his arm was still in a sling; he therefore chose to don a leather jerkin instead, which he draped over his injured shoulder. Sigbert had also put on his war gear and brought his bow, a quiver of arrows and a spear, all of which he placed in the back of the cart.

Osric himself came to see them off as did Oswald and, of course, Odelia, all of them certain that such an organised and well-armed escort would deter unwelcome attention. Having said their farewells, the small party moved out in single file with their shields strapped to their backs as they crossed the open heath. When they reached the edge of Wareham Forest, Edward had them close up to form a regular column with two guards at the front followed by the cart carrying the priest and Sigbert, with him riding Fleet alongside them. Edmund was left to stumble along behind with the four remaining guards marching in pairs on either side of him. It was the guards' job to hustle him along as best they could given that he was in no hurry to reach their destination knowing the fate that awaited him.

As they entered the forest, Sigbert insisted that Edward dismount and walk in the midst of the escort party so as not to present an obvious target. 'Remember, not all the robbers are accounted for,' he warned. 'At least two are still at large and a single arrow loosed from behind those trees is all it would take to see you killed.'

The guards were therefore ordered to remain especially watchful for any signs of trouble and to raise their shields in order to deny any would-be assassin a clear shot.

*****

Mayda and Cedric saw the column approaching from some way off and remained hidden as they watched it pass.

'There's more of them than I expected,' noted Cedric. 'But what's worse is that if they march so close together like that it will be all but impossible to hit Edward. It would be better for us if he was actually riding.'

'But at least he isn't wearing mail,' suggested Mayda, sounding hopeful. 'Surely that will make it easier?'

'Perhaps,' agreed Cedric. 'But that leather jerkin will be hard to penetrate with an arrow unless you can get much closer than this. Even without that it would take a very good shot to kill him from here.'

'But you could manage it, could you not?' asked Mayda.

'No doubt I could but, like I told you, I've no quarrel with the boy,' Cedric reminded her. 'I'll help you to prepare yourself but have neither cause nor inclination to kill him myself.'

Mayda picked up the bow.

'Don't even think about it!' he warned, fearing she might be tempted to risk a shot. 'All you'll do is throw your own life away, not to mention mine as well.'

'But he's not so far away,' pleaded Mayda. 'Surely even I can manage to shoot that far?'

'You couldn't manage to strike a target with an arrow at anywhere near that distance,' he assured her. 'In fact, you'd be lucky if it even reached him, never mind killed him. And wherever it lands, they'll be upon you before you know it. There's too many of them and they're all so well trained that we'd both be killed or taken for certain.'

Mayda shrugged. 'So what? I've nothing to live for anyway so would at least die having avenged my sister.'

'Only if you manage to kill him and, like I said, you haven't a hope in hell of doing that. Anyway, I still don't see why you're so intent on revenge. After all, both your mother and Hild are dead and killing that boy won't bring them back.'

'It's not him. It's what he stands for that so enrages me,' she explained. 'He was born to privilege and wealth whilst we scrabble around with nothing but the clothes on our back and not enough food to fill our bellies.'

'He wasn't born to wealth or privilege,' corrected Cedric. 'I heard that he was just a stable boy and born as a bastard to boot. Not much wealth and privilege there.'

'Well, he has more than he needs now. Look at him, with his magnificent horse and a body of men all sworn to protect him! At his age, Hild had already been whoring for several years whilst I begged for scraps of food or rummaged through the waste others had thrown away.'

'Killing him won't change that,' said Cedric as Edward's party disappeared from view.

'That's true. But I shall feel better knowing that he and all the others who had a hand in this are dead. And if I'm going to die as well, I'd as soon do so here, in the forest, just like Hild. We might as well share that fate as she and I shared everything else whilst we were together.'

* * * * *

Having returned to the glade, Cedric began to teach Mayda how to use the bow. He started by indicating a tree stump and inviting her to strike it with an arrow. Before allowing her to try, he first gave her a band of leather to place around the lower part of her arm lest the bow string should graze it when the arrow was loosed. Having put it on, she looked at the target which didn't seem to her to be too far away, so set the arrow, drew back the bow string and then released it. The arrow landed harmlessly on the ground having gone but a very short distance. She looked at him helplessly.

'You must use all your strength to bend the bow as much as you can. The more you manage that the further the arrow will fly,' explained Cedric.

'But that took all the strength I have!' pleaded Mayda.

'If that's so,' teased Cedric, 'you may find it easier to run up to your target and use your hand to plant the arrow directly in his chest!'

Mayda scowled at him, unamused by what he'd said.

'Look, I suggest you keep practising whilst I go to find something for our supper tonight. And don't worry about hitting the target for now, just try to get an arrow to reach it.'

Mayda did as he said but, by the time he returned, she had made very little progress. 'It's such hard work,' she complained. 'Already my arm is aching.'

'Well, we have the best part of a week for you to get used to it.'

She made to try once more and Cedric was pleased to see that she was at least drawing the bow back further than before. He went across to stand beside her and put his hand on top of hers on the shaft of the bow whilst his other arm reached around her to hold the arrow in place. As he did so, Mayda could feel the warmth of his breath on her cheek and felt curiously aroused. Whilst serving her sister, she had learned much about what was needed to please a man, but Hild had never once allowed her to put that into practice. What intimacy she had enjoyed had all been with her sister, the forbidden love of another woman. Yet this was somehow different. She felt strangely protected with his body standing so close to hers, but no guilt for the thoughts which briefly crossed her mind.

Cedric must have felt it as well for he stepped away. 'Your feet should be further apart so that you keep yourself steady when you release the arrow,' he advised, trying to ignore whatever had passed between them.

Mayda seemed to take strength from that and, for once, the arrow flew much further than it had before though still fell short of its target.

'That's better,' encouraged Cedric. 'But you need a lot more practice. Shooting at tree stumps is all very well for they don't move. Trying to shoot a man, particularly one on a horse, is much more difficult.'

*****

Having left the forest, Edward's party carried on until late that afternoon when they made their camp for the night. Edward took that opportunity to speak again with Edmund who had been bound to a tree to keep him secure, with the guards taking turns to watch over him. Much of what Edmund could tell him about his family he'd already learned from Alfred, Ethelnorth or Osric, but he was pleased to hear it confirmed nonetheless.

'You should first know that our family enjoys a very noble lineage,' advised Edmund. 'Your grandfather was a kind but firm man, fiercely loyal to Alfred and with a reputation for having been a very good warrior in his younger days. For that, he was well rewarded with lands and honours. As a gesture of their friendship, Alfred also gave him a very valuable ring, which is the one found with the other items Byram had squirrelled away in that hollow tree. I have no idea how it came to be there but, by rights, that should now be mine as my father promised me that, as his eldest son, I should one day have it. However, if I'm to be executed, as I fear will be the case, be sure to ask for it to be given to you instead – not because of its value, but because it's an important part of our family's heritage.'

'So, what of my father?'

'As I said when we spoke whilst in Wareham, he was given to the church just before I was taken by the Vikings, hence I know little about his life after that.'

'But what happened that resulted in you being taken by the Vikings?'

Edmund hesitated as if not quite sure where to start. 'With most of the other realms having fallen into Viking hands, Alfred was obliged to defend Wessex virtually unsupported,' he said at last. 'Raids were commonplace at that time and, apart from the main force led by a jarl named Guthrum, there were Viking warbands seeking to plunder the rich Vills and the monasteries, plus others raiding settlements and farmsteads as they scavenged for food and supplies with which to feed themselves. One such band struck at my father's Vill. As the eldest son, I managed our family's estates whilst my younger brothers were both away – Edwin fighting alongside Alfred and your father already taking instruction at a monastery. When the attack came, I did what I could but we were completely overwhelmed and many of those who served us died, as did both my father and my mother. I and my sister, Edwina, were both taken for slaves. I'm told that she died somewhere in the northlands having been traded many times and forced to become a whore. For my part, I was taken back with the raiders and set to work on a farmstead. Mostly it was hard labour or work the Vikings felt was beneath them but, when it was found that I had some knowledge of managing the land, I was sold to a bastard named Borg. It was he who eventually brought me here, not expecting me to survive long given my age.'

'That all sounds very cruel,' observed Edward.

'Aye, but others suffered worse. Most of those who were taken when I was didn't even survive the journey across the sea. I saw several bodies tipped overboard, not all of them dead at the time.'

'Why would they do that?'

'To conserve their supplies. Life was cheap and they had no cause to preserve the weak, for they'd fetch little or nothing at the slave markets. Anyway, it was what it was. I made the best of it I could but those who have never had to endure enslavement cannot know what it is to lose your freedom. It somehow burrows deep into your very soul and fills your heart with hate.'

* * * * *

WINCHESTER

Having made very good progress, the escort party reached Winchester without incident late the following afternoon. As they entered the settlement itself, Edward found that not much had changed since he was last there. It remained a thriving and busy settlement, particularly given that more people than might normally reside there had gathered as Alfred was in residence at his Royal Vill. His presence always attracted a good many petitioners as well as those hoping to earn contracts to supply merchandise and items he'd need both for his army and for the many projects he'd initiated in order to improve his realm.

Being armed, the escort party was stopped at the main gates and then again at the entrance to the Vill compound itself, but not detained at either. Then, as they reached the

Great Hall, one of Alfred's reeves came out to meet them. He barely recognised Edward as the pathetic stable boy who had been taken away to tend Governor Osric's wilful stallion but was much impressed that Edward had not only managed to tame the horse but was actually riding it! He made no mention of that and instead greeted them all warmly. Whilst the guards then took the prisoner away to be detained, Father Cuthbert was shown to his lodgings and both Edward and Sigbert were invited into the Great Hall where they found Alfred was expecting them. He insisted they join him in one of the small side chambers where they were offered refreshments.

'Sire, may I first offer my condolences for I hear that Lord Ethelnorth has been slain,' said Edward.

Alfred acknowledged the point. 'He was indeed a great man, a good friend to me and also a loyal Saxon. My only consolation is that he died as he lived, fighting for the Saxon cause, although I doubt that we shall see his like again.' For a few moments Alfred seemed lost in the memories he had of the warrior but then stirred himself. 'So,' he said, looking at Edward's arm in a sling, 'what have you done to yourself this time? It seems that every time I see you you've managed to harm yourself in some way or other.'

Although Edward knew that Alfred was teasing him, he felt obliged to explain in detail what had happened. 'Sire, I took a fall whilst riding Fleet,' he said. 'But it was neither mine nor the horse's fault. It seems that Edmund had bribed someone to cut the girth strap to my saddle so that it worked loose and eventually slipped off altogether. We believe that they intended that I would not survive the fall, which very nearly proved to be the case.'

Alfred had clearly received a report about the incident already. 'But I gather that Oswald and some of the guard managed to capture Edmund and I assume you've now brought him here for trial?'

'We have, Sire. One half of me hopes you won't treat him too harshly as he is, after all, my only surviving kin. The other half is so angry at all he's done to harm me that I would wish that you let me kill him myself.'

'I can well understand that,' noted Alfred. 'Whatever wrong he's done you, you still share the same blood.'

'Also, he suffered much whilst being held as a slave by the Vikings so, not surprisingly, he's grown bitter. I now realise why he would wish to risk everything to secure what he sees as his rightful inheritance.'

'Do I then take it that you and he have now spoken?' he asked.

'We have, Sire. In fact, twice since he was captured. He has explained much and I dare say there's now a measure of peace between us.'

'What about you, Sigbert?' said Alfred. 'How do you see him as things now stand?'

'Sire, I am for giving any man the benefit of the doubt and he has been at pains to convince us of his intention to repent his actions, but there is something about him which seems less than sincere. I cannot say exactly what beyond my own suspicions.'

'Thank you for speaking plainly,' said Alfred. 'No doubt we shall see what he has to say for himself. I'll leave you and Sigbert to settle into your lodgings here at the Vill then we'll interrogate Edmund tomorrow. In the meantime, you can both dine here tonight. I regret that I cannot join you, for I have official duties which I must attend to.'

'Sire, may I ask what news there is of the invasion fleet?' asked Sigbert.

'I wish I knew,' replied Alfred. 'We have reports of strikes here and there along the coast but it seems that many of the ships have gone to Essex to join what's left of their army after the battle at Buttington. We believe they will strike north from there but have forces watching their every move, just in case.'

'God be praised,' muttered Sigbert.

'Aye, God be praised indeed. Although we may be a little premature in acknowledging our deliverance. Vikings have a habit of doing what you least expect. And at present they are camped very close to the borders of my realm.'

* * * * *

The next morning Edmund was taken into the Great Hall looking very despondent. Alfred was seated on his grand chair with several guards in attendance whilst Edward sat to one side of him. Sigbert and Father Cuthbert were also present in the Hall, as were many other people who had come to listen to what was said, mainly out of curiosity rather than with any particular interest in Edmund's fate.

'So,' began Alfred. 'You now appear before me charged with treason, two murders and several counts of attempted murder. I gather you also took to robbing travellers in the forest at Wareham, including a priest. How do you plead?'

By virtue of his bloodline, Edmund had been allowed to remain standing rather than kneel in Alfred's presence, but his hands were still tied. 'Sire, I refute these charges and ask what proof can be levelled against me,' he announced boldly.

'The proof is in the word of witnesses who claim otherwise. We shall come to that, but let us first deal with the most serious charge of all. That of treason against your King in that you fought with the Viking raiders against the Saxon forces at the battle near Twynham.'

'Sire, all that was debated whilst we were at Wareham. I explained then that I was a slave and therefore had no choice but to stand with them against you. As I told you, I played no part in the battle itself, rather I simply waited for my chance to escape.'

Alfred considered that, carefully weighing it all up as he always did. 'I allowed that the charge of treason could be set aside if you served the Saxon cause to prove your allegiance. You were given coin for that very purpose but saw fit to break away and went instead to hide out with the robbers in Wareham Forest. That being so, I must insist that the charge of treason still stands. As for the murders, what have you to say for yourself on that account?'

Edmund was quick to answer. 'Sire, I deny those charges. Those who have spoken against me are mistaken or have lied.'

It was a serious accusation to make and Sigbert positively bristled when he heard it. 'Sire, may I speak?' he asked.

Alfred held up his hand to stop him. 'What Sigbert wants to say is that he was witness to the fact that you murdered the man who you hired to kill my loyal subject, Edward. I am also persuaded that Father Cuthbert here described you most particularly after you robbed him in the forest at Wareham where he watched as you ruthlessly murdered his guard. Is that not so? Or are you accusing these two men, both of whom are of impeccable reputation, to be liars?'

Sigbert was anxious to qualify what he'd said about that. 'Sire, I was close enough to see him kill a man at Wareham, but cannot confirm that the victim was the assassin who had attacked Edward.'

'Nonetheless, you are certain that Edmund, who stands before us, is the one who killed him, whoever he was?'

'I am, Sire.'

Alfred then turned to Father Cuthbert. 'And Father, are you certain that this is the man who robbed you and killed your guard?'

'I am indeed my Lord. I shall not easily erase the memory of such a brutal and callous act from my mind and have asked God to give me the strength to forgive him.'

'Then is there any man here who will speak for the accused?' asked Alfred loud enough for all within the Great Hall to hear him.

Only Edward raised his hand but Alfred seemed ill-inclined to hear what he had to say. 'I have heard your testament, Edward, and acknowledge that you would have me show mercy, but it seems to me that even if we allow some grounds for doubt, this man is guilty on most counts, if not all.'

'My Lord, he has acknowledged his crimes against me and shown repentance, does that not count for something?'

Alfred saw that as a very important point and took a few moments before he responded. 'It does, as indeed it should,' he agreed at last. 'To that end I shall pray that when he stands before St Peter to be judged for his sins on this Earth, full account will be taken of his repentance. However, I cannot discharge him in this world on that basis alone. I can only dispense justice in accordance with the law of this land; anything more than that must be decreed by a much higher authority than I.'

Edward could think of nothing more to say then remembered the ring which Osric had given him to show to Alfred. 'Sire, Governor Osric would have me show you this ring. It was found among the loot that had been taken and hidden by the robbers in Wareham Forest. We have no information as to how they came by it but Edmund claimed it is the one which you gave to his father, Lord Edwulf.'

Edmund suddenly stood up straight. He had been waiting for his chance to mention the ring but had assumed that Osric had not sent it with them.

Alfred took the ring and then nodded as if to acknowledge that it was indeed the one he'd given to Lord Edwulf. 'But what does it prove?' he asked.

'Sire, it proves that I am who I claim to be,' insisted Edmund.

'I was already convinced of that,' replied Alfred. 'But it takes nothing from the crimes you've committed. I shall therefore gift this ring to Edward for it was his grandfather's and is thus now his by right.'

At that, Edmund looked despondent, his last hope having been dashed.

On seeing that, Alfred then spoke again. 'Although it grieves me to pronounce sentence on one whose family has served my cause so well, I have no choice but to sentence you to death on several counts. Unless you can now show just cause as to why your execution should not proceed, I rule that you shall be taken from here tomorrow at first light and be hanged.'

Edmund looked ashen faced although he must have known all along that it would come to that. 'My Lord, if you will not show mercy, then I must ask that as the son of a noble family, you spare me the rope. My birth right entitles me to a quicker death at the edge of a sword.'

Alfred was impressed with his sudden show of courage, as were others, so nodded his agreement.

'Sire, given my family's service to you over several generations, I would also prefer that I am executed in private so as not to compound the disgrace I have brought upon us. I would also prefer that my head is not removed from my body, for I would wish to be buried intact.'

The last point was something which Alfred understood all too well. It was a courtesy which could be extended to a condemned man, although it was never given lightly. However, in recognition of Edmund's father having been both a friend to him and a true supporter of the Saxon cause, he was minded to agree.

'Thank you, Sire. If it pleases you, I should like a priest to attend me that I may make a full confession before I die,' he added.

Alfred first looked towards Father Cuthbert but then thought better of it. He therefore motioned to one of the priests from Winchester who was there to witness proceedings. The priest bowed to acknowledge his instructions in that respect. With that, Edmund was led away to await his fate.

*****

'Sire, he acquitted himself well,' said Edward when he and Alfred were alone together after the hearing had finished, having asked if he could remain once the others had gone as there was something he wanted to ask.

'He did indeed,' agreed Alfred. 'In fact, much better than I expected. Perhaps some element of his noble bloodline still persists. Will you come to witness his execution tomorrow?'

Edward had no wish to attend but felt obliged to be there.

At that, Alfred produced a very fine sword which he examined briefly then passed to Edward. 'This is the sword I promised to return to you; the one which has been wielded with pride by so many members of your noble family, including your father. It should now, by rights, be yours.'

'Thank you, my Lord. I have been learning how to wield a sword albeit my practice sessions were interrupted following my fall from Fleet.'

'What about your schooling? There can be no excuse for you not continuing with that.'

'I have, my Lord. Both Father Emmett and Odelia have helped me much but I must confess that I'm not a ready learner.'

'Odelia?' said Alfred smiling. 'I imagine she was your favoured teacher?'

'Of course, Sire. In fact, it brought us closer together and leads me to ask you something of great import.'

'I think I already know what that is,' said Alfred.

Edward hesitated, not sure what to say.

'I have a feeling that you and she are wont to wed and you have quite correctly come to first seek my consent to the match.'

'That's exactly so, my Lord.'

'She is of a good family but there are others in this realm of even higher status and at least as much charm and beauty. Given how young you are, should you not wait—?'

'No, my Lord,' said Edward interrupting him. 'My heart and mind are set on this course.'

Alfred was actually delighted, for it was a match which he had long anticipated and wanted to encourage. 'I stalled your father when he sought to marry your mother and, consequently, caused much harm. I would not repeat that mistake, so therefore willingly give my consent and my blessing provided her father and Governor Osric are of a similar mind.'

'They are, my Lord. And thank you.'

'That leaves several matters we need to consider.'

'Such as, my Lord?'

'Well, for one thing, you are entitled to the lands which I promised to restore to you. I have several vacant seats which might interest you and we must discuss these that you may choose which of them best suits your needs.'

'I think Odelia would wish to stay close to her family whereas I have no kin so would live wherever she chooses.'

'A wise decision. Your affairs will take up a good deal of your time so it would be as well for her to remain close to her mother. We'll discuss that more over the next few days. However, there is also the question of the bridal settlement.'

Edward looked bemused.

'It is the custom within noble families to gift some measure of wealth to your bride,' explained Alfred. 'This is because in these unsettled times so few men make old bones having succumbed to the rigours and dangers of battle. Therefore it's only right that you should bestow some of your fortune on your wife to sustain her if and when you are no longer able to provide for her.'

At that, Edward looked a little concerned. 'But Sire, as yet I have no fortune!'

'Oh yes you do. In fact, you have a great fortune as you stand to inherit all that which is yours as of right. We also need to resolve that but it will take more time than we have at present. However, I shall ensure that you are able to offer a generous provision to Odelia. I shall also grant a regular stipend to cover your expenses until such time as all that's yours has been agreed and given over.'

'Thank you, Sire. But my expenses are modest.'

'Tell me that again once plans for your wedding get underway! But is there nothing you wish to purchase?'

Edward thought for a moment. 'There is one thing, my Lord. I should like to buy ten horses. Not for me, you understand, but as a gift for Governor Osric to replace those which were killed in the battle.'

'That was hardly any fault of yours,' said Alfred.

'It was in part, my Lord. Besides, I owe Governor Osric much and would value the chance to repay him. I will also get to look after them until I'm wed…'

Alfred laughed heartily. 'I'm sure that will prove a welcome gift. You do realise that propriety requires a betrothal of several months at least between noble families?'

Edward looked disappointed. 'Is that so, my Lord?'

'Aye, it is. And these things are best done right. But you'll find there is much to be arranged so the time should pass swiftly enough.'

*****

WAREHAM FOREST

Mayda had spent the past few days practising with the bow to the extent that Cedric soon realised that she had become obsessed with the prospect of killing Edward. In fact, it seemed to him that she could think of little else. Despite her enthusiasm, she showed little natural ability and even when she managed to release the arrow with some element of force, it passed woefully wide of the target.

Having trapped a hare out on the heath, Cedric skinned and gutted it, then cooked it on a makeshift spit over a small fire. 'We should now eat,' he suggested. 'You need to keep up your strength and a rest from all this practice will do you good.'

They ate the hare hungrily, tearing off strips of flesh with their fingers until they had cleaned the bones completely. Afterwards, Mayda went to the stream and washed herself. She wasn't sure why she had done that as it was not her usual practice to wash until morning.

That done, she returned to sit with Cedric beside the fire. 'I recall that you were among those at the camp who visited Hild when we were last there,' she said.

'I think most of the men did as much,' he noted, wondering why she had raised the matter.

Mayda was suddenly quiet.

'I did visit Hild then and on several other occasions as well,' confessed Cedric. 'She always said I was the best she'd ever had, but I assume she said as much to all the other men as well.'

'I'm afraid that was the way of it,' Mayda said, laughing. 'She would always say that you men were so simple as to believe anything she told you.'

'Yet you and she were more than close, or was I not right in thinking that?'

'No, it's true,' admitted Mayda, seeing no shame in what she and Hild had meant to each other. 'But how did you know that was the way of things between us?'

'I just guessed,' said Cedric, preferring not to mention that all within Byram's camp had assumed as much as well.

'Is that why you have not asked to lay with me since we've been here? Most men would have insisted on that in return for helping me to learn how to shoot a bow.'

He was quiet for a moment. 'You're not much older than my daughter,' he said as if that was all the explanation that was needed.

'Your daughter? You have a daughter?'

Cedric nodded. 'Aye. Her mother and me have been parted for many years now and she has another fool who breaks his back trying to provide for her. I'm pleased to be free of her but I miss my daughter. As I say, she'd be near enough your age by now.'

'When did you last see her?'

'It must be ten years or so now. Too long, but that's the way of it.'

'And is that why you've stayed your distance from me?'

'No, I've made no advance to you because you're grieving for your sister, so it wouldn't be right,' he explained. 'Besides, I assume that you have never lain with a man and, so far as I know, have shown no inclination to do so.'

'That's true. At least in part.'

Cedric was surprised by that but said nothing. Only when Mayda drew closer to him and put her arm around him did he realise what it was she had in mind.

Chapter Fourteen

Shortly after dawn the next morning, Alfred and several other men of great import waited in a small courtyard which had been selected as the place for Edmund's execution. Both Edward and Sigbert were there as well, as was Father Cuthbert who was anxious to see that justice was done on his account

Edmund was led out under guard with his hands tied behind his back and accompanied by a priest who was still reciting something from the Bible even though it seemed doubtful that Edmund was paying him much mind. Instead, he walked with firm and deliberate steps, his head held high until they reached the small area where the ground had been covered with straw. There he turned and bowed his head to Alfred in respectful compliance, knowing that, in deference to his old friend, Lord Edwulf, the King had mercifully consented to him being put to the knife rather than the sword.

Edmund was dressed in a loincloth but with a cloak around his shoulders lest he shivered in the early morning air whilst the list of charges against him was read aloud. That done, he was asked how he pleaded.

'Does it matter?' was all he said. 'You're intent on killing me whatever I say.' With that, he straightened his back as though determined to meet his fate with dignity. When ordered to do so by his executioner, he shrugged the cloak from his shoulders and dropped to his knees. One of the guards stepped forward intent on holding Edmund's head high enough for the blade to do its work, but Edmund scowled at him. The guard looked to Alfred who simply nodded to confirm that he should step aside. Edmund then knelt there with his back straight as the executioner moved in behind him.

'Is your blade keen?' asked Edmund.

'Keen enough,' quipped the executioner. 'Leastways, I've never yet had anyone come back to complain about it.'

Such black humour caused Edmund to smile briefly but the executioner knew better than to dally. He tipped Edmund's head back and laid the edge of his knife against his throat as he waited for Alfred's order to proceed. When it came, he uttered something which only Edmund could hear then dragged the knife virtually from ear to ear in one swift and easy motion. Edmund's body slipped away from his grasp as the blood welled up from the gaping wound, spilling out and staining the straw. That done, two guards went with a cart to take Edmund's remains away for burial.

He died well,' observed Sigbert. 'I didn't think he had it in him.'

Alfred overheard him. 'It's no more than his dear father would have expected of him. It's just a pity he didn't show that much courage earlier in his life. Things may well have ended very differently if he had.'

Edward just stared at the blood-soaked straw and considered what Alfred had said, knowing that he was right. Matters could have ended very differently, not only for Edmund but also for himself.

*****

WAREHAM FOREST

That same morning, Mayda and Cedric lay together beside the stream with nothing more than leaves and bracken to cover them. As far as she could tell, Cedric was still sleeping and she had no intention of waking him as there was so much she needed to think about. Laying with him had seemed almost inevitable, yet her natural inclinations hadn't changed. She would have gladly exchanged her new bedfellow for her sister but, of course, that was not to be. Despite that, sleeping with Cedric had been pleasurable enough, so much so that she had found herself confused at having been so eager to please him.

As he at last stirred, she wondered whether he would offer her coin for her favours as men usually did with Hild, but knew that even if he did, she wouldn't take it as she needed him to teach her more about using the bow.

Cedric sat up quite suddenly and glanced at Mayda but said nothing. That they were both naked didn't seem to concern him, he simply walked down to the stream where he knelt and washed himself before returning and starting to dress. Mayda took her cue from that and soon they were both up and, with nothing left from the night before they could eat by way of a breakfast, drank some water from the stream and then made ready to do more training with the bow. Without so much as a word being said about what had happened between them, Cedric began to pace out a suitable distance from the tree stump they'd used before as a target.

Mayda waited until he returned then selected an arrow, set it in position, then drew back the bowstring before letting it fly. It was still no better placed than before but at least it would have easily reached its mark.

'It seems you've improved whilst we've been sleeping,' remarked Cedric.

'Is that what we were doing?' joked Mayda as she selected another arrow.

As she did so, Cedric took it from her and examined the head. 'I'll need to sharpen these, they're beginning to blunt with so much practice and, having now seen the leather jerkin he's wearing, they won't suffice as they are. I'll see to it later.'

*****

WINCHESTER

Alfred was anxious for Edward to remain at his Vill for a few days more but knew that the boy was keen to return to Wareham where he could now formally propose to Odelia and begin to make arrangements for them to wed. 'My Lord, if you agree, I'll leave tomorrow but then return again soon so that we may speak of any matters which remain to be resolved.'

Alfred understood his impatience. 'Very well, but you must take care. The journey is still not without danger so you must keep the guards close about you at all times.'

'I will, Sire. But with Edmund now gone there is less danger than there was.'

'Good, but before you go, I want you to see Martyn, my stable boy. He has someone you should meet.'

'Who is it, my Lord?'

'It's a horse trader. A man by the name of Elmer who I've asked to attend us with some horses for you to inspect.'

'Horses, my Lord?'

'Yes, horses. You're not going to tell me that with all these thoughts of marriage you've forgotten what horses are!'

'No, my Lord,' said Edward, laughing. 'But why am I to inspect them?'

'You said you wanted to buy ten to give to Osric as a gift, so I've had him sort out a dozen or so from which you can choose. Martyn has already looked them over although I'll warrant he'll defer to you on the matter of which are best suited to your needs.'

'But Sire, as yet I've no money to pay for even one horse, never mind ten!'

'Don't worry, I'll take what's due from that which I owe you. God knows there's reserve enough to buy a hundred horses and still have more left over than most men will see in a lifetime.'

'Thank you,' said Edward, already excited.

'I've also been considering what lands might be suitable for you to govern.'

Edward looked at him expectantly.

'You still have much to learn about how to manage lands and deal with administrative matters, so I'm going to suggest that you remain at Wareham for a while longer and learn all you can from Governor Osric. That would fit well with your marriage plans and when Governor Osric retires you can then take over his role within the settlement.'

Edward was speechless. Remaining at Wareham was the perfect solution so far as he was concerned.

'There will be those who might argue that you deserve a more prestigious post but I would advise that you first learn what's needed, and there's no better teacher than Osric who I regard as one of my most trusted and able Governors. Also, you will have Oswald on hand to assist with military matters. More importantly, I gather that having proved your worth, you are now much loved by the people of Wareham so they'll willingly accept you as Governor when the time comes, despite you being so young.'

'Thank you, Sire. The posting is much to my liking.'

'I thought it would be. And looking further ahead, Lord Aelfric is now getting on in years and has no heir so, in time, you might replace him as Ealdorman of the Shire. Now, go to the stables to see Martyn. I assume you can still remember the way?'

* * * * *

WAREHAM FOREST

Mayda loosed two arrows in quick succession, both of which found their mark.

Cedric was impressed and said as much to encourage her. 'We now need to teach you to hit your target from as far away as possible and still strike it cleanly. You'll be afraid when you come to take the shot but fear is something which you can manage only for yourself.' He then told her to take a few steps back and then try again.

'Will you not now remain with me?' she asked, hoping that what had transpired between them the night before might be enough to persuade him.

Cedric was not sure how best to answer that. It was true that in Mayda he had found a woman he was pleased to be with, but anything more than that troubled him. 'No, I've no wish to stay here only to watch you die,' he said, a little more bluntly than he intended. 'Now keep practising and with each shot move back three paces. Keep doing so until you miss and, when that happens, move forward and start again.'

As he watched her, Cedric realised that she looked stiff and rigid so was holding the bow awkwardly as she tried to align it with her target. He corrected that and advised her to stand tall and straight, but to relax her shoulders. She did as he advised and over the course of the day her aim and range both improved considerably.

'You're all but ready,' he assured her as they settled down to rest. 'By my reckoning, they could be passing through the forest soon so, if you're still intent on killing the boy, we must prepare ourselves. We'll stay here one more night then tomorrow we'll move back to wait for them beside the track.'

'And what do we do whilst we're waiting? By your earlier reckoning it could be several days at least before they return.'

'We practise of course. And you must become familiar with that part of the forest so that once you've had your revenge there is a way in which you might escape if the chance arises.'

'And what about you?' she asked. 'How long will you remain with me?'

'I shall remain only until Edward and his escort are sighted. Once they are, I'll take my leave of you as, like I told you, I'll have no truck with the murder of an innocent boy.'

Mayda was disappointed. She had come to enjoy his presence but it was a feeling which was born out of neither lust nor love. It was simply the first time in her life she had felt safe, even though with all she intended to do she was far from being so. 'Then I shall have to manage on my own as best I can,' she said. 'Although I'd persuade you to stay if I could.'

Cedric was surprised to hear her say that. 'With what intent?' he asked.

Because her natural inclinations hadn't changed, Mayda couldn't answer that.

'How you were with Hild is one thing, how you are with me is another,' said Cedric, apparently understanding her misgivings and sensing her confusion. 'Yet these "preferences" are seldom set in stone, they are simply different sides to the same coin and you can freely choose one over the other as your inclination allows.'

She was not sure if she fully understood what he was trying to say so just smiled and nodded as if she did. After all, there was much which had happened that she didn't fully understand.

*****

WINCHESTER

Edward took Sigbert with him to meet Martyn at the stables. They found him sweeping out the stalls.

'My Lord,' said Martyn, bowing his head respectfully. 'I'm very honoured that you should visit us in person, for I gather you were once a stable boy here?'

'Indeed I was,' admitted Edward. 'Albeit that seems a lifetime ago.' So saying, he glanced around the stables. 'However, I see that not much has changed.'

Martyn took that as a compliment. 'My Lord, I was instructed to have Elmer, a horse trader of some repute, come here and bring a dozen horses for you to inspect.'

'Thank you. Have you done so?' asked Edward.

'I have, my Lord. They're in a pen we formed in one corner of the pasture.'

'Good. Have you yet inspected them yourself?'

'I have, my Lord, and have selected the best of them. I gather you require ten mounts in all?'

'That's true. Hence I'm looking forward to seeing what Elmer has to offer.'

'Then shall I have him bring them over one at a time, my Lord?'

'No, I'd first like to see them all together,' said Edward. 'That way I can determine which are dominant within the herd.'

With that, Edward, Sigbert and Martyn walked over to the pen where Elmer was waiting. The horse trader bowed his head respectfully when they got there but clearly saw it as being beyond his station to address Edward direct. Both he and Martyn then watched as Edward carefully inspected the horses.

'Which ones were you thinking might suit?' asked Edward once he'd finished looking them over.

Martyn immediately pointed them out.

'I agree,' he said. 'Although I fear that bay mare is somewhat headstrong.'

Martyn laughed and Edward turned to look at him.

'I'm sorry, my Lord. It's just that you managed to ascertain that so readily.'

'Why, do you not agree?'

'No, my Lord. Far from it. It's just that it took us both so much longer to reach that same conclusion. She's certainly headstrong, but we think she's not beyond restraining and seems to have both strength and courage. The grey on the far side is also single-minded but may still suit as she seems much faster than all the others.'

'Good,' said Edward. 'Bring the ten you've chosen to the stables so I can check them over more closely.'

Having done that, they all watched as Edward assessed each mount one by one. There were several that he wanted to ride but Sigbert dissuaded him from doing so. 'You'll not be used to them and can't risk another fall, not with your shoulder as it is,' he advised.

Edward realised he was right so had Martyn ride each horse in turn so that he could watch how they moved. Then, satisfied that all the ones they'd singled out seemed calm enough and well settled, he agreed they were all ideally suited for his purpose. 'You ride well,' he said to Martyn. 'And I'm pleased to find that you're diligent in your work.'

'Thank you, my Lord. We'll groom them all and ensure that they're well fed and watered. Would you like me to attend to your horse whilst we're about it? He's truly a magnificent beast.'

'No, I'll attend to Fleet myself, but thank you both for your help. I'll tell Lord Alfred that these will suit us well. Can Elmer supply saddles and bridles for them all?'

Elmer stepped forward and this time answered for himself. 'I can, my Lord. When are they needed by?'

'I'm intending to leave tomorrow. Is that too soon?'

'No, my Lord.'

'Good. Then I'll send my guards to see you directly so that you can help any who have never saddled a horse before.'

'But they can ride, my Lord?' asked Elmer, clearly worried by that.

Edward laughed. 'I think so. If not, by the time we reach Wareham they'll be expert horseman. Either that or they'll be very stiff and sore.'

*****

'How will we get all the horses back to Wareham?' asked Sigbert.

'We'll ride them of course. I would have you take the men to the stables where Martyn and the horse dealer will help you get everything sorted. The priest is going on from here in order to return to his parish and will take the cart with him, but we now have eleven horses in total. I shall therefore ride Fleet whilst you and the guards each ride one of the new mounts, leaving the others to carry our supplies. The journey will be that much quicker if we all ride and I've cause to make what haste I can.'

'Then I take it that your conversation with Alfred went well?' said Sigbert, grinning.

'It did,' confirmed Edward. 'In fact, it went better than I could have hoped. It seems I'm to stay at Wareham for the time being at least, then succeed Osric as Governor when he retires.'

'I was thinking more about your plans to wed,' said Sigbert.

Edward found that amusing. 'Of course, but that's not yet settled.'

'But I thought that was the reason for us coming here?'

'It was. And I'm pleased to say that I now have Lord Alfred's blessing and consent from both Governor Osric and Oswald.'

'So why is it not yet settled?'

'Because Odelia has yet to formally accept my proposal and I've already learned that it's best not to take such matters for granted. At least, not where women are concerned.'

Chapter Fifteen

WINCHESTER

Having drawn fresh provisions from the stores at Alfred's Vill, Edward's small party prepared to set off the following day. All the guards were happy enough to ride as all of them knew how. Indeed, three of them had been part of Oswald's elite squad. Thus at first light they were all mounted and ready, waiting only for Edward who was still speaking with Lord Alfred.

'Take these letters which confirm all we discussed yesterday about your future role at Wareham,' said Alfred. 'One is for Lord Aelfric who you will need to send word to before re-entering his shire whilst accompanied by men bearing arms. It's but a formality given who you are but one which it would be as well to observe.'

Edward acknowledged the advice.

'The other letter is for Governor Osric.'

'Thank you, Sire.'

'I see you have your family's sword at your side. That pleases me for it somehow seems to signify that your great line lives on. That can only be of benefit to this realm, so wear it with pride.'

'I will my Lord. Although I hope I shall not need to draw it just yet for, with one arm in a sling, I doubt I could wield it as I should.'

'From what I know of you, you'll wield it well enough if you have to,' said Alfred. 'Now, God speed. And please give my best wishes to Odelia. I hope that by the time we next meet you and she will be betrothed.'

Sigbert helped Edward to mount Fleet and the small party then set off. As the men were not used to the new mounts and Edward was still wearing his sling, they rode slowly at first and stopped often to rest the horses and to refresh themselves. They made camp the first night and ate a meagre supper and, as they sat together around a fire, Sigbert related a tale that, as always, most had heard before but which all agreed was worthy of being repeated.

'There was once a man who was thought to be a skilled warrior, but who was by no means as good as some of the others in the fyrd,' Sigbert told them.

'What was his name?' asked one of the men.

Sigbert had to think hard. 'I believe he was called Aelwyn,' he recalled. 'He was older than many of the other warriors and had served more often than most yet had managed to survive every fray unscathed. The problem was that after each battle it concerned him that he couldn't expect to survive forever and feared that his luck must therefore change sooner or later. He thus set about trying to avoid taking his usual position in the front row of the shield wall, hoping that in moving to the back he would be safer.'

'Was he then a coward?' suggested another man.

'No, not a coward, for he'd always taken his place in the battle lines readily enough. But he'd reached an age where he felt it would be fair if he let others serve their turn in taking the brunt of any assault. He thus feigned an injury to his back and asked their Lord if someone else could be detailed to take his usual place. He stressed that he would still do his share of the fighting but from further back. Their Lord was wise in such matters and saw at once what Aelwyn was trying to do. Even so, he agreed at once, saying that he needed an experienced warrior to stand beside him at the rear to help deploy the men once the battle was underway.

'Aelwyn was delighted as that role was surely a much safer one in which to serve. When they next went into battle he therefore took his place beside his Lord and, as the fighting got underway, spent his time running messages to those in the shield wall before returning to safety behind the line. Of course, whilst he'd managed to convince everyone of his intent, fate is not so easily fooled. As the battle unfolded things did not go well for the Saxons and it quickly developed into a particularly bloody fray. As a result, the shield wall broke up and, as it did so, the enemy charged through their ranks hacking and killing at will. Aelwyn and the others were forced to retreat to make their last stand beside their Lord, most of them praying for mercy or preparing themselves to die. Their Lord had more sense than Aelwyn had given him credit for. He stepped forward and told the men to leave the field whilst a few selected warriors bought them enough time to reach safety. Inevitably, he chose Aelwyn to be one of those who were to remain on the basis that he was the least tired as he'd not been fighting and, as one of the oldest, could be sacrificed to save the lives of the others. Aelwyn soon found himself confronting the enemy with no hope of surviving the onslaught which was about to unfold. He died bravely enough but the story proves that you can never cheat your fate; all you can do is meet it as best you may, for there's nothing you can do to change it.'

The men all understood the story but still debated it late into the night. Most thought that it meant that fate cannot be avoided, others simply that courage is always the best option when facing an attack – after all, the braver soldiers had been spared whereas by being afraid, Aelwyn had ended up among the fallen.

* * * * *

As they continued their journey the following day, Edward had one of the men ride on ahead in order to advise Lord Aelfric of their coming. He returned soon after midday to say that the Ealdorman had asked to see them and offered to provide them with supper and beds for the night.

Edward struggled to remember the way to Lord Aelfric's Vill but, fortunately, the Ealdorman rode out to meet them as he had done before.

'You look well, young Edward,' he roared. 'Although hopefully whatever damage you have done to your arm is not serious.'

'Thank you, my Lord. My shoulder was displaced when I fell from my horse, but it seems to be mending well enough.'

'I'm pleased to hear it. Now, come all of you. You'll no doubt be glad not to spend another night in the open.'

That was indeed true, although the weather was kinder than it had been when Edward went to Lord Aelfric's Vill on his way to Wareham for the first time, all of which seemed to have been a long time ago.

Once there, Sigbert and the men took all the horses to the stables and were shown to a large barn which was to be their quarters for the night.

'Do you still have the same stable boy as when I was last here?' asked Edward, having first remembered to remove his sword before entering the Hall.

'I do,' said Aelfric, more interested in examining the sword. 'Is that a concern for you?'

Edward recalled how the lad had been less than diligent in the way he cared for horses given to his charge. 'Not really, my Lord,' he said tactfully. 'It's just that Fleet is a very finely bred stallion and I would like to ensure that your stable boy knows how best to handle him.'

Aelfric seemed to find that amusing, but whether he understood Edward's concerns or not he didn't say. However, he remembered how particular Edward was when it came to looking after horses. 'Then do so,' he said warmly. 'When you're finished, join me back here where I'll have food prepared for us both. And don't worry, I'll see that all your men are well looked after.'

As Edward entered the stables the boy looked very sheepish. 'Is it really you?' he asked.

'It is. I've been restored to my rightful place but don't worry, I well remember how it was to be a stable boy,' he said, petting Fleet. 'I must urge you to be more diligent with these horses than you were inclined to be when last I was here. I know that means a lot of extra work for you but rub them down well and see they are all properly fed and watered, particularly this horse as he belongs to me.'

The boy acknowledged the instruction and Edward handed him a small coin as an incentive for him to do his best.

'My Lord…' said the boy, astonished at his generosity, for stable boys usually worked for nothing more than board and lodging and were seldom given coin.

'Take it,' insisted Edward, knowing that the boy would be up all night looking after so many horses. 'But I shall expect all our mounts to be ready to complete our journey tomorrow.'

With that Edward returned to the Hall where Aelfric was waiting to receive him.

'Here, sit and eat,' offered the Ealdorman. 'I would hear what news there is from Winchester.'

Edward gave him the letter from Alfred then explained what had become of the robbers and how his treacherous uncle had been executed for his crimes.

'His poor father will be turning in his grave, I'm certain of that,' reflected Aelfric somewhat wistfully. 'Mind, I'm equally certain that he would be very proud of you. I wish I'd known of your true lineage when first we met, for I also much respected your grandfather, your father and, of course, your uncle, Lord Edwin.'

'Thank you, my Lord.'

'From what you say, not all the robbers have yet been accounted for. You must therefore take great care, particularly when passing through the forest at Wareham. There could still be those seeking vengeance.'

'I will, my Lord. But as you can see, I'm well guarded.'

Lord Aelfric said nothing but knew well enough that there was little to protect Edward from a determined assassin. 'Keep the men close around you as you follow the main path,' he advised. 'There's safety in numbers and that way you'll make a less obvious target. Even so, you must remain vigilant at all times.' Having said that, Aelfric looked at the message which Edward had given him from Alfred. When he'd finished reading it, he placed it on the table and smiled broadly. 'So, you are to be advanced in station?' he noted.

'I am, my Lord. And I trust I may serve you well in my new role.'

'You'll do well enough, I've no doubt about that. And Osric is a good man to show you what's needed. If I'm not mistaken, Alfred intends that in time you will take my place here when I'm gone – or when my mind has become addled with age. I see that as a wise decision and would welcome it, for none of us live forever.'

'I hope that will not be for some time, my Lord.'

'Well, if there's anything you need, you have only to ask. Now, what's this I hear about you wanting to wed? I take it the lady in question is the fair Odelia?'

'It is my Lord, if she'll have me.'

'That's a good match and I for one welcome it. To see two such noble families united can only bode well for our Saxon cause.' He raised his goblet. 'I drink to your health and to hers,' he said, then drained the cup.

*****

WAREHAM FOREST

Having returned to where they intended to set their ambush, Mayda and Cedric prepared themselves as best they could. Whilst they couldn't be certain as to when Edward and his escort would arrive, they had identified what they thought would be the perfect spot – a place which he and his escort would almost certainly have to pass. It was where the track was relatively wide as it rounded a bend, a point where the column would inevitably spread out a little thereby giving

Mayda a clearer view of her intended target. There was also plenty of cover, including a thicket behind which she could conceal herself yet remain close enough to use her bow with some hope of success. Cedric seemed pleased with that and even prepared a crude path beyond it which she could use to make good her escape if the chance arose.

'Remember,' advised Cedric. 'You'll get but one shot so make it count. If you miss, there won't be time to shoot again as they'll react at once which is, after all, what they're trained to do. Whether your arrow hits home or not, you must retreat immediately into the forest. Once there, you can hide and pray they don't find you.'

Mayda was already worried. Although still intent on going through with it, she had come to like Cedric and still half hoped that he'd change his mind and remain with her, at least until the deed was accomplished – and who knows what after that. 'So where will you go?' she asked.

He didn't answer.

'If I do manage to get away, can we not then agree to meet up again elsewhere?' she pressed.

'There's nothing more to be said about that for you won't survive,' he warned harshly. 'Even if you manage to achieve your objective and kill the boy, the chances are you'll be killed yourself or be taken back to Wareham to be hanged.'

'But if I do, could we not go far from here and find a place where no one knows us? I can't return to Wareham because I'm banished but there must be somewhere we can live our lives in peace.'

'If there is, then I've not heard tell of it,' he sneered. 'All we could do is carry on as we have been – me stealing from unwary travellers until I'm eventually caught. And what will you do then? You'll be alone and destitute and quite possibly with child, so you'll be forced to follow in your sister's ways by selling your body just to put bread in your belly. Isn't that the sort of life you're trying to get away from?'

Mayda said nothing.

'You said it yourself and in a way you're right,' continued Cedric. 'It's surely better to die here rather than starve.'

'But there is another way,' she pleaded. 'You can shoot a hundred times better than me and could kill enough of them to give us both a chance to get away.'

'I told you, I want no hand in what amounts to cold-blooded murder. Whether you loose the arrow or I do, we'll both hang if we're caught and, if I'm to meet my maker, I'd prefer to do so with my soul untainted. Besides, I still don't fully understand why you've become so obsessed with killing Edward. That notion seems to have possessed your very being and, in so doing, has obscured all reason. No, if you'll not give up your thirst for vengeance, you're on your own. I'll have no part in it.'

Mayda thought about that. 'No,' she decided at last. 'My sister must be avenged. Her death was not the boy's fault, or at least, not directly, but his mere existence so troubles me that I must kill him and thereby set matters to rights.'

* * * * *

It was only as they reached the part of the track which led through Wareham Forest that Sigbert began to feel uneasy. 'This place reeks of danger,' he muttered as they began to make their way between the trees.

Edward overheard him and knew better than to scoff at his concerns, for he'd found often enough that Sigbert's instincts were not to be denied. He therefore ordered the guards to close up around him and sent two men on ahead to check for any signs of danger. On finding nothing untoward, they returned and reported that the way ahead seemed clear.

Cedric and Mayda had seen the two riders and hence they knew that Edward's party was close by. As it rounded the bend where they waited, Cedric realised at once that all was not as he expected. 'They're all of them now mounted!' he whispered, anxious lest they should hear him. 'We hadn't bargained on that!'

'What difference does it make?' asked Mayda as the small party drew closer.

'The difference is that you'll not be able to pick him off when they ride so close together like that!'

'I'll take my chances,' said Mayda, raising the bow.

Cedric was having none of it. 'Don't be a fool,' he warned. 'You're wasting your life for nothing. Let them pass and we'll go together and see what fate has in store for us.'

Mayda took careful aim. There was one point when the man riding beside Edward got a little way ahead of him, leaving Mayda with a clear shot. She hesitated for the merest moment. 'You said "together",' she said, her bow still raised.

'What?' said Cedric.

'You said, "*We'll go together*." Did you mean it?'

As she spoke, she looked at him and he nodded. With that she lowered the bow and allowed Edward to ride safely past, still closely surrounded by his guards.

*****

WAREHAM

Once back at Wareham, even the guards on duty at the north bridge welcomed them home and sent word to the Vill. By the time Edward's party had ridden through the settlement they found that Osric, Odelia and both her parents were waiting to greet them.

Edward turned first to the guards. 'Thank you,' he said. 'You have all done well and I shall be sure to tell Oswald of your good services.' With that, they and Sigbert took all the horses away to be attended to. As there was not enough room in the stables, all the new horses were turned loose into the pasture.

'So, what news from Winchester?' asked Osric.

As Edward dismounted, he gave Osric the message from Alfred. Osric thanked him but didn't read it. Instead, he led the way into the Hall where Edward, Oswald, Eanflead and Odelia were all offered seats at the table.

'Edmund was found guilty on all counts and was executed,' reported Edward. 'He claimed noble privilege so was put to the knife rather than the sword but I'm bound to say that he died bravely enough, although there's little consolation in that because he was still disgraced.'

'And your journey was safe enough?' asked Osric. 'There was no sign of the remaining robbers?'

'Not that we saw, my Lord. It all went much as we would have wished.'

'But you returned with additional horses? How did that come about?' pressed Osric.

'They are a gift from me,' said Edward. 'Intended as thanks for all you've done to help me. I selected them myself.'

Osric sat back in his chair. 'Then I'm very grateful,' he said. 'I look forward to—'

It was Oswald who interrupted him. 'Uncle, will you please shut up about the horses? I'm every bit as pleased to see them as you are but that was not why Edward went to Winchester, if you recall. There was something he wanted to ask Lord Alfred.'

Everyone laughed.

'That's true,' said Edward.

'So, what did he say?' pressed Oswald. 'Has he given his consent for you to marry my daughter?'

Edward looked at Odelia who was blushing. 'He said that he would not only welcome it but would also bless our union,' said Edward. With that he took Odelia's hand in his. 'I would therefore like to formally ask you to be my wife.'

*****

It was later that Osric, Oswald and Edward sat together, celebrating what they all regarded as excellent news. Eanflead and Odelia had gone off to consider what arrangements needed to be made in order to announce the engagement. Despite her earlier reservations, Eanflead seemed more at ease with the prospect knowing that Alfred had approved it, for there was no higher endorsement than that of the King.

'But we have yet more to celebrate,' said Osric. 'In the message I received from Alfred he has appointed Edward to become Governor here at Wareham in my stead.'

'Not yet, he hasn't, my Lord,' corrected Edward. 'I am to shadow you to learn what's needed to govern here and then take over when you see fit to retire, but not a moment sooner, for he values all you've achieved here.'

Oswald raised his goblet. 'Nonetheless, that's a wise decision as I see it. And one which I welcome, for it means that my daughter will not move far from us even once she's married.'

'However, I think Alfred plans that there is more to this appointment than for you to replace a humble Governor,' added Osric. 'Eventually he would see in you a worthy replacement as Ealdorman of the Shire, albeit not until Lord Aelfric has renounced the post and retired, as must we all in the fullness of time.'

Having spoken, Osric struggled to his feet, tired but joyful. Both Oswald and Edward stood as well. 'I raise my goblet to a union which was truly forged in Heaven,' he said. 'I am of an age when I cannot expect many more days upon this Earth but in the time I have left I shall take much comfort from knowing that two such great families will be thus united.'

Conclusion

WAREHAM – ONE YEAR LATER

Edward stood beside the willow tree where he and Odelia had so often embraced whilst they were courting. He was dressed in his finest tunic, had his family sword at his side and was wearing the ring which Alfred had first given to his grandfather many, many years before. Like others, he had been to attend the funeral of Governor Osric. His sorrow at such a sad occasion was shared with virtually all those who resided within Wareham, and many people had also come in from the smaller settlements and farmsteads to pay their last respects to a man who was well loved by them all.

No secret had been made of the fact that Edward would be appointed as the new Governor despite being so young. Lord Aelfric, who had troubled to attend the funeral ceremony in person, had also confirmed his support for the appointment. Even Alfred himself had planned to attend the funeral but was unwell and could therefore not be present.

'So, this is where you're hiding,' said Odelia.

Edward smiled and put his arm around his wife's shoulders to draw her close.

'You have a look about you which reminds me of when you first came to Wareham,' she said.

Edward laughed. 'I was terrified,' he recalled.

And are you terrified now?'

A little, perhaps,' admitted Edward. 'But I'm more daunted than anything else, worried lest I cannot live up to what's expected of me and the example set by your great uncle.'

It's not yet two years since you first arrived here as a lowly stable boy, yet look at what you've achieved,' she said proudly. 'You're loved and respected by all. You have great wealth, a family which has embraced you, a fine sword and a magnificent horse. Should you not take confidence from having managed so much?'

I also have a beautiful wife who I am sure will help me to shoulder the burden I must now carry if I am to be responsible for the lives of so many people.'

'Ah,' admitted Odelia. 'Then I'm afraid that your beautiful wife has something to tell you which may only add to that burden.'

Edward looked at her, not sure what she was saying. She took his hand and placed it on her belly. 'Yes,' she said softly. 'I am with child.'

Glossary

Whilst not all universally accepted, the following is an explanation of some of the terms as used in this story:

BESERKERS Feared Viking warriors who were said to work themselves up into a frenzy prior to fighting, often by imbibing some form of hallucinogen. They fought bare chested or wearing a symbolic bear skin and were said not to feel pain or fear anything, even death.

BRETWALDA A mainly honorary title given to a recognised overlord.

BURH A fortified settlement forming part of a defensive network of others, each sited close enough to reinforce the one nearest to them in the event of an attack.

CEORL The lowest rank of freemen.

EALDORMAN A high-ranking nobleman usually appointed by the King to oversee a shire or group of shires.

FYRD A group of able-bodied freemen who could be mobilised for military service when required.

JARL A Viking nobleman or chieftain.

REEVE An official appointed to oversee specific duties on behalf of the King or an Ealdorman. These included administrative and sometimes judicial responsibilities.

SEAX A short single-edged sword.

THANE A freeman holding land granted by the King or by an Ealdorman to whom he owed allegiance and for whom he provided military support when needed.

Acknowledgements

The Prodigal Son is intended to be the final part of *The Shadow of the Raven* series but, in saying that, I realise that I may have inadvertently left scope for further instalments to be written. It is, nonetheless, a good point at which to acknowledge the many people who have helped me to create the series.

First and foremost is my wife who has encouraged me to continue writing even when I was tempted to stop. She has also been responsible for checking my work prior to submission, clearing up all the typos and spelling mistakes. It never ceases to amaze me how many times I can read something and fail to notice errors which should have been all too obvious!

I should also like to thank Patrick Knowles who has designed the very striking covers for all my books, and Joey Everett who has produced the various maps and diagrams.

It goes without saying that research has always been an important part of my writing and I have enjoyed that aspect immensely. There are too many people who have helped with that to thank them all individually, but they will know who they are. I am grateful for the insight and information they've provided.

Finally, and perhaps most important of all, I am grateful to my many readers and to the people I've met at the various talks, writers' groups and book clubs I've attended. It has been a great pleasure for me and I've valued their feedback – most of it positive, but sometimes giving me cause to think more deeply about what I'm writing. That's something which I think all writers need from time to time.

Writing the series has been like a voyage for me – a long and sometimes difficult one, but a voyage nonetheless. I'm not entirely sure where it started and certainly have no idea where it will end, but the journey has been very rewarding in itself – as has been meeting so many interesting people along the way.

CJB

Author's Notes

Given that this story follows on chronologically from all the other books in The Shadow of the Raven series, it's not surprising that much of what I wrote in previous author's notes is equally relevant here. I therefore make no apology for repeating at least part of what I've said before.

One of the many challenges facing any author of historical fiction remains that of achieving a balance between fact and fiction, whilst not losing sight of the need to tell a good story. That's certainly true of any story set in Anglo-Saxon England as many of the "facts" have been lost to the mists of time and even those which have survived need to be treated with caution as we have relatively few unbiased contemporary accounts to rely on. The mist thickens considerably where intervening generations have added embellishments of their own, which certainly seems to be the case with such an iconic personage as Alfred the Great.

Given that I am a writer and not an historian, my task has therefore been to sift through all the available and sometimes conflicting information and carry out a huge amount of research. This, for me, has been a labour of love since I have a lifelong interest in all things Anglo-Saxon. However, it has also given me the task of deciding what to leave out as much as what to include. I must therefore not only confess to having taken a few "liberties" with the perceived facts, such as they are, but also own up to some omissions as well.

For example, the area which I've referred to as Wareham Forest was, at the time the story is set, probably not quite as vast as I've implied. More likely it was mostly open heathland by then, which was replanted by the Forestry Commission about a hundred years ago. The heathland originated in the Bronze Age when farmers cleared the trees for agriculture, but the land was of such poor quality that it was used for grazing instead.

However, I had good cause to choose Wareham as the principal setting for both *Bloodlines* (Book 4) and *The Prodigal Son*. It was indeed one of Alfred's fortified settlements (or burhs) and retains considerable evidence of Anglo-Saxon occupation – not least of which are the earthworks which formed the basis of the fortifications and which (at the time of writing) you can still see and actually walk around. As such, it is still possible to envisage some of the tactical issues facing those defending the settlement and you can also get a very good impression of how Wareham might have looked at the time.

That said, *The Prodigal Son* remains predominantly a work of fiction albeit one woven around the events which occurred during the Viking invasions – a time in which many people would indeed have lived in fear under "the shadow of the raven". The sequence of background historical events I refer to are largely based on the perceived facts insofar as I can interpret them but, as with all the books in the series, almost all the characters spring from my own imagination rather than from the pages of history. However, sometimes fact and fiction merge and so it was with one of my characters, Lord Ethelnorth, who I introduced in *Blood and Destiny* (Book 1).

Whilst he was initially inspired by a man reported to have played a key part in Alfred's defeat of the Vikings in 878, his exploits throughout the series have been largely fictitious. Yet, whilst researching the battle at Buttington for *The Prodigal Son*, I was surprised to find mention of a man of that name listed as being present. I remain uncertain as to whether or not it is the same "Ethelnorth" who had originally inspired my character but couldn't resist using the coincidence (if, indeed, that's what it was) for my own ends. Hence my Ethelnorth did not survive the battle despite having come so far in the series and playing such a pivotal role.

I am often asked about the details I include in my work and have said before that these are drawn from a store of "snippets" gathered over many years of research and general reading, so much so that I've no idea where most of them came from. Whether true or not, they hopefully help to bring the story to life.

For my part, I never set out to write a history book as such, but rather to relate a story, the initial part of which came to me all but complete and which then continued to flow seamlessly from my pen as the series evolved. I've tended to follow that inspiration even though it means the series must sit on the fiction shelf of the bookcase rather than alongside the weightier tomes written by the many eminent historians whose work I have much admired and enjoyed but not had the wit or inclination to emulate, preferring instead to rely on my own interpretation of events.

Doubtless there are therefore errors and inaccuracies for which I apologise and must acknowledge as my own.

Finally, throughout the series I've tried to reflect not just the huge social divide between the nobles and the common people (the "have" and the "have nots") but also how harsh life was, how difficult just to survive. But survive they did. To that extent, perhaps they were not so different from us, albeit they faced very different challenges and had more limited resources at their disposal. And therein lies what I feel is the relevance of history – it reminds us of the fortitude of the human spirit and the resourcefulness of people to get on with their lives regardless of what confronts them.

As I said earlier, this is intended to be the last in the current series but my interest in the Anglo-Saxon era remains undiminished, so much so that I may not be able to resist writing a further book. Who knows?

Nonetheless, I very much appreciate your interest in my work and hope you have enjoyed the series.

CJB

About The Author

Chris Bishop was born in London in 1951. After a successful career as a chartered surveyor, he retired to concentrate on writing, combining this with his lifelong interest in history. This is the fifth book in his **The Shadow of the Raven series**. The others are *Blood and Destiny*, *The Warrior with the Pierced Heart*, *The Final Reckoning* and *Bloodlines*.

Visit his website at www.chrisbishopauthor.com and sign up to his mailing list.

Follow him on Twitter at @CBishop_author.

THE SHADOW OF THE RAVEN • BOOK 1
BLOOD AND DESTINY
CHRIS BISHOP

THE SHADOW OF THE RAVEN • BOOK
'Brilliant, brutal and bloody ... told with Viking cunning'
Cassandra Clark
THE WARRIOR WITH THE PIERCED HEART
CHRIS BISHOP

THE SHADOW OF THE RAVEN • BOOK 3
'Amazingly vivid ... completely believable'
Historical Novel Society
THE FINAL RECKONING
CHRIS BISHOP

THE SHADOW OF THE RAVEN • BOOK 4
'Breathtaking ... like stepping back through time'
Mary Anne Yarde
'This is an outstanding piece of historical fiction'
The Book Magnet
BLOODLINES
CHRIS BISHOP